T0208970

Sweet Strawberry Sunsets

A Tennessee Hometown Romance

CALEB WRAY

WESTBOW
PRESS®
A DIVISION OF THOMAS NELSON
& ZONDERVAN

WestBow Press books may be ordered through booksellers or by contacting:

WestBow Press
A Division of Thomas Nelson & Zondervan
1663 Liberty Drive
Bloomington, IN 47403
www.westbowpress.com
844-714-3454

Because of the dynamic nature of the Internet, any web addresses or links contained in this book may have changed since publication and may no longer be valid. The views expressed in this work are solely those of the author and do not necessarily reflect the views of the publisher, and the publisher hereby disclaims any responsibility for them.

Any people depicted in stock imagery provided by Getty Images are models, and such images are being used for illustrative purposes only. Certain stock imagery © Getty Images.

ISBN: 978-1-6642-3535-9 (sc)
ISBN: 978-1-6642-3536-6 (hc)
ISBN: 978-1-6642-3534-2 (e)

Library of Congress Control Number: 2021910318

Print information available on the last page.

WestBow Press rev. date: 08/25/2021

Contents

Prologue

"Wait for me!" The cry rang out over the open baseball field. Seven-year-old Amelia Allen desperately tried to run and catch her teammates following the final game of the season. As the only girl on her team, the other members attempted to get away as quickly as possible. Amelia stumbled over a rock while trying to catch them and fell flat on her face. Laughter sounded from all of her teammates as she laid on the ground, embarrassed and upset.

"Here, let me help you." Amelia lifted her face as her eyes began to fill with tears, to see a boy from the opposing team offer his help. She grabbed his outstretched hand and allowed him to pull her up off the ground. She then proceeded to wipe the tears from her eyes and dusted herself off. "You played really well."

Amelia looked back at the boy to search for any hint of ridicule. His face seemed genuine, so she shrugged. "Thanks. I'm not sure why they treat me that way. Girls can play baseball as good if not better than boys can."

The young boy shrugged and nodded his head, "I guess so. You played better than several on our team."

She smiled at the boy, "I'll show them just how good I can be."

He grinned back at her and said, "I'm sure you will. I'm Ian. Ian Reynolds."

"Amelia Allen. I appreciate your assistance in getting me off the ground, but I could manage on my own."

The young boy dug his hands into both pockets of his uniform. "I am sure you could, but it doesn't hurt to have a little help."

The young girl looked at him quizzically. *Did he not understand that I can take care of myself?* "Yes, I guess so. I do thank you, Ian."

The Allen and Reynolds families had slowly approached the children as they continued their conversation. The heat of the summer was starting to get to everyone, so the two families gathered their children and proceeded to head home. Ian and Amelia continued getting to know each other, even if only briefly. Mrs. Allen revealed that Amelia was going to be in Ms. Travis's third-grade class, and Mr. Reynolds commented that was who Ian had as well.

"Amy, did you hear that? We are going to be in class together, so let's sit together."

Amelia stopped walking. "My name is Amelia. Not Amy."

Ian shrugged and gave a wide smirk, "I like Amy. It's short and sweet. You should try being that sometime."

Amelia huffed, ignoring his comment. "Well, we can be friends, I guess. Just know that I'm going to be the best in everything!"

As the families reached their vehicles, Ian called out. "Nothing's gonna stop you!"

Chapter One

Twenty-One Years Later

"Frank? Frank? Where are you Frank?" Amelia Allen's voice rang out through her condominium. She was standing in front of the mirror, ready to head in for a day's work. Glimpsing at the reflection on the wall, her eyes wandered over the long, voluptuous strawberry blonde locks of hair cascading around her face. The clothes she had chosen, a bright emerald-green top with plain khakis, failed to show the frame of a once agile tennis player. She longingly thought of days past, her racket against that of her former best friend. "No time for trips down memory lane," she muttered to herself, shaking her conscious mind back to the present.

She readjusted her hair, pausing momentarily as her bold, warm brown eyes noticed a flickering of orange in the space behind her. "Aha!" She spun around to give Frank a scolding, but he had already dashed down the hall towards the front door. Amelia sighed, deciding that there was no sense in chastising him at this point. She'd wait until he wanted something tonight and then let him have it.

The drive into the heart of Nashville took only thirty minutes this morning. Amelia was more than pleased with her commute in the hustle and bustle of one of the fastest-growing cities in America. "Good morning Ms. Hopkins!" The friendly parking garage guard waved back at Amelia with a bright smile. Debating whether to climb ten flights of stairs in the place of a routine workout that afternoon, Amelia headed straight inside of the elevator, clutching her morning shake.

The exchange of pleasantries was routine as well, and at fifteen minutes until eight, she pulled the blinds in her office to see the capitol building in the distance. Buildings blocked her ability to see the Cumberland River, located only six blocks away. She gazed out at the crowded buildings, lines of cars, and never-ending people. "All the beauty of this city, hidden by its traffic." She murmured to herself before heading to start her day.

The bright pink shake before her had a hypnotizing effect, taking her back to days past of a simpler life in the confines of her small hometown. There, nature's beauty was all around, and one could enjoy the quieter blessings of life. A knock at the door brought her back to the present time. Before looking to see who had entered the office, she silently reminded herself that the luxuries of a major city could never be found in a town of less than ten thousand.

"I see you are still drinking those pink shakes. Ever try a donut instead?" Bradley Winters had entered her office and seated himself as if the chair belonged solely to him. As she prepared to dispute his annoying question, she thought about how grateful she was when her collegiate-best friend agreed to move back to Nashville and work alongside her.

"A strawberry shake is better than a donut any day of the week," Amelia stated matter-of-factly. The shake was a true treat that started her morning every day at work. On the weekends, she might splurge for a full breakfast, but a shake was much more practical during the week.

Bradley snorted before picking up a paperweight on Amelia's desk and tossing it in his hand. "Sure. Whatever you say."

Amelia snatched the paperweight with a scowl and began reading through her emails. "Any thoughts as to why Director Jones wants to see me in his office at 10:00?"

Bradley looked sheepishly, tugged at his collar, and rose from the chair before replying, "I think I hear my desk phone ringing. I'll catch you at lunch, ok?"

Her eyes sharpened as he attempted to leave the office. Before he could get to the door, her voice rang out, "Bradley Joseph, get back in here right now."

Amelia knew that outside of his mother, she was the only one who would call him Bradley Joseph, and always when he was in trouble. As he made his way back to the seat, she noticed how he began to squirm and tug more at his collar. Her glare, inherited from her mother, was making the man in front of her crumble before even the first question could be asked.

Approaching him slowly, like a predator catching a glimpse of its prey, she noticed how flushed he was becoming. Internally, she thought, *this must be where the phrase in the hot seat originated.* "So, Brad." He seemed to relax under the use of his nickname, but Amelia was merely turning on her sweet Southern charm. "Tell me what you know."

The sigh that left his mouth sounded full of exaggeration, and if possible, lined with guilt. "Director Jones asked to know how many employees were about to lose vacation time. He was not surprised to learn that most department heads and assistant directors had much of their time still accumulated. He's going to be talking with all of those who have excess time built up."

Amelia narrowed her eyes at the man sitting before her. "Did the Leave Administrator offer any commentary on this list?" Amelia and Bradley both worked for the state government as the Assistant Director of Benefits and the Leave Administrator, respectively. Bradley avoided the question, and Amelia watched on as he adjusted the pale blue suit that perfectly accentuated his athletic frame, blonde-brown hair, and gray eyes. She noticed him pick at his pants leg as if there was a speck of dust. Tiring of his silence, she repeated, "Did you comment about the names on the list?" Amelia frequently fought off Bradley's attempts for her to take a long weekend or even a trip home. Nothing was stopping Amelia from getting the promotion to Benefits Director when Mr. Hansen retired later this year.

"I did not. Director Jones was curious to see that you haven't taken any time off in the past year and made a comment to me, but I shrugged and walked out of his office." Amelia knew Bradley would never purposefully harm her chances at the promotion, but she wondered if the close sibling-like friendship would cause him to speak up about his concerns. She relented and returned to her desk before narrowing her eyes once more at Bradley.

"Why did you look so guilty then? Not commenting about my leave is exactly what I would've expected you to do." Bradley began squirming again in the seat.

"Before he commented about you being on the list, he asked for the Leave Administrator's input about the situation. I suggested that the roughly fifteen names each take a week off to take care of a little excess leave."

Amelia sat, shocked. She hadn't had a day off of work, outside of government holidays, in three years. Every day she arrived early, left late, worked at home, etc. Every action had one goal in mind — a director's position. She dreamt of one day being Director Jones, the head of Human Resources for all state government.

Bradley left a little while after this revelation, and Amelia attempted to return to work. "I've got to convince Director Jones's to let me continue working. I can take time off after I'm the director."

Amelia continued muttering these statements to herself until it was time for her meeting.

Knocking on Director Jones office, Amelia headed inside after hearing a gruff, "Come in, Ms. Allen." As she sat down, she muttered to herself, "No Southern tricks." Director Jones had come to Nashville from Minnesota. His style was blunt, say what you mean, and move on with it. Southern tricks and mannerisms held no sway over the man, and Amelia knew reasoning was her best route.

Twenty-five minutes later, Amelia realized she must sound like a crazy person. She was arguing about having to take time off of work. Most people would jump in a heartbeat to take a vacation, and if work were pressing the matter, they'd be out of the office in a flash. Amelia Allen was no such person. She had few friends from the young professionals' circle she associated with, her best-friend Bradley, Frank, and one or two from her hometown that was still in constant contact. She saw her family maybe twice a year, using work as an excuse to stay in Nashville.

"Director Jones . . ." her following reason never had the chance to leave her tongue as he held up a hand to stop her.

"Ms. Allen. I've heard enough of your reasons. I admire your enthusiasm towards state government, and your work is indeed exemplary." Amelia smirked slightly to herself, *I've got it!* He continued, "Nonetheless, my decision stands. Take at least five days off. Ten if you'd like. Later this year, I will meet with the division heads to find our new Benefits Director. You are at the top of that list, but to take care of our employees, you first have to take care of yourself."

The wind felt knocked out of her, but she reasoned that five days couldn't be too bad. "Thank you, Director Jones." *No sense in arguing anymore.* Amelia headed towards the door as he called out, "Amelia, it's Friday. Why don't you head home now and take the next week off." *Might as well get it over with.* She nodded her agreement and headed out of the office.

Returning to her office, Amelia began to handle a couple of files before leaving. Turning on her email responder, she headed home, changed her clothes, and went for a run to clear her head. Amelia talked to herself the entire time she was running. "Five days . . . what am I supposed to do with five days?" *You could always go back. . .* "No!" Amelia verbally stopped the thoughts that were plaguing her mind. "That place is in your past. A holiday or two, and no more!" For the next forty-five minutes, Amelia consumed herself in an attempt to schedule her downtime.

Back home, she showered and changed before sitting down to order supper. *Bringing an early supper.* She smirked at the message from Bradley. *Guess he does know me well.* A flash of orange went by her, and she jumped to follow it. "Frank! Come back here, Frank." She found him resting on the bed, giving her an apathetic look. "It's about time you showed up. It's been a long and bad day." Frank gave off no response. She continued droning on about her day and finally said, "You could show a little compassion. At least we get to spend next week together." He turned his head away from her, ignoring that last comment especially. "Fine, you can't have any of the food Brad's bringing." Frank finally made his first sound for the day, "Meow," although it sounded much more like "Meh."

Amelia huffed as she left the room. "Get a cat they said. Much less maintenance than a dog. More independent. They're smarter. Blah Blah. I knew I should have gotten a dog." At those words, Frank ran after his owner. "Meow!" She picked up the orange tabby and stroked his fur, gaining a growing purr. *Works every time. Remind him of a dog, and he's all over me.* "You're lucky you're cute." "Meow."

Brad arrived about twenty minutes later with a large pizza in hand. He had something in a large brown bag with handles, but she couldn't distinguish what it was. "Got your email's auto-response. I never thought you'd be starting vacation today." Bradley lifted the lid to show Amelia's favorite -- Spinach pizza with alfredo sauce instead of tomato.

"Mhm." Amelia was absorbing as much of the flavor as she could in one bite. Then another and another before the piece was gone and another in her hand. Before beginning on the next slice of this masterpiece before her, she interjected, "I tried to reason with him into letting me work instead of taking time off. That may have caused me to be the first off, now that I think about it."

Bradley laughed, "Probably so. He sent two others home today, too, and I know for a fact that Roberts tried arguing that he was too valuable to take time off. That didn't go over well."

Amelia snorted, "I imagine not. Director Jones doesn't care for that whole 'I'm irreplaceable' attitude. My biggest concern is that I don't know what to do for the next week."

"Sorry. I knew you didn't want to take any time off work, but maybe this will be good for you. Your hometown festival is only a couple of weeks away, right? You can see the town setting up for it before the crowds of old friends arrive. You constantly talk about that Festival and haven't been in over a decade."

Amelia stared longingly out the window. She did miss portions of her home — the food, shops, and especially the Festival. There were hints of red and green all around her condo, giving glimpses of the place once called home. The bad memories outweighed the good ones. "You know I can't do that."

Challenging, Bradley quirked an eyebrow, "Can't or won't?"

Instead of a glare, Amelia sent him a look of longing coupled with hurt. "You know why I don't go home. Everywhere reminds me of him and our time together. Everyone in town looks at me like there should be someone standing beside me, and he's not there. They look as if I've done something wrong when I wasn't the one who skipped out without saying anything. I go home long enough to visit for a holiday and then right back here. It's been this way for a while; no need to change it now."

Bradley began to argue when Amelia's phone rang. A long groan filled her living area, "We talked her up." It was Bradley's turn to snort when Amelia turned the phone around so he could see displayed plainly, Mom. She pressed the speaker button before greeting her mother.

"Hi, mom. How are you?"

"I'm doing good dear, I was about to serve dinner and wanted to know if you were almost here or if it would be later before you arrived."

The phone nearly dropped from her hands as Amelia struggled to respond. She mouthed at Bradley, "You told my mother?"

He held up his hands in surrender, "Not me, I swear!"

"Who else knows my mom? What did you do, Bradley Joseph?"

"I promise you that I didn't say anything!"

"Amelia, are you there?"

"Sorry, mom, the phone cut out." She could feel the reproving look through the phone as she lied to her mother. "What did you ask?"

There was a slight hesitation before her mother continued, "I said, are you almost here? I forwarded you an email this afternoon, and I accidentally sent it to your work email. When I got the automatic response, I saw you were off for the next week. You always say the first chance you had off you'd come to visit for more than a day, so I just assumed... "

The remainder of Susan Allen's words missed the ears of Amelia & Bradley. First, Amelia mouthed an apology at Brad, who waved it off in return. Second, Amelia wished that her mother would stop emailing the work email about personal things for the millionth time. Thirdly, she devised another lie to cover. "Mom, of course, I'm coming!"

Susan Allen responded timidly, the accusing tone noticeable by both parties, "So you are on the way then?"

"No, sorry. I wanted it to be a surprise. I'll be there Monday morning. I can only stay until Wednesday morning, though. Brad needs my help doing some project at his apartment Wednesday night." She threw a demanding glare at Bradley, daring him to challenge her statement.

"Oh." The tone of her mother had changed from accusatory to a mixture of sadness and disappointment. "You're a good friend to him. You sure you can't be here for Sunday church services?"

Amelia's last desire was to attend church services with her family. Everyone there knew her and would look longingly at her for being close to thirty and still single. The church she was a part of here, while more modern than she wanted, was a better fit for her. She mouthed quickly at Bradley, who nodded his head in agreement before responding.

"Sorry, mom. I told Bradley that I would visit his church Sunday before heading west." This statement was not technically a lie but was highly deceptive. Amelia would not dare use a lie to get out of church services. Her faith may not be as strong as it once was, but she still drew the line at places.

"I understand then, dear, although you could visit with him any Sunday." Amelia rolled her eyes at her mother's use of Southern guilt.

"You and dad did always raise me to stay true to my word, something not everyone in my life has followed, so I try especially hard to keep my word."

"Glad to hear it, dear, and you are doing that with this trip home. Bring Frank too dear; I've got some mice I need him to catch. Bye, dear."

Shocked for the second time that day, Amelia hung up the phone. "She got me there. I did promise to come home. Frank, want to go vacation in small town, USA?" Frank perked up at this question and seemed to gladly respond, "Meow."

"She spoils you, yes I know." Amelia rolled her eyes at the cat. Remembering the mice comment, she quivered. "Sounds like you've got a job there too." *Always loved living close enough to the country that mice were just an issue bound to appear at some time or another.*

Bradley took another slice of pizza, bit off a large bite, and said, "So, since I need you to help with a project Wednesday, that means you're helping me with my garden, right?"

Amelia smirked, "In your dreams. You need help with a chick flick marathon. Maybe then, you'll understand us enough to get a date."

"Funny."

The weekend flew by, and soon it was time to head back to her hometown. She loaded Frank into a carrier, finished loading the car before muttering, "You're only going home for about forty-eight hours. You can handle this." The entire way home, Amelia muttered reassuring words to herself. "There's no way I can avoid people in town this time. No holiday to distract everyone with their own families."

She jetted down I-40. As always, the road trip felt as if she'd been in the car for six or seven hours. Time seemed to pass slowly as she neared the exit for her hometown. The dread she felt with each trip home only added to her wish to stay in Nashville. Twenty minutes off of the interstate, making the total drive only two and a half hours (though feeling immensely longer), she saw the large strawberry, symbolic of the week that gave her town their few minutes of fame each year. Written across it was the words she saw each time, yet somehow it was shinier than ever before. "Maybe that means this will be a good trip," Amelia whispered as her eyes darted back to the road, looking away from the three words: Welcome to Humboldt.

Chapter Two

*H*umboldt, Tennessee: A town where close to eight thousand people call home. It was also her birthplace and the location of so many memories, heartaches, friends, and rivals. As she drove towards her family home, she thought of former neighbors and friends. She noticed repaired buildings and vacant homes lining the streets. The town had seen a lot of change through her life, but it was still in many ways home.

Amelia drove up to her parents' house and noticed the freshly manicured lawn. The home was a simple yet elegant, white house trimmed with red and slight hints of green. It resembled everything the town was famous for — strawberries. Amelia exited her car and breathed in the local air. She was finally home. She gathered her luggage and went through the front door. "Mom, guess who?" Amelia gladly called throughout the two-story house.

"Amelia, so glad to have you home, dear!" Her mother's voice called from upstairs. Mrs. Allen descended the stairs in no time and hugged her daughter. She stood as tall as possible at an even five feet. Her perfectly groomed, greying red locks fell just right around her face. Amelia took in her mother and noticed that she was looking a bit paler than usual.

Relishing in the embrace of her mother, she quickly enveloped her mother in another hug. While their relationship had waned over the years, Amelia savored moments with her mother. Once Frank had been freed from his carrier, he happily rubbed against Susan Allen's legs. Frank loved her parents' home. He had plenty of space to hide and lots of places to play "I guess dad is downtown?" Susan gave a slight uptick with her lip and a knowing look towards her daughter before saying, "Of course, always working at this time of year. You know, as May gets closer, it is harder and harder to pull him away. Maybe you should stop in and visit him at the office. Oh, and dear, while you are downtown, I need you to run some errands for me."

Amelia stopped admiring the beautiful vase filled with fresh flowers on the kitchen table and spun around to face her mother. "Mom, I got here only moments ago, and you already want to send me away?" Her daughter's statement did not fool Susan. She knew Amelia liked to avoid the townspeople every time she came, and Susan Allen was determined to stop that. "Well, I need your help, and besides, we've got plenty of time to catch up. Now here is everything you need to do, all organized on a list, as I know you'd prefer. While you are in town, you should stop and have a bite of lunch. We can catch up at dinner tonight. Your siblings are coming over then as well." Amelia was excited at the thought of her two younger brothers. Both lived in town and worked in the area. Jason had gotten married back this last fall while Eric was engaged to be married next spring.

Without any further discussion, Susan had picked up Frank, and the two went off into another part of the house. Amelia had not even gotten a real chance to argue or smooth talk her way out of this. She dropped off her luggage in her room without paying much attention and started out the door.

Once she had her seat belt buckled, she took the list from her pocket and examined her mother's chores. The two words lining the top of the page let Amelia know that this was most definitely premeditated.

Amelia's List

- *Pick up a Welcoming Gift for the County Mayor*
- *Pick up Dad's Prescriptions*
- *Drop off Books at the Library*
- *Renew Newspaper Subscription*
- *Pick up Flowers*

Attached to the list was her mother's card and account information for different businesses. Amelia noticed the lack of specific places to accomplish some of the goals and wondered where the library books were. Before she could reach the door, her mother ran out with a bag full of books. Amelia chuckled as her mother frantically handed her the bag before rushing back into the house. "Let's knock this out quickly," she muttered to herself while resettling into her car. Amelia had brought a few letters to mail, so she decided to start at the Post Office.

Two years ago, Amelia had a bad situation with the outside drop box and mail getting lost. Ever since then, it was her goal to place all correspondence in the hands of a postal clerk. She entered the tall building across from the local police department. Inside the post office, it was just as she had always remembered it. The walls were lined with post office boxes, and the blue background brought her back to the many trips she would make with her parents here as a child. Amelia also remembered the countless trips she made for her parents once she began driving. This place reminded Amelia how she had gone from her parents doing everything for her to running their errands around town. Laughing at the memory,

Amelia moved through line. She stopped to chat briefly with Kelly, a member of her parent's church. She exchanged pleasantries with a few others and then started back down the steps of the tall building.

As she exited and turned towards her car, her breath hitched when she heard an all too familiar "Amy?!" Amelia considered her options once more: feign hearing loss, pretend to have a heat stroke, running into the road, or smiling with as much Southern charm as she could muster. The first option only meant a visit to her house later by said individual, the second would prove problematic on a mild-Tennessee day with the weather in the low eighties, and the third would spread that she was in town to even more people, so option four was, unfortunately, the only way to go.

Amelia's veins turned to ice as she turned to find herself face to face with Ian Reynolds. "Amy, it's so . . . It's been. . . Why are. . . How are. . ." She had never seen Ian so flustered. Admittedly, she was somewhat satisfied seeing him flounder like a fish out of water. He stopped speaking and took a moment to collect himself. "Amy, never thought I would run into you here."

She smiled and said, "Ian, it has been a while. I got into town only an hour ago for a short trip, and mom has me running errands everywhere."

Ian spluttered for a moment more and then said, "Well, how have you been?"

Amelia thought for a moment and said with a little too much enthusiasm, "I am fantastic. I love my job, friends, and social life. With a busy schedule, it can be so hard to take a break. What are you doing back in town?"

Ian looked at her with a little bit of shock and said, "Amy, that is great. I moved back a few months ago. I recently started working nearby and am trying to get reacquainted with everyone."

"That sounds great," she replied curtly.

Amelia began to glance off at the strawberry decorations

making their appearance everywhere. While looking off in the distance, she heard Ian mutter, "Did you bring anyone with you?"

Amelia sharply turned her head back towards Ian. Assuming he was asking about a significant other, she hastily replied, "Well, I did bring someone home. We've been together for a few years now. I met him one day and couldn't resist making him a part of my life. He listens to everything I say, and while he appears to be rough and tough, he's extremely caring." Once the words left her mouth, she couldn't believe what she said. *Where did that come from?* Subconsciously, she must have wanted to impress Ian. She noted his look and was puzzled by the expression on his face.

"What is this wonderful man's name?"

"Frank."

He smirked and said while exaggerating the name, "Oh, Frank sounds wonderful. I must meet him. Will he be joining you in your town excursion?"

Could he know who Frank is? Deciding to continue the fabrication, she remarked, "Unfortunately not. He gets tired very easily with the work he does. Most likely, he is hope taking a nap right now."

Ian continued that incorrigible grin and said, "Oh, that is just too bad. Napping on a beautiful day like this? Well, at least bring him to the Festival."

It was now Amelia's turn to smirk. "Unfortunately, I am not going to attend this year. Work always keeps me so busy." Even after this revelation, Ian's grin failed to falter.

"You're off now. Are you sure you can't get away for a day or two? It's the Festival, after all."

Amelia decided that since she'd already dug the hole, she might as well jump right into it. "Either way, I have unfortunately already accepted an invitation to my friend Brad's family gathering the same weekend." Amelia's face was brighter than the sun when she believed Ian's happiness to vanish.

"I cannot believe you are going to miss our class reunion. The class president missing the first reunion? Your uncle is even hosting the event at his barn."

Amelia's face dropped as she considered what he'd just said. She did remember that it was their 10th anniversary. While truthfully she wasn't keen on seeing her former classmates, she'd actually forgotten the reunion was the same week as the festival. She was confused on how to answer since no one had informed her that Uncle Kent was hosting the gathering. It made sense because his daughter Jessie graduated with them as well. His barn was out on the Medina highway, and he had been busy setting it up as an event and wedding venue. She realized no one in her family had even told her that the venue was finished.

Amelia responded, "I was unaware he was hosting. I perhaps can change things to make it, but I cannot say with any certainty yet."

She glanced at her watch as an excuse to getaway, even though the conversation had not been long. "Oh no, I have got to run! This list is not even close to being done, let alone started."

He laughed as she hurried to her car. As she jumped in, he hollered, "It is good to see you, Amy. Maybe I can see you again soon."

Amelia was never so glad to escape. She headed over to Serene Strawberry 'Scripts to pick up her dad's prescription. It was so lovely to see familiar faces behind the counter that did not pry into your personal life. The same could not be said for when she dropped off the library books. What should have taken five minutes took forty-five. It seemed that every member of her parents' church was in the library at the same time looking for some new book.

As she exited the library, her mind pondered why she had not used the big orange box outside. The library's front was one main area that had seen several changes and improvements over the years. Gone was the giant dogwood outside of its front door. As a teenager, she would often leave the building with a new book and sit down under its shade to enjoy a thrilling tale. Ian would often join her, and they would seem to lay there for hours or until someone came and ran them off. The tree had started dying a few years ago, and the library decided to take it down. A new internet garden, full of flowers and excellent connectivity, stood in its place. The landscaping was beautiful. She remembered how one of the library's patrons had taken extreme care in tending to the plants. This front resembled what she wished Humboldt would always be like – finding new beauty in the old surroundings.

She got back into her car and reviewed her mother's list once more. She still had to pick up a gift, the flowers, and renew the subscription. She settled on finishing the beginning item of the list first. As she drove through downtown Humboldt, she smiled at the strawberry scenes painted on the business windows. It was a tradition that the high school art class would send students to paint "Berry Scenes" in the storefronts. She thought fondly of trips into old businesses like the Robbin's Nest, Mrs. Cyrus' hat shop, and who could forget the Red Door Cafe. The thought of the cafe' had her wanting one of their grilled chicken Caprese sandwiches. Their pesto sauce was one of the best she'd ever eaten. She was sad to think of businesses like these that were no longer there but excited about recent developments.

She pulled into a spot right outside of the red-bricked building. *This is different.* Her mind wandered to when this store was two blocks down in what was now a dance hall. It once had a pharmacy to go with the store and it was always one of her favorite spots. She and Ian would take a stroll through the store, and always find each other's gifts there. Stepping out of her car, she took in the facelift of downtown with the trees and metal strawberries and filled with a foreign emotion. She looked at the shops, and as scenes of a decade prior swarmed her mind, the feeling was identified. *I'm home.* Even with her run-in this morning, it was heart-warming to be in a place that could settle her. As she entered Berry-Exciting Gifts, she was greeted by several warm, familiar faces.

Amelia considered how strange it was that one could be gone so long, and yet minutes after stepping into the past, everything seemed as if it was only yesterday. That was the beauty of living in a small town. Sure, she had groaned and moaned about it already multiple times this week, but everyone knew everybody, and the city always supported their own. When anyone took the time to consider the charm of a small town working together, it could warm the heart of even the coldest snowman.

Inside the store, she chatted for a while with Ms. Gretchen, the worker behind the counter, and then went off searching for the perfect gift. Her parents had a tradition of giving the county mayor a token of appreciation each year to commemorate the festival. Her mother's rules were simple: It had to involve strawberries, and it could not have been given to this particular mayor before. "Maybe that was more challenging than simple," she said to herself while perusing the shelves.

One of the reasons she stopped in the store was somehow the staff always found new strawberry-themed gifts. The items were guaranteed best sellers in town, so the team always searched far and wide for strawberry-themed gifts. Amelia was so engrossed in all of the things that she failed to notice a person in the aisle. The woman was stopped, admiring her potential purchase. "I am so sorry," Amelia hastily said after bumping into the individual. She looked up to see the face of Ellen Louise Hart, best known as Lou.

Lou smiled as she responded, "I heard you were back in town and hoped to bump into you, but not this way." The two ladies laughed, then hugged, and started to chat about their lives. Here was yet another example as to how it seems one's home never truly leaves them. Lou and Amelia were the closest of friends throughout school. Even while taking different tracks in high school, the two girls were as close as sisters. Since the days of Ian, Amelia had distanced herself from practically all high school friends. Lou was one of the few she talked with still, but only once in a blue moon. Lou told Amelia all about her two twin girls at home and invited her over to see them. Amelia agreed to catch up with Lou the next night over take-out from their favorite local restaurant with the most enormous and best-tasting salads and sandwiches in the city.

Amelia finally found what she was looking for — a set of strawberry cufflinks for the mayor and a unique strawberry necklace for his wife. This necklace was made of several small strawberries in a circle around the map of Gibson County printed on the white face. These items would be the perfect gifts for the mayor and his wife. She checked out at the register, spending a few more moments with Gretchen, and then headed out the door.

She decided to call ahead to the florist and see if her mother's favorites were ready. The list stated to pick up flowers but not what kind or for what occasion. Amelia knew that her mother wanted a centerpiece for the dinner table, and so what better than her mother's favorite flowers — pink roses. She dashed by the florist and gathered the flowers, thanking them for their outstanding work. After renewing the Chronicle subscription, loading everything back into her car, and checking off the last box, Amelia was happy that the list was complete. It was nearing lunchtime, so she popped into one of the now three Mexican restaurants to order lunch for herself and her father. As she drove over to the parking lot of his office, she was eager to see her dad at work.

She glanced up at the tall, proud building that read City Hall and went on inside. Newcomers to town would often be confused by the writing on the building. It was the original city hall that had since been vacated. Entering his office, her father's secretary informed her that he would be of a call in about ten minutes, so she strolled across the way to the incredibly famous Strawberry Festival Museum. The local Festival was so renowned that it had to have its own exhibits inside the building. While some would jest at the idea, she loved taking a stroll through the town's history. This annual event was the one gathering that united this community like no other. It seemed there were no trivial problems for one week, only a tiny community sharing in their history with thousands of guests. She resolved to come back to take a tour of the art gallery, located down the hall, before leaving town as she headed back into his office.

"Busy day?" Amelia called from the door. Her dad looked up first in a state of shock and then with a face of total delight to see his daughter.

"Milly! As I live and breathe, I cannot believe you stopped by here. I thought I would have to wait to see you until tonight." His daughter laughed at the old nickname, as he was the only one who could get away with it.

"How could I miss seeing the Chamber of Commerce director in action?"

Roger Allen believed in this town more than the average resident, and it showed through his life's work. Mr. Allen had started as a business executive in Nashville when he met Susan Tomlinson from the little town of Humboldt, TN. He instantly fell in love with her city and moved to be the finance director for a local company. When the company sold, Roger turned his attention to non-profits. He worked for himself as a business consultant and had built an impressive set of clients. Throughout the years, Roger Allen had built not only an excellent brand but an extremely successful hometown consulting business.

Three years ago, the local chamber director moved to another area, and he decided to apply for the position. Mr. Allen still owned the consulting business, but his team had taken over much of the work. When the chamber director applications opened, no one even applied against Roger Allen. He loved this town more than many others. Several thought he might run for mayor, but his belief was in bettering the city outside of politics. He was content in helping local businesses and individuals while trying to attract new people and jobs to the town.

Roger smiled at his daughter's question and beckoned her into his office. "Well, you should have made it about thirty minutes ago. I was passionately working on this year's festival logo."

Amelia rolled her eyes at her father, "Let me guess . . . it involves a strawberry."

He returned the classic Allen smirk to her, "No, I decided to use a grape this year, you know — spice it up." She laughed at the sass that she had so obviously inherited from her father. Amelia was a mixture of her parents. On the one hand, her mother was very stoic and prim, while her father was a character (and then some). One parent could be stubborn enough for the both of them while the other was as tender-hearted as they come. The combination could be dangerous, as was evident in the package known as Amelia Allen.

Her dad filled her in on his day as they sat down to enjoy their lunch. "We have been working with a new graphic artist recently. The 81st Annual Strawberry Festival doesn't happen every year. You know the 75th brought back the Clydesdales, and what a treat that was. We decided to give the signage a facelift this year. The graphic artist recently opened shop in town, and he's amazing."

"Sounds like it," she quipped as she ate her lunch. The two chatted and visited for at least two hours before Amelia decided to return to her mother with all of the fruits from her labor. Amelia's eyes warmed as she drove through town, though changing to slightly sad as she passed by the nearly vacant hospital. While some areas were seeing new development, others stood trapped in vacancies from days past. She decided to take the highway around town before going back home. Once she pulled into her parents' home, she sat in the car for a quick moment and quietly said to herself, "It feels like I never left. I guess you can always go home. Maybe, this time will be different."

Chapter Three

*A*melia had settled into her old room. She took in the awards lining her old desk and dressers. It was as if she was still in high school, and nothing was different. Picture frames cluttered one spot, and her mirror had notes and pictures taped all around— several featured Ian and herself at various events, dinners, and school functions. *I guess I haven't come home much if these are still here.* She started to take them down as her mother called up the stairs, "Amelia, come help with dinner." She sighed and resigned herself to tackle this project later.

As she headed down into the kitchen, she could almost taste her mother's pasta sauce due to the strong smell. It was the old family recipe, tweaked from generation to generation. She often wondered when the torch would pass to her, but her mother wouldn't budge on her family secret. Each generation added, without taking away, one ingredient to the sauce, thus continuing the family's legacy. Her mother smiled at her, "Thank you, dear, for doing all the work in town today as well as the lovely roses. They are beautiful. Come, we need to start cooking. I decided to make lasagna."

Lasagna was Amelia's favorite. The perks of coming home

rarely were that she typically got her favorite dishes of her mother's cooking. Her mother set her to work making the homemade pasta. They made idle chit-chat as they worked together in the kitchen. After working on the dough, Amelia decided to be brave, "So, when do you think I might get to learn the recipe?"

Susan Allen continued stirring her sauce at the stove. She chuckled, "It is the same answer as the last time you asked, dear. You know that it is passed from mother to daughter once the daughter is engaged."

Amelia despised the answer, as she believed it to be an old worldview. She could not understand how being engaged would be the reason to learn the sauce. Amelia started to argue with her mother, but one stern glance was all it took to signal that the conversation was over. Once the lasagna was assembled and baking in the oven, the two began to work on the strawberry cake and muffins. "So, how was your day in town?"

"It was nice to see so many familiar faces. The city has changed more than I thought it would. It hurts to see so many former businesses gone, but the new ones look exciting! I wonder if they will ever use the hospital at full capacity in some way again. Dad seemed to be enjoying his work, oh, and I'm having dinner tomorrow at Lou's."

"I am so happy to see you two girls getting together. She's missed you and could use the company. Her girls are only a few months old. Her mother helps as much as possible, but with her husband deployed, it gets difficult. I've watched the girls a time or two for her. They are such dolls."

Amelia had forgotten that Justin was in the Marines and learned that he is deployed for eighteen months. Justin and Lou had been high school sweethearts who stayed together through several rough spots. Justin had enlisted right out of high school and was able to complete his education. The whole town admired his determination to serve his country. His unit had recently been activated for an extended overseas deployment. He ended up having to leave right after the babies were born. Lou moved back to Humboldt for her mother to help as she could. Amelia felt sorry for her friend and thought she might go a little bit earlier and see what she can do to help.

Her mother continued the light-hearted interrogation, "Anything exciting happen in town?" Amelia cut her eyes towards her mother, who appeared to be as innocent as a mouse, "Why did you fail to mention that Ian moved back to town?"

Her mother looked highly smug. "Maybe I wanted it to be a surprise, like your trip, dear. Besides, I thought you were over him." Amelia started to interrupt, but her mother turned to the fridge and kept on talking, "I mean, you two broke up nine years ago, right after you left for college. You've not mentioned him in years, so I just assumed he was long forgotten. Is he looking good?"

Amelia's mouth flew open. She had not considered how long it had been. She closed her mouth abruptly, but not before her mother caught the action. "Of course, I am over him, and yes, he seems to be doing well." She did not want to discuss Ian's looks, although at six foot two, lean and muscular with sandy-brown hair and piercing grey eyes, he was what many considered dreamy. "I only meant, by my question, that it would be nice to know what all is going on in town. I mean, yes, we dated through high school, but that ended a long time ago."

Now it was her mother's turn to cut her eyes towards Amelia. A mother could always tell when her daughter was feeding her a story. Susan Allen did not believe Amelia one bit except for the "doing well" line. "You are so interested in what goes on in town, huh? I guess that is why you make so many trips down here to venture into town. Or maybe is that the reason why you call so often to discuss folks in town?"

Amelia withered under her mother's intense glare. Medusa and her snakes did not hold a candle to the ire-filled gaze of Susan Allen. Amelia felt ashamed of herself and meekly retorted, "Touché."

As dinner finished in the oven, Amelia began to set the dining room table. "Make sure you set enough for eight," her mother called out. "Your dad is bringing the new graphic designer to dinner tonight as a thank you for his hard work." Amelia added an extra spot while silently hoping that this was not another of her parents' many attempts to set her up on a date.

Initially, she had refused all of the potential suitors found by the Allen parents but eventually caved under their pressure. That was until Leo, Lucas, & Tom all turned out to be "great" catches. Leo was the one that tried to plan their wedding on the first date. She finally walked out when dessert came around, and he asked what her favorite cake flavors were. While he likely was interested in ordering their dessert, this seemed to be the straw that broke the camel's back in the context of their date.

Lucas had brought up children's names on their second date. The first one had seemed so magical that she believed this might be good for her. When he said the words, "Little Lia, named after you!" She excused herself to the restroom and never looked back. Tom had invited her over for dinner for their first date, which seemed to be romantic. He offered to make them a nice, elegant dinner to be followed with homemade cheesecake. When she arrived, she found it was an elegant candlelight dinner . . . at his mother's house with her in attendance. The food was delicious, so she stayed through the entire evening thinking the cheesecake was a terrific consolation prize. When he called her the next day, she had Bradley act like a jealous boyfriend after bribing him with hockey tickets. After that third failure, her parents were no longer allowed to set her up on any dates.

Donna, Jason's wife, had done slightly better than Amelia's

parents. She had set her up with Chase right before her wedding. Chase was Donna's younger brother who lived in Nashville and worked as a marketing specialist for a top consulting firm. They had dated from the wedding in September until February 13th. Yes, they had broken up the day before Valentine's Day. Most of her friends despised Chase for the break-up, primarily due to when it fell. None of them believed her when she said it was a mutual decision. Chase was a great gentleman and good friend, but neither could imagine a future with the other.

Amelia always remarked it was the most successful set-up, even if it ended with an undesired result. The two were very well suited for each other. She missed the many events they would jointly attend. They still occasionally ran into each other at one of the Nashville Young Professionals events. They shared a similar taste in movies and music, which made her miss going to all those types of events with him. Luckily for her, she could drag Bradley along, especially if he had irritated her. Amelia was a wizard at inter-office relationships and assisted co-workers with problems, even if her specialty was employee benefits. When it came to relationships involving the word love, though, Amelia could write a thousand stories on how not to do it, but unfortunately for her, she had yet to find one way to accomplish it.

Amelia headed upstairs to change out of her work clothes. Just like her mother, she typically cooked in older clothes and changed before eating. That made it easier if you spilled a little something or the preparation caused you to be extra warm. After slipping into something more pleasant, she decided to give Bradley a call. "You'll never guess who I ran into in town today. . . Ian!" Bradley gasped on the other end of the phone, knowing how volatile their history was. He chatted with Amelia for a while, trying to encourage her to enjoy the time off. He refused to answer any work questions.

"You've only started your vacation. Don't think about work!" The two continued to talk until Amelia heard the downstairs door close. She hopped off the call and headed to see who was here. While heading downstairs, Amelia noted how refreshing it was to hear Eric's voice fill the air. She ran behind him and grabbed her youngest brother in an enormous hug.

"Whoa, sis! Calm down a little bit. It's good to see you too!" Eric Allen grabbed his sister and gave her a real hug. Then she greeted his fiancée Emma. Emma was the younger sister of her classmate Jenna. Jenna had been her rival in practically everything during high school. They had become somewhat friends during their senior year, but Amelia adored Emma. The two of them chatted about the wedding coming next spring when Jason and Donna walked through the door. She spent time hugging and catching up with each of them before Donna pulled Amelia aside.

"I am so sorry that it did not work out between you two. Chase assured me the break-up was mutual, but I still hate that it happened." Amelia had been expecting this conversation the next time she saw Donna, but it still was slightly uncomfortable.

"It is perfectly fine, Donna. He and I are still great friends and see each other around the area. There was no harm done."

Donna smiled at her sister-in-law. "That is wonderful to hear. I know you are only in town for a short while, but I was hoping you could meet a new guy from work. His name is Ben, and he is very handsome, although please keep that to yourself. Jason has been more and more protective lately."

Amelia quirked her head at the last comment but let it pass. "Donna. . ." she started before being cut off.

"No, let me finish!" She exclaimed with a little more force than Amelia had seen before. "Sorry, I am not sure what came over me. Anyways, he is one of our new doctors and is a huge cat lover. He loves to spend time reading a good book, and he is living in Humboldt. He is very involved in the community here already and has a terrific personality."

Amelia had to admit that he sounded great by Donna's recommendation alone. "Donna, thank you, but I am not ready yet. Maybe another time." Donna looked slightly hurt but nodded her head in agreement. Just then, Roger Allen walked through the front door. "Sorry that I am a little late, everyone. Our guest will be here in about fifteen minutes. Let me put my things away, and then we can get started."

Roger Allen returned to the dining room about ten minutes later, missing the work materials he had brought home and sporting a light, thin red sweater instead of the dress shirt and tie from moments ago. Susan Allen had just called everyone to dinner and sat each in their proper place. Amelia inwardly groaned as she noted that the seat was empty next to her. She knew it made sense being the only single person at the table, but it felt more and more like a set-up.

After everyone was seated, Jason spoke up. "While it is only the family here, Donna and I want to share some news." Everyone glanced at Donna in anticipation as she pulled out a sonogram and laid it on the table. Roger and Susan Allen leaped out of their chairs with sheer joy on their faces. The first Allen grandchild was on its way, due to be here around New Year's Eve. Amelia's mind clicked all the clues into place from her conversation with Donna. It now made sense why Jason was so protective and Donna's earlier mood swing. The happy couple passed the picture all around the table, and everyone was hugging and congratulating them.

Amelia was taken aback by all the surprises today: Errands all over town, running into Ian, the conversations with both her mother and Donna and now the baby. It was one crazy day that was only about to get crazier. The doorbell rang, and Roger Allen took time away from the celebration to answer the door. Amelia was so excited that she would be an aunt and had Donna's ear asking how the pregnancy was going. A few moments later, Roger walked back into the dining room and said, "Now that our guest is here, we can eat." The Allen family settled back down and returned to their chairs. Amelia looked for the guest and realized her dad's stocky frame blocked him. As her dad moved to get his seat, the person came into complete focus. Out from behind Roger Allen was standing Ian Reynolds.

Amelia now understood why her mother was so vague in announcing who the guest was. None of her family seemed phased by his presence. "Ian, so lovely to see you again," her mother called to him. Ian smiled and hugged her mother as he sat down beside Amelia. She was taken aback at the familiarity between her mother and Ian. While Ian had spent many times in this very house, she was under the impression her mother had not seen him since he moved back. Why else would she ask if he looked good unless. . . Oh, meddling mothers.

"I thought dad invited the new graphic designer," Amelia decided to inquire of her mother. Susan glared briefly at Amelia, who couldn't care less that Ian was standing right here as she questioned her family.

"Did I fail to mention that Ian's new business is as a graphic designer? He's helping the Festival, City Hall, and several surrounding businesses and communities. He has a real talent for the work." Susan Allen said as innocently as she could manage while passing the salad bowl.

"Yes, mom, you did fail to mention that. I am surprised to see him at the house; it seems like it was so long ago when we sat here at this table together. I wouldn't think he would be coming over here any."

Jason was not as oblivious to the issues going on between his mother and sister as others might be. He, like all the rest of his family, felt as if Amelia should travel home more. Jason, like Amelia, tended to speak before thinking and decided to take his older sister to task a little bit.

"Well, Mills, if you'd get home more often, it would be a more regular occurrence to see and eat with Ian." Amelia may not have had the same death glare as her mother, but she mustered all she could as she attempted to scare Jason. Whenever he called her by that horrid childhood nickname, it meant that he was either mad at her or picking with her. The trouble was, she was unable to tell which type this could be. She considered it was likely a part of both.

"Jason, you know I am busy with work and cannot always leave. I try my best to be here for family gatherings and holidays, but with my schedule, it gets hard. Oh, and will someone explain what he means by a regular occurrence? I thought you said this was to reward his hard work, mom."

Ian sat in silence as he watched the family dynamics play out. He had become much wiser than in his high school days and for once knew when to keep silent. His ego was slightly — alright largely — bruised by her reaction. Their history had played out so long ago that he had hoped they could start over fresh. He contemplated getting up and leaving to save the family some trouble. He realized it would probably only add fuel to the fire. He and Jason had grown a lot closer since moving back. They had made amends for perceived wrongs and worked past them. He knew Jason was in a way defending his friend while criticizing the sister who was always absent.

As Amelia waited on someone to answer her question, she noticed the looks on the faces of her family. There was a mixture of disbelief in her reaction, hurt that Jason's words were valid, and shock that this was playing out at the dinner table. In regards to Jason, his face told all of his emotions. Amelia no longer had to wonder why he was using her nickname. "Well, Mills, Ian joins us for dinner most Friday nights and special occasions. It is nice to have someone here since you seem always to be working. I know that your job is important, but my friends in the state government tell me they are generous with granting time off, so either you are the only overworked state employee, since most do nothing, or you don't care about us in little Humboldt, TN. I'm guessing you don't care about us here in small-town, USA. We don't fit into your city life anymore."

"Jason Denver Allen!" Susan and Donna exclaimed at the same time. As both women began to scold Jason profusely, Amelia suddenly found she had no appetite. Instead of being filled with the delicious food, her body became overcome with a fit of raging anger burning at her brother, fiercer than ever before. She usually would have exploded on him, but the statements he made broke her heart. Everyone joked that state jobs were these cushy, pencil-pushing careers. Honestly, she dared any of her family and friends to work a day in her shoes. It was not glorious trips across the state, meetings, and tons of holidays. There were late nights, weekends, hard decisions, budget cut concerns, and more work added with staff reductions. While that irritated her, she was mostly upset by the accusation that she cared very little for her family and that Ian was here to take her place. She excused herself from the table and headed up the stairs.

Moments after locking herself in the room, she heard three knocks at the door. "Go away, Eric," she called out. She curled up on the bed and grabbed a pillow to hold. As the first tear escaped, three knocks rang out once more. "I said go away." This time the knocks came again, and her temper began to rise once more. "Eric, GO AWAY!" She knew it had to be Eric because the two of them were so close. She may not make the trip home regularly, but she talked with Eric almost daily. He would tell her how much he missed her, but he'd long given up talking about Humboldt. He learned how painful it was for her, and honestly, it was equally difficult for him to be without his sister. Her mind quickly turned off the sorrow as she wondered why he failed to warn her about Ian. What had started as one tear was now a cascade running down her face. *I was foolish to think this trip could be any different.*

It was, though, because never before would she have guessed that the heartache felt would come from inside her own family. When the knocks came one more time, she decided to confront Eric about it. He was the one family member she could take out her anger on, and he did not get belligerent back.

"Eric, what do you not understand. . ." she screeched while opening the door. Her rant ended when she came face to face with Ian.

"May I come in?" Ian asked gently.

She stood speechless but allowed him to enter the room. He glanced around, admiring the decor before settling on the bed and beckoning her over to join him. "This room has not changed one bit. There are our old pictures everywhere too." Ian was always skilled at defusing Amelia by distracting her. It was not working as efficiently this time. "Well, as you probably know, I'm never in town long enough to have noticed it before now." He pulled a photo of the two of them fishing at Lake Graham from off of the dresser. "Remember when my dad took us fishing this day? We were what, nine? I begged him not to take you because you would talk and scare all the fish away."

Amelia laughed somewhat fondly through her tear-stained face at the memory, "Is that the reason why? I thought you might have heard that country song and wanted anyone to go but a girl. Well, I seem to remember a certain young boy trying to show off on the side of the bank that day. He tossed his line out so hard that it tipped him over the bank and right into the water."

Ian grinned, "Wow. You are so young to have dementia already, seeing as that never happened." Amelia jabbed at him, and they discussed old memories. *Why am I feeling like this? It's as if we are still friends, and he's the reason my family is upset with me.* No matter the internal conflict, she could not find the anger that should be directed at him right now.

He handed her a handkerchief from his pocket so that she could cleanse her face. After all these years, he still carried one. That was something he learned from her father to always have handy. Roger taught that it could help you in some situations, but especially to let a lady use it if needed. After twenty minutes of reminiscing, she realized that yet again, he had succeeded in distracting her. It irritated her to no end that this boy — man — could get into her head that way.

"Amy, I am truly sorry for the trouble I caused tonight. I thought you knew I was coming, or at least that I was working with your dad. I am sorry to cause a rift between you and your family."

Amelia let the nickname slide. "Ian, it is partially your fault..." she smirked towards him. At first, he looked at her in slight shock and then smiled at her. "No, the fault is all mine," she continued. "I do avoid coming home and, in turn, avoid my family. I love and care for them deeply, but it has been hard coming home for short periods here and there. I am only here until Wednesday morning, and I just had hoped we could avoid this conversation. Jason is wrong because I do care, but his reasoning is right. I have been horrible to my family."

"Why are you only staying for such a short time?" Ian inquired of her. She rubbed Frank's spine and decided to ignore the question. "We need to rejoin everyone; come along." She exited the room first, and he lagged behind just a moment. He smiled fondly at the photos of their life story all around the room. She was not the only one who was hung up on the past. He took in the pictures of their senior year and felt a little shame and guilt begin to rise in his conscience. By the time he left the room, she had already walked far enough ahead down the hall that she never saw him rub Frank and say, "Susan was right. You are a pretty cat, Frank."

Chapter Four

As Amelia and Ian returned to the dinner table, tension still filled the air. The eight individuals ate the delicious dinner made by the Allen ladies in complete silence. When the time came for dessert, Susan cut a larger piece of cake for Amelia and an extremely small portion for Jason. A complaint started to leap from his mouth, but he ultimately decided it would be wise to keep quiet this time. Once the dinner ended, the group retired to the living area for some conversation.

When she had first seen Ian at the dinner table, Amelia had felt awkward. She assumed it would be the same in her return to the table, but the earlier feeling quickly seemed warm and fuzzy compared to now sitting on the loveseat with everyone else in the room staring at her. The deer in headlights look could only be effective for so long. Chivalrous Ian tried to distract the whole family, although his skill worked mainly on Amelia. After a few failed attempts, he finally made some progress. "Roger, how are things at your office? I heard you were talking of expanding."

Roger Allen shook his head out of a daze as he considered Ian's question. "Uh, yes . . . right . . . we are considering adding a marketing sector. We currently consult with a few marketing executives, but our company does not offer those services. We started with business restructuring, organizational management, and human resources. Over time, we added accounting, financial, tax consultants, and supply chain and operational logistics. The main branch we are missing is marketing. It would be wonderful to be a one-stop-shop for our clients' needs. This type of service allows our business to grow even more. Any progress for our company is progress for Humboldt." Allen Inc., over the years, had become a staple in the small community. They had sponsored countless programs and events and had brought several well-paying jobs to the moribund economy.

Roger was keeping it a secret that he had already moved forward with the expansion. His trial run had been using Ian to do graphic design work for him and several clients. The response had been excellent, and so Roger ran with the idea. He hoped Ian would consider being a permanent contractor with this section. His work was superb, and his marketing skills were outstanding even outside of graphic design.

Jason seemed engrossed in his father's words, as was Amelia. The two of them realistically were trying to avoid the other and the family's eagle eye. While Amelia was impressed in her dad's operation, she wanted nothing more than for the evening to be over. Roger Allen realized that just the two of them were listening, and he finished his talk. Ian tried again, "Mrs. Allen, those strawberry muffins were exquisite. You should consider entering them into the recipe contest at the festival."

This time Susan turned towards Ian to comment, but Amelia laughed at him first. Eric took note of his sister's laugh. He tried to remember the last time he had heard her laugh that genuine. She liked to joke and play with everyone, but there was a noticeable distinction in what he called her "half-laugh" and a laugh from her soul. If Amelia wanted everyone's eye off of her, she made the wrong decision in laughing. Everyone focused on her, and she decided that it was best to make the most of the moment.

"Ian, you think my mother's muffins could win the contest?" She inquired about her high school boyfriend.

Ian looked puzzled towards Amelia, "Yes, Amy, I do. Why is that so funny?" The family carefully turned their heads back to Amelia, considering Ian had just used her hated nickname. Like earlier, Amelia let it simply roll off of her. Ian was attempting to help her horrible situation, so she decided the guy could get off a little easier. "Ian, I think it is wonderful that you are so confident in mom's award-winning strawberry muffins."

It took Ian a few moments to piece together Amelia's exaggeration of the words "award-winning," and then it dawned on him. "Let me guess. The award was the Strawberry Festival recipe contest?"

Amelia smiled back at him, enjoying his slight discomfort, "That and the county fair, of course. I'm sure the committee would frown upon re-entry of an award-winning recipe, right mom?"

Susan Allen was a terrific chef and baker who had won the contest a time or two. Now instead of competing, she worked as the head of the event. She, as well as the whole room, laughed at the situation. Amelia gazed towards Ian, who was deep in conversation with Emma. He had diffused the case at his own expense. She figured Ian must be feigning memory loss, as she remembered how engrossed he was with her mother's muffins years ago. He was the one that convinced her to enter them one year. She always tried to go with something more extravagant and assumed the muffin recipe to be too simplistic. After his goading, her mother finally relented. Ian had worked to assist Amelia even though she had been somewhat hostile towards him since his return. Amelia's emotions continued to be conflicted, as it irritated her that he thought she needed assistance (at least to her), and she was impressed how he took a little heat on her behalf.

Ian glanced over at Amelia and caught her staring at him. He smirked as she quickly turned away from him. *It feels like we are back in high school.* Amelia wondered what today would be like if they had stayed together. Would they still complement each other? Would it be fun? Would it have ended worse than it already did?

As the evening ended, Ian excused himself to head home. Amelia walked him to the door, thanking him for his assistance this evening. "Ian, I appreciate what you did tonight. I wanted to offer for us to grab a bite to eat tomorrow and maybe work towards civility?" It took a lot out of her to admit this to the bane of her existence for years now. He carefully considered her words and replied, "Amy, I too want to start over. Can we do lunch tomorrow, and we will talk then?" Amelia agreed to meet him the following afternoon for lunch. Considering her options and feelings, she failed to catch that he had called her once again by her nickname.

Once Ian had left the Allen home, Amelia headed back towards the living area only to be stopped by Jason, "Can we talk?"

Amelia wanted nothing more than to avoid her brother after his statements tonight. Her heart was on the verge of breaking due to his horrible accusations, but she knew that ignoring him would only add fuel to the fire. She beckoned him into their father's library, and the two siblings began to discuss what had happened earlier.

"I went too far. It is frustrating only to see you at random times throughout the year. I miss my sister and wish you were here more often." Jason was trying not to look Amelia in the eye. She was unsure at the moment if it was because he was truly upset or if looking at her might rekindle his anger.

"How could you think I don't care about this family?" Amelia heard how heartfelt he had sounded in his almost apology, but she was not caving and admitting her wrong that easily. She was deeply hurt and wanted him to know.

"I used the wrong words, Amelia. I was mad and frustrated at you for questioning why Ian was here. What else could I say? You rarely come home, and yet Ian comes by regularly. Did you know that his parents moved to New England to be with his sister's family? When Ian moved back, all he had was local friends. He always felt like a part of this family, so when dad ran into him in town, Ian received a standing invitation to join us. Did you know that for the first month, he refused to attend? Only when mom found and coaxed him into attending did he show. He was worried that something like tonight would happen just by his presence."

"After all that he did to me, after the heartache and the pain, you just let him eat here like family?"

Jason sighed. "Mom explained that there's always more to the picture. It took a little time, but eventually, Eric and I were comfortable being with him. It felt like something was always missing, and while it was never the same without you here, having him seemed a little bit more normal."

Amelia considered all that her brother had just revealed. It must have been hard for Ian moving back to town with no family left here. She attempted to see her brother's reasoning. It was as if she took their family for granted when Ian's was miles and miles away. "You have yet to explain how you think I don't care about this family."

"Amelia," his voice called as he lifted his head and stared directly into her eyes, "It was a poor choice of words. I know that if something happened to one of us, you would be here in a quick minute. Instead of not caring, maybe considering us an inconvenience is a better statement." Before she could interrupt with her anger, he simply continued, "Eric is your closest family member, and I understand why. You two have always been inseparable with all of the similarities between you. I think it hurt Eric when you were not here for the engagement. I know you saw him in Nashville a week later, but he wanted his entire family here for the weekend, and yet you made up an excuse not to come. In that moment, I realized that you must dislike us for something we did, or there was something more important than us at play. If you failed to come home for Eric, what chance did I have when we announced the pregnancy? Then, just to my surprise, mom stated you were coming in today, and Donna and I agreed it would be the perfect time. I suspect mom used guilt to bring you home since she described an awkward phone call with you. No matter the reason, I was grateful to know my entire family would be here for this occasion. Then just as soon as we have shared our wonderful news and sit down to dinner, you act like a spoiled child. You are never here, and you had the nerve to complain to mom and dad about the guest they asked into their home. I just had to say something."

Amelia stood in shock at her brother's words. While these words were tamer, they had cut her heart even more than the last. A tear rolled down her left cheek, and Jason immediately regretted this conversation. He sat down in one of the chairs and folded his head into his hands. "Here I go making everything worse. Amelia, I am trying to tell you why I feel this way. I want my sister back more than just once or twice a year, if that. I want my child to have their joke-loving, fun, inspiring aunt in their life. I am not trying to upset you, but you need to know how we all feel."

Amelia's family had been mostly quiet about her frequent disappearances. Like most Southern families, they were upset yet tight-lipped. It was easier to ignore the problem and bottle up the feelings than to face it head-on. Most Southerners kept issues to themselves. As a child, you learned to solve your own problems and not burden anyone else, including other family members. She could tell that her family was trying not to upset her, but her short trip likely upset them in reality. Her mother would disagree, being happy for even a moment with her daughter, but all would wish that she come for regular trips. It may seem almost like teasing with a spontaneous trip here or there and no commitment to being fully involved with this family.

"Jason," Amelia started with a shaky voice, "I hurt you and everyone. I have only been concerned with how I feel about this town. It is hard coming back to town as if nothing happened. I envisioned my future here until all of those plans got shredded to pieces. I am sorry for the decisions I've made, but maybe we can work together on being a better family?"

Jason half-smiled at his sister. "I would like that, Amelia, but forgive me for being hesitant towards a total reconciliation until I see how things will improve. As mom and dad have always taught us, actions speak louder than words." Amelia inwardly hurt that her brother could not yet fully trust her but nodded her head in agreement. The two left the library better than they had entered and went to rejoin the family. Everyone stopped talking as soon as the two re-entered the room. Anticipation filled the air as everyone wanted to see if the two siblings had reconciled.

As the eldest Allen siblings sat down, neither spoke. After an eternity — or at least that is how it seemed — Susan questioned her children. "Did you apologize to your sister?" Before Jason could comment and complain that the blame was always on him, Amelia spoke up first, "We apologized to each other and made amends." Susan nodded her head sharply, glad that her children were working through their issues. The room delved back into several conversations, and Amelia went over to take Eric's attention.

"So, little brother. Any reason why you failed to mention Ian Reynolds in our regular talks? It seems like the two of you have been having dinner together a lot." Eric took in his sister's face for a moment before responding. "Well, I could have told you, true. I seem to remember you failing to take me to TPAC as promised for a show. I decided I'd rather see this one play out in front of me when you found out. It was a true tear-jerker. I was deeply moved by you tonight, although I think you forgave him way too easily. I never liked that in stories, so you only get four stars for the performance." Amelia slugged him with a throw pillow as he grinned in triumph. "Cheeky, now are you? How would you like me to tell Emma about what was her name again, Sarah? I think Emma would love to hear how you declared your undying love through song in the ninth grade." Now was Eric's turn to bash Amelia with a pillow, "Brat."

"How do you feel about being in town with Ian?" Eric asked once the two had stopped laughing and play fighting. This was a complicated question. Amelia glanced around the room and saw that everyone was deep in their conversations. She gazed at the ceiling before settling back on her brother. "It feels weird. You know that I normally avoid coming home because it is too painful. All around town today, especially after running into him, I saw our memories. Then tonight, we get along as if nothing ever happened. I even agreed to lunch tomorrow with him to try and bury the hatchet. I want to be able to come home more often, so I am trying to move on from the past."

Eric sat in silence for a few moments. Amelia was about to speak again when he finally commented. "Amelia, I know that things ended badly between the two of you, but give him a chance to explain. I want you to have no regrets after discussing the situation with him. You know, more than one heart was involved in your relationship. Maybe his was hurt too." Amelia raised one eyebrow at her brother. She never imagined that Eric, of all people, would be arguing Ian's side of the situation. Before she could comment, Eric ruffled her hair and stood. "Enjoy your date tomorrow." He smirked and dodged as she launched another pillow in his direction.

The following day, Amelia awoke at 7:00 a.m. Throughout the night; she had tossed and turned more than a boat on rocky waters. Her mind refused to shut down as she contemplated the argument with Jason, the conversation with Eric, but especially the upcoming lunch with Ian. Leaping into the shower, Amelia attempted to find some vigor for the day. As the showerhead blasted her with ice-cold water, her body jumped, and she became definitively more alert.

She changed outfits only five times this morning. She simply did not care for one; another was too loose; one was basic; the last was highly flirtatious. Eventually, she settled for something in the middle. As she headed down the stairs for a quick shake, several thoughts ran through her mind: *Why am I even concerned with what I wear? Remember Amelia — this is a meeting between old friends, not a date. Be careful not to fall for his charm. He can be a friend, but nothing more. Don't be a fool!*

Likely, her mind would have continued to slip down this path if not for her accidentally tripping over Frank. Once again, he cried his displeasure, and her mother came from around the corner. "Oh, you poor dear, are you ok?" Amelia had caught herself and straightened up, "Yes, mom. I am . . ." Amelia trailed off when she saw her mother walking away holding Frank and rubbing him with loads of affection. *Look at that. I almost fall, and my mother is more concerned over the cat.*

Amelia mixed her shake, which seemed to be extra delicious. These locally grown strawberries had the best flavor. No one could come close to Green Acres strawberries. After cleaning her small mess, she headed out the door and into town. Amelia decided to head over to her father's company and visit her soon-to-be sister-in-law at work. Emma was the head human resources consultant's executive assistant. Her dad was actually in the process of revamping the human resources sector of the company. They had grown to the point of having fifty employees. With the proposed expansion, they had already brought in a few contractors, like Ian, and hired another five staffers. His current plans were to have a staff of sixty-five by summer in addition to the contractors.

For the past few years, the head human resources consultant for their clients doubled as the internal director of HR for Allen Inc. With the continued growth, Roger wanted to split the position into a dedicated director who consulted on occasion and a head consultant. Mr. Timmons, the current head consultant, did a fantastic job, but he was not always well-liked. He had moved to the little town of Humboldt three years ago from New York City as one of Roger Allen's newest recruits. While being a terrific consultant, his northern politics and mannerisms did not always align with southern ones. His brash attitude could rub their clients and other employees the wrong way on the best of days.

Amelia smiled at the front desk receptionist and thanked her for directing her path to Emma's office. "How is my favorite almost sister-in-law today?" Amelia called out to lure Emma up from a stack of papers. "I'm still your only almost sister-in-law Amelia unless another Allen boy is hiding in the background. That, or you finally found someone to marry! What brings you here?"

The two chatted for a while over random events. Eventually, their conversation led to Jason's outburst last night and how Donna had informed Emma that he was in the proverbial dog house for the foreseeable future. Emma also told Amelia that her father had posted the job description for the new human resources director this morning. Amelia was so glad to hear that her father's plan was coming together. Amelia was about to head out to meet Ian for lunch when Mr. Timmons barreled out of his office. "Emma, send this over to Roger ASAP!" With that quick order, he was gone. Emma waved goodbye to Amelia and headed over to the chamber to deliver the envelope she'd received.

Amelia drove over to the former Red Door Cafe. Someone

had painted the door with new signage all around. What had once been the cafe was now the town's Italian restaurant. Inside, Ian was waiting for her. He had dressed in a bright, bold blue dress shirt with grey slacks. She was briefly taken aback by how handsome the man before her was. He beckoned her over to his table, and she sat down to join him. "I went ahead and ordered for you. I hope that is alright."

"A little presumptuous if you ask me. Who says that my taste buds are the same as when we were together?" Amelia said with a little too much snark. Seeing the look on his face, she chastised herself. *Way to work towards civility.* So far, her wish at resolving old issues was right on a track to crash. The salads had come and gone with little discussion. If anyone were listening to their conversation, it would almost appear as if two strangers had sat at the same table in a crowded restaurant to avoid a long wait. In reality, the tables were pretty scarce on a Tuesday afternoon. The silence of the restaurant only amplified the awkward setting.

Amelia decided that it was time to take the strawberry by the cap. "Ian, we came here to resolve our issues." Ian took several drinks of his sweet iced tea before making any acknowledgment of her statement. "I hope the food is about ready." Amelia was getting annoyed at him for avoiding the conversation. "Ian, for the sake of my family, I think we should at least discuss what happened." Ian snorted at her, "I'd like to move past the mistakes of our youth. Before yesterday, I cannot recall hearing your voice or even a text message in the last nine years. I am almost certain that the last time we did have a conversation, you told me to never speak to you again. While I know I made several mistakes, including one large one, I thought we'd at least talk again."

Amelia's temper was rearing its ugly head. Her face would have matched the festival decorations if she had only dyed her hair green. "Don't call me Amy. I have not used that nickname in years. My name is Amelia, and Ian, I was crazy about you. We had grown up together, spent holidays with each other's family, were sweethearts as everyone would say, and I thought we were going to keep experiencing life together. Can you imagine how I felt once college started and you never showed at Belmont? How about when I called you, and you refused to answer the phone? Can you imagine my surprise when I learned my best friend had changed universities right before the semester began and never told me? I never understood why you were mad at me or what I had done, and then I get a letter saying goodbye. There was no explanation other than you just didn't feel like being with me anymore. You broke my heart. You wanted me to speak to you again? Why? Why should I have gone down that road when it led only to hurt memories?"

Ian could not meet her eyes. "Refusing to use the nickname I gave you? You always loved being called by it, and maybe I handled things the wrong way. I truly am sorry for hurting you the way that I did. If it is any consolation, my mother scolded me fiercely before grounding me, and I was away at college! If I was any closer, I imagine I would have felt a few switches too. She could not believe that she'd raised a child who would act that way." Amelia smiled very meagerly at the scene. It satisfied her to know that Mrs. Reynolds had given him plenty of grief, but her heart still hurt. Still not meeting her eyes, he asked another question, "Why have you taken so long to return to Humboldt on a non-holiday? Everyone has mentioned that you never come around anymore."

Ian finally faced Amelia as he awaited her answer. When she caught him staring, she decided it was her time to glance away. "It was too painful. I left here full of passion and dreams, and you stole that, Ian. A couple of times, I did come home freshman year, everywhere, and everyone around town reminded me of us. It was hard enough being here and experiencing everyone's sympathy. You know how this town is. Everyone knows everything. People thought you and I would be married with kids at this point. It was hard to see all the faces as if somehow, we were letting everyone down by not being together. Then, Bailey Park, where we used to jog, or the library where we would sit for hours under the dogwood. How could I forget about all the dinners at local restaurants or playing ball over by the old armory? Then there was where we grew up at church together, and well, you get the picture. Every place reminded me of you, and with each memory came more pain. Now, it brings me sadness and anger. I cannot believe that I let our silly teenage romance control my adult life. I'm filled with anger at myself for giving power over to you even years after our end."

Ian could no longer stare at Amelia. When she glanced back, she saw the shame and despair on his face. She cared little for upsetting him as she needed to say what was on her mind.

"This was the first trip where from the beginning I started to feel at ease. Honestly, it feels like I'm back in freshman year, and everything is bubbling to the surface. I want to see my hometown friends. I want to be able to enjoy spending time with my family. For years I thought I needed to move on from Humboldt, but I just needed to move on from you."

Ian watched the birds flying by outside and muttered, "Never thought you'd let anyone get in your way, especially me." After saying all she wanted and needed to say, Amelia seemed a lot calmer. His words, however, took her ire back to full force. "Then I guess you never did know me."

Ian jerked his head in her direction. "Amelia, whether you think so or not, I have always known you better than anyone else."

Amelia scoffed at his remark, her anger dissipating. "You sure knew how to show it."

Ian rose from the table just as the food was arriving. "I see now that no matter how I apologize, you will always hold this against me. That is my cross to bear but do not for one moment think that

I still don't know you. We may have had our bad times, but we also had a lot of great ones." He handed the waiter some cash, asked for a to-go carton, and quickly stuffed it with his meal. "I don't think I'm hungry anymore. Amelia, have a nice trip home."

As he went to exit the building, Amelia called out, "You always run from your problems. I see nothing has changed." Ian sauntered back over to their table and stared at Amelia with a look she could not quite figure out. "I see you still don't know me. Oh, and Amelia, for the record: I'm not the one running away tomorrow; I'm still in town. One last thing — your heart was not the only one involved in our relationship. Sometimes saying goodbye is just as hard, Amy." With his final words spoken, he rushed out of the building and walked down the sidewalk.

Amelia considered his words and then finally decided she would not waste the food. As she glanced down at what the waiter had brought to their table, she found herself genuinely shocked. Looking down, her eyes stared at a small bowl of three cheese tortellini soup with a side of antipasto squares filled with pepperoni, salami, pepperoncini, and her favorite cheeses. She asked the waiter how long they had served the antipasto squares this way. He remarked that the gentleman special ordered them and the soup. The chef was happy to oblige due to the small crowd and figured the connoisseur having the meal was someone with impeccable taste. As the waiter walked away, she sat in an even deeper level of shock.

The sight of the dish before her transported her back to a dozen years ago, seated around Ian's grandmother's kitchen table. *"Amy, here is my signature soup just for you, my dear." Amelia was never the type to happily try new dishes, but Ian had encouraged her into trying this dish. "Amy, you'll like it, I promise." She spooned a small amount into her mouth and was overwhelmed with the delicious flavors. She began happily devouring the bowl before her. Constantine,*

Ian's grandmother, smiled as she sat down the antipasto squares. "Ian told me all about your favorite foods. Give this a try as well." Amelia eagerly agreed and was amazed by the flavors. "This is delicious, thank you." As the meal ended and Ian cleared the table, Amelia talked with Constantine. "You know, my dear, all my grandson ever talks about is you. He spent all day yesterday quizzing me on what I was preparing to ensure you would like it." Amelia blushed and thanked the lady for her hospitality. Every time Amelia visited Constantine after that, the two enjoyed soup and the antipasto squares.

Amelia took the first bite, and more memories of days past flooded her mind.

Chapter Five

*A*melia's mind was still spinning after she returned home from the unusual lunch. Her mother asked her how the day had gone, but Amelia was in such a daze she missed her mother's words. Somehow she ended upstairs, sitting on her bed. Finally reawakening, she decided to grab the wooden box hidden in the sock drawer. It was a beautiful cedar jewelry box with a heart carved on the top. She opened the box and took in the contents: her grandmother's emerald ring, a few pairs of strawberry items, a folded piece of paper, and a beautiful oval garnet ring. This piece of jewelry was a simple silver band with the garnet held just right by the ring's design.

She used to wear it so much that people assumed her birthday fell in January due to the stone. Those individuals would be wrong in their assumption. Her fingers delicately caressed the ring, and she decided to try it on for just a moment. As she slipped the ring on her finger, more memories flooded her mind.

A distant voice called, "Garnet symbolizes friendship and trust." *The memory seemed so distant and yet so close at the same time. She had replied to the voice, "It also happens to be your birthstone." The other figure had laughed and slipped the ring on her finger. "Well, then call it a promise."* In her memory, she giggled as she lifted her hand for the gem to catch the light. *"A promise for what?"* The image became more apparent as she noticed Ian's face pop into view, *"A promise of me. Trust that your best friend loves you and wants to promise himself to you."* The two had hugged and kissed the remainder of the afternoon. She had been thrilled to show everyone the promise ring.

Amelia quickly tugged the ring off of her finger and laid it back in the box, wondering why she had held onto it for so long. The item was nothing more than a reminder of broken, empty promises. Her mind was attempting to show her Ian's romantic side, but she wanted no part in that. Slamming the box shut, she stashed it back in the drawer. Attempts to reach Bradley were futile as he was busy with a work project. She had forgotten that it was the middle of his workday, pleasantly surprised by her ease at having time off.

Amelia headed downstairs, where she found her mother hard at work. As Amelia approached the busy woman, she was astounded to see how frail Susan was looking. "Mom, is everything ok?"

Susan smiled up at her daughter, and her body seemed to improve physically. She caressed her daughter's face, "Of course, dear. Now, how was lunch?"

Amelia chose not to go into too much detail. She could tell that her mother knew there was much more to the story but was glad when the woman decided not to pry. "Mom, you look like you are a little under the weather. Are you sure everything is alright?"

Her mother turned towards her stovetop to begin the evening meal. "Yes, dear, it just takes a little more effort to do things now and then. I'm not as young as I once was, you know."

Amelia accepted the answer but only for a moment. Her mother could be as stubborn as she was, and there would be no use in discussing this any further. She decided to try and interrogate her brothers to find out their impression of the Allen matriarch. Amelia noticed the time and decided to head over to Lou's. She pulled into the red-bricked home just ten minutes later. It was amazing how quickly you could reach someone across town in Humboldt. It would have taken her at least twenty minutes to get half as far as she had today in Nashville. She could not wait to meet the twin girls. Amelia hardly ever checked her Facebook, and other than being told of the new children, she did not even know their names.

Lou called from inside, "It's open, come on in!" Amelia walked into the home and took sight of Lou attempting to bottle feed both kids at once. She rushed over to grab a child and a bottle to help out. Lou thanked her for the help. "It gets hard at times. Tonight, they both started crying at the same time for food. I try to do what I can, but sometimes I just want to join in on their crying session." Amelia felt bad for Lou and was determined to help while she could tonight. It had to be hard being alone while raising two twin two-month-olds. *Lou is an amazing woman to be doing this so Justin can serve our country.* The baby in Amelia's arms seemed to take to her quickly. Lou looked over and smiled at her old friend. "That's a good picture of you two. I wish I had extra hands to take a picture." Amelia smiled and promised to have a picture taken before leaving town.

Amelia watched and admired her friend's mothering skills. Lou took extreme care in tending to her babies. Amelia wondered what it would be like to be a mother one day. She knew her time would eventually come, but she hated hearing the inside clock ticking away. She decided to bring herself out of her self-induced pity party and asked, "So which darling do each of us have?"

Lou smiled brightly down at the bundle in her arms. "This is Kathryn Jane after my mother and Justin's sister." Amelia loved the names and smiled adoringly at the infant. Lou glanced over at Amelia, and her smile seemed to magnify. "You are holding Daphne Amelia, after Justin's mother and the closest person I have to a sister."

It was good that Amelia was sitting while rocking the child. Amelia froze, thankful to not be standing lest the child fall to the floor. No one had mentioned to her that she was a child's namesake. How could such important news not reach her? Had distancing herself from the town led to missing essential milestones in the lives of her friends?

Tears welled up in her eyes as she thanked Lou. She didn't trust herself to speak, so she merely mouthed the words. Emotions ran rampant inside of her body. She felt a special connection to this little girl and wanted to be a good role model. She thought if someone named their child after her, then the least she could do was put forth the best example for them. Then she considered that this child was already two months old, and she did not even know they shared a name. She wondered if the lack of trips home was stopping them from already having a relationship. The emotions did not end there. How could they when someone just called you a sister, and you have hardly spoken to them over the last decade? What type of role model was she currently, and how could she continue this way?

Amelia decided to save her plans for redemption until later and instead cherished the current moments with her now pseudo-nieces. Once the children had settled down and fallen asleep, the two ladies loaded them into their cribs. Lou informed Amelia that instead of having take-out, she had decided to make her chicken casserole. Amelia immediately agreed that Lou's casserole was a better option. The local grill had a fantastic menu, but nothing could beat the home-cooked meal of Lou Hart. The two ate their dinner and reminisced about their high school days. Lou told Amelia all about married life with Justin, and it was evident that Lou loved him with all of her heart.

The two retired to the couch after dinner, and Lou was ready for some more vigorous conversation. "Alright, Amelia. I've told you all about my life, so now it is your turn. How's life in Nashville?" Amelia smiled at her friend. The evening now felt like the old slumber parties where they would sit and share about all of their life issues. Amelia started to tell Lou all about her Nashville life. She spoke of her boss, work, and friends before telling funny stories of times in Chicago and moving back to Tennessee. She showed pictures of Frank and spoke of all the arguments she would have with the feisty cat. Lou laughed and smiled like an old friend would and then decided to take the "slumber party" to the next level. "Alright, alright, that is enough work and general talk. You sound like an old maid. How about your love life?"

Amelia snorted and said, "Talking about that will solidify me as an old maid." Lou could hardly believe it was that bad. Amelia began with Chase, and by the time she'd gotten to the trio of dates set by her parents, Lou was crying with laughter. Lou thought that Chase sounded intriguing from the start and was disappointed to hear that it did not work out. She could not believe how bad Amelia's luck had been in the dating world. "You didn't mention Ian," she carefully stated. "I went to lunch with him a few weeks ago, and he wouldn't say anything about the two of you. The whole town knows there is bad blood there, but you've never told even me about it."

Amelia wondered when this would stop getting brought up. She was tired of the Ian situation and ready to move past it. As much as she told herself these statements, she did want to talk to someone about today's events. Ian Reynolds had sent her mind into orbit with all that happened. Lou saw the trepidation on her friend and asked her to start at why the two broke up.

"Honestly, Lou, I still have no idea where things went wrong. You know that we had planned to go to Belmont together, graduate with business degrees and then look for work back in this area. He had even given me a promise ring, I think you saw it, and we planned to be married right after our college graduation. The day before we planned to move, he kissed me and said that he loved me more than anything in the world. The next morning my parents moved me into the dorm, and I texted Ian to see if he was settling into his room. He never responded, so I walked across campus to his dorm to see if he'd checked in yet. The head RA informed me that there was no Ian Reynolds on his roster. I tried calling Ian, but he never picked up. My dad finally got ahold of Ian's parents, and they informed us that Ian had changed his enrollment at the last minute. They had just settled him into his dorm in Knoxville. When dad handed me the phone to speak to him, all I heard was a dial tone. A week later, there was a note in my campus mailbox with a postmark of Knoxville, TN. I ripped it open, eager to hear any news. Inside was a letter stating that our relationship was just a fling and that he couldn't be with me anymore. I tore the letter to shreds and sobbed into my pillow for hours. My entire future had vanished before my eyes."

Lou was utterly heartbroken at Amelia's story. She could never imagine Ian being so calloused towards Amelia. She saw the way he looked whenever someone mentioned her name. His face was always a mixture of remorse and desire. "So, I guess that's why you never come home."

Amelia felt no accusation in the statement but rather understanding. "I've never felt so bad in my life. Then when I came home for fall break, Thanksgiving, Christmas, and spring break, it was too painful. Ever since that spring break, I have limited my time in this city, which has led to fights with my family and losing touch with dear friends." Amelia filled her in on the drama that had occurred at the Allen home the previous evening. Lou noticed how Amelia described Ian's presence, assistance in dealing with the issues, and him in general.

"So that means you had lunch today with Ian," Lou commented

as she innocently sipped from her glass. It was times like these that Amelia wished she had something more substantial than strawberry lemonade. Amelia told Lou all about the lunch and argument that had ensued, including Ian's cryptic statements and even the meal description. "Amelia, it almost seems as if you're mad at him one moment, missing him the next and daydreaming about him in between."

Amelia burrowed herself into the couch and let out a groan of frustration. "That is precisely what is going on, and I cannot stop it." Lou patted her friend's knee while trying to stop herself from laughing. Amelia seemed like a high school kid again, confused by her feelings. Lou figured Amelia was still fascinated with Ian deep down beneath all those levels of heartache. She comforted her friend and played the role of a sounding board. Eventually, though, she was unable to continue the silent method once Amelia asked for her advice.

"I think you miss your old friend Amelia. Remember that before you two dated, you were the best of friends. The two of you got into more trouble as kids than the whole rest of our class and would constantly pull pranks on teachers and family members, and each cast suspicion on the other. It was years before people realized you were a team. From the time you met as kids, you were inseparable. I was your closest female friend, and I can count on my hand the number of times we spent together without him present. No one was closer than the two of you, and when he broke your heart, you lost your best friend. Just remember, though, he lost his too."

"Why does everyone keep bringing that up? He broke my heart, not the other way around. Everyone wants me to feel sorry that he broke my heart. Why?" Lou stared at her friend, deciding the best way to tackle that question.

"No one has ever looked at me the way Ian looked at you except my husband. Everyone in town saw how deeply in love he was with you. I would almost wager he still loves you even all these years later. True love never ends. It must have been hard for him to break up with you, and I'm sure that letter was a completely false reason. I guess that he was too afraid to share the real reason behind the split. Remember that while he was probably wrestling with the decision, he couldn't speak to his best friend because it involved her." Suddenly one of the girls cried out after waking up from the short sleep.

"Well, the therapy session is over. Time to be a mom again." Lou laughed as she rose from the couch. Amelia sat in silence, taking in all that Lou had shared tonight. She considered that things weren't always black and white. Then and there, Amelia resolved to try and move past her hurt feelings and visit more often. As the other girl cried out, she rose to help her friend. After settling the children back into their cribs, she hugged her friend and promised to visit again soon.

The next morning came quickly for Amelia. She rose from her bed and began to pack her bags. She lugged them down the stairs to see her mother holding Frank and her father eating breakfast. "I'm going to miss you so much," her mother said to the cat while rubbing his chin.

"What, not going to miss your daughter?" Her mother laughed and sat Frank down on the floor to hug her. Amelia loaded her car with all but Frank. She decided to take a quick trip down to the Art Exhibit for a short walk-through before leaving. Returning to the Allen family home from the art gallery, it took only a few moments to load Frank back into the car. She could have sworn that he was more displeased in leaving than he had been on their trip to Humboldt. In some ways, she felt similar. Her mother made her promise to call after she got home. Susan reminded her daughter that she would be at the ladies' Bible study during lunchtime and leave her a message. Amelia pulled out of her parents' driveway and headed down the road.

Amelia stopped in Jackson for what she hoped would be a special treat. One of the benefits of coming home was she could stop at one of West Tennessee's premier bakeries, located near the interstate, for some delicious desserts. Only after pulling into the parking area did she remember that the bakery was closed on Wednesdays. *Maybe I can come by here on my next trip to town.* As she drove back to Nashville, she was already considering another trip home. She figured the best way to move past the trouble was to face it instead of hiding in another city.

Traffic on the interstate was moving at an incredible pace. As Amelia reached the Benton County line, she began to consider coming back for perhaps a day or two of the Festival. She figured spending time at her favorite event would be great therapy for her soul. There was slight worry over running into Ian again, but Amelia figured the odds were better since the town would have so many more people. This time, she would make sure it was a surprise for her family. She figured this would also help them all in moving forward.

Amelia had made it past the exit for I-840 when her car's Bluetooth began to ring. She noticed the caller-id was Eric and gladly picked up the phone. "I've only been gone for two hours, and you miss me already?"

"Amelia," he started, but she kept going.

"Oh, don't tell me I forgot something. I have almost made it home."

This time Eric loudly interrupted his sister. "Amelia, there's been an accident. You need to come home right away." Amelia's happiness drained in an instant. She nearly hit a car herself in losing awareness of her surroundings. The words created a tunnel vision, and she decided to pull over into the emergency lane out of safety.

"What happened? Who's hurt, and where are y'all?" Millions of other questions ran through her mind, but these were the best and most important starting place.

"Mom was leaving her Bible study, and all we know is that someone found her car smashed into a large oak tree. They've taken her to the Jackson hospital, and she is currently in surgery. I just got to the hospital with dad, and Jason and Donna are on their way. Emma is finishing things at the office and then headed here. I thought it best if you heard from me."

Amelia thanked Eric for the information and stopped everything to pray for her mother. "Lord, please heal my mother. I promise to be a better daughter to her. Please give me the opportunity to do so." Amelia got back onto the interstate and turned around at the next exit to head west.

The drive to the hospital seemed much longer than any she'd taken before. With every mile, her mind wandered with thoughts of horrible outcomes. She worried over her mother and the whole family and continued to pray to God. She arrived in Jackson and found difficulty in parking. As she exited the car, she saw Lou getting into a car. Lou looked shocked to see Amelia here, and with the look on Amelia's face, she knew it couldn't be good news. Lou had just left visiting her uncle in the hospital. Amelia caught her up on the situation, and she offered to say plenty of prayers for Susan. When Lou asked if she could do anything to help, Amelia asked her to take Frank, to which she happily obliged.

Amelia ran into the hospital to find her family. The hospital had set them up in a private room awaiting information from the trauma surgeon. She hugged each family member and sat holding hands with Eric and Jason. Roger Allen admired his three children comforting each other, but he worried more and more for his wife with each passing moment. Susan had been in surgery for four hours when they finally got word that the surgeon was making good progress. His nurse informed the family that he would go over all of the injuries after the surgery.

"Allen Family?" A police officer entered the waiting room.

Roger and his children gathered around the officer. "I'm the responding officer to Mrs. Allen's accident."

"Thank you, officer, for helping my wife. Do you know what happened?"

"From eyewitnesses, she was driving down the road, not swerving or showing any issues. Suddenly, the car veered off to the side of the road before entering someone's yard and striking the tree. One of the eyewitnesses ran to her aid and noted that she seemed dazed. We are unsure if she fell asleep at the wheel or if the dizzy feeling was due to the accident itself. Have you noticed any issues with her lately?"

The family talked about how pale she had looked and tired she was. "She has a lot on her, and she often doesn't rest as much as she should."

The officer nodded his head. "I'll wait to hear from the doctor, but it seems as if this is all just a bad accident." Roger pulled his children aside, and they chatted about Susan's health. The four agreed to try and work on getting Susan to relax a little more and help with her jobs."

"Officer, the bystander who helped her, what do you know about him?"

Once the officer had rejoined the family, he shared, "The man helped your wife tremendously. She had a deep wound on her forehead, and he tore his shirt to use as a make-shift wrap to stop the bleeding. The paramedics told us that she could have lost a lot of blood if not for his reaction. He wanted to follow us here to the hospital, but being the only eyewitness that approached the vehicle, we had to question him about the accident."

After six and a half long hours of surgery, the nurse finally called to say Susan was in recovery. The family anxiously awaited the doctor's visit. Almost thirty minutes later, the doctor came through to share his notes. "Mrs. Allen appears to have passed out from dehydration and low blood sugar. My best guess is she has not been watching her diet and has been overworking herself. I need you all to be watching her, or else the next time, things might end worse. She will make a full recovery, but she's got a long road ahead. The gash on her forehead was pretty deep, but we were able to stitch it up. Someone tried to stop the bleeding, and thankfully they did a good job. She could have lost a lot of blood from that wound. She has a broken femur in one leg as well as a damaged tibia in the other. The accident smashed one of her hands which resulted in several broken bones. She has bruised and cracked ribs. She will need to be immobile for a couple of weeks, and then she can start working through therapy. We will evaluate her in the morning and go from there." Roger Allen thanked the doctor for all of his work as he left the room.

The police officer finished gathering all the needed information and informed the family he would send them a copy of the crash report. Jason spoke up to ask for the name of the bystander. He felt as if the family should thank the gentleman for his assistance with their mother. The officer flipped through his notepad before finally finding the gentleman's information. He handed the pad over for Jason to copy down the information. Amelia glanced a peek at the note pad and to her surprise, it read, *Ian Reynolds*.

Chapter Six

Susan Allen did not awake until the following day. Amelia spent the night propped up in a chair beside her bed while Roger Allen laid across the couch. Amelia had sent her brothers and their loved ones home to rest while agreeing to take the night watch with their father. She barely got any sleep. One would think a hospital to be a peaceful place at night so that patients could rest, but there were always alarms and bells going off down the hall. Though weary from the long night, Amelia continued stroking her mother's hand while taking in the image of her hurt mother. She wished she had pressed her mother hard the last few days and learned about the trouble. Hearing her family members talk, it seemed Susan had not been well in months. The news was yet another blow to Amelia's self-esteem. She wondered if she had made more regular trips home, could this have been seen and treated in time.

When Susan awoke, it was only for a moment. She smiled at her daughter and rested once more. Roger told Amelia to take a walk around the hospital and stretch her legs. Amelia agreed and walked down the hall to where she knew there was a coffee pot. Halfway down the hall, there was a room with a sign that read *chapel*. She remembered the Humboldt Hospital having one across from the cafeteria, but she could not recall seeing one ever on a patient floor.

Deciding to walk into the room, Amelia sat down to pray. She prayed for guidance and a healed heart, knowing that her life needed change. This trip had shown her several hard truths in more ways than one. Throughout the long night, Amelia wrestled with what to do. Deciding to turn it over to God, Amelia promised to do what it takes to help her family. There were so many things she wanted to make right, starting with her mother. She thanked God that she still had an opportunity, and as she considered what the outcome could have been, tears rolled down her face. She dried her eyes and decided before leaving the room to add, "Thank you, God, for Ian."

Amelia returned to the room with two coffees in hand, one for herself and her dad. She figured Roger had no idea how long she had been gone as he hadn't commented one bit. She took in how her father was caressing her mother's face and patting her arm. Despite the circumstance, Amelia's heart delighted in her father's love, care, and compassion. She still considered how thoughtful and sweet he was to care for his wife like this. Here was the picture of true love staring her right in the face.

Eric stopped in a little while later. He finally persuaded Amelia to let Emma give her a ride home and get some rest. Eric had decided to take the late-morning to early-afternoon shift, and Jason would come after work to switch out. He asked Amelia if she needed to get back to Nashville, and she loudly refused to leave until they knew more. Emma drove Amelia's car home while Amelia slept in the passenger seat. The drive only took around twenty minutes, but all of the stress had finally caught up with her.

When she awoke several hours later, Amelia's memory was blank on leaving the car and getting into bed. She rolled over to see a note from Emma on the dresser, "I turned off your phone so that you *could get some rest. If there's any major news, I will bring it over myself. Your mother will be fine; you know how much she likes a good fight."*

Amelia smiled at the note and decided to take a quick shower. Twenty minutes later, she was dressed and back downstairs. She wandered into the kitchen to fix some food not only for her but also for her family. She bagged up a few sandwiches while talking with Bradley over the phone. The care and concern he showed for her family warmed her heart. She mentioned Ian, and he began to question until she realized how late it was getting. After promising to catch up with him later, she headed out the door to bring Frank back home before heading to the hospital.

Upon arrival at the hospital, Amelia was pleased to learn her mother was in a step-down room. She eagerly made her way up to the new space. Inside, Susan Allen was awake and talking with Jason, who had gotten off early. Roger was asleep on the couch, and Amelia was grateful that her father was getting some rest. "Now, all three of my children are together again." Susan smiled as Amelia walked into the room. Eric reminded her that they had been together just a few days ago. "True, but you were fighting. When I'm sick, fighting is not allowed, so I can enjoy having you together without any fights, right?" All three nodded their heads while Eric grumbled under his breath that he had no part of the fight. Susan cocked her head his way. "Want to repeat that, dear?"

Eric withered under his mother's glare. He said with a bright red face, "Just said, glad to see you being your normal self."

Their mother nodded her head triumphantly, although not without wincing in pain, "That's what I thought you said." Amelia wanted to both scold and embrace her mother, but neither would be best at the moment. She was thankful that her mother was alert and talking, so the scolding was trivial at this point. With bruised ribs, a hug would not be the best gift in the world. Amelia shared the sandwiches with her brothers as her mother ate from the hospital tray. Her mother wished for something other than hospital food, but Amelia was hesitant. When pressed, Jason reminded their mother that Amelia always played everything by the rules, and there was no way she would bend them until approval from a doctor.

Susan grimaced and tried her best to eat the turkey and green beans. Once everyone's meal was gone, a handsome doctor walked through the door. "Hello everyone, I am Dr. Taylor, Mrs. Allen's new orthopedic." Roger had woken up and inquired where Susan's regular doctor was. "Dr. Farley is out of town for the next few weeks, so for now, you are stuck with me." He introduced himself to everyone in the room, shaking each one's hand. He stared a little long at Amelia, who did not mind the attention at all.

As he was examining Susan, Eric caught Amelia staring heavily at the doctor. He elbowed his sister and said, "Wish you were in the hospital bed?"

Amelia stomped on his foot hard enough that he cried out in pain. When everyone turned to look at her, she merely tilted her head innocently, "Sorry, Eric. I thought I saw a spider." Susan Allen fired off one of her piercing glares, but Amelia didn't seem to care. Eric had gotten exactly what he had coming to him.

After the examination, Dr. Taylor gave the family some news, "Well, she will make a full recovery. As the surgeon told you last night, she is going to be down for some time. I want her immobilized for at least one to two weeks, and then Dr. Farley and I will consult from there. Since she will be unable to walk, I would prefer she go to a rehab facility unless someone can be home to help her. I also want to start physical therapy on her hand before the muscle loses too much mass." Susan Allen decided to put her two cents into the conversation, "Doctor, I can look after myself. I do not want to go to a rehab or a nursing home, so please let me go back to my house. Are you sure about being immobilized and down for that long too? That will cut right into the Strawberry Festival, and I've got so much to do to get ready for it."

Dr. Taylor tried to reason with Susan, but it was a losing battle. As he battled her ever-growing strong will, Roger Allen pulled his children aside for a discussion. Jason and Eric were texting Donna and Emma to figure out who could help where. Roger wanted to honor his wife's wishes, but now it was just imperfect timing. As his sons tried to come up with a schedule, Roger dropped an additional bombshell, "Timmons quit yesterday as well. He's taken a job back in New York to be closer to family. He asked to leave right away, and I agreed. Diana is taking on more Festival work, so I'd plan to split my time between the chamber and the office. Emma agreed to help where she could and is already sorting through resumes for the two new positions in HR. Luckily there are no projects that require Timmons' experience, just the company dynamics, and interviews."

Amelia decided that she was being allowed to redeem herself, "I'll stay and help." Her brothers stared at her in disbelief while Roger began to argue with her. "Let me help, please. I may have fudged the truth a little bit, as there is nothing planned for the rest of my vacation. I can stay with mom when needed, and I can assist at Allen Inc. It would help me get over some of the guilt I've caused here."

Surprisingly enough, it was Jason who questioned her, "Amelia, this is your vacation. Are you sure you want to spend it working for dad?" Amelia nodded her head, yes, and while not thrilled with the idea, Roger had to accept. The family turned back to Susan and Dr. Taylor to see the poor doctor on the receiving end of one of Susan Allen's Medusa glares.

Amelia admired how he was not backing down even amidst the razor-sharp eyes. She stood there taking in his tall, tan, and handsome self. His eyes were as blue as a clear sky, and his chiseled features accentuated his smile. She was dragged forcibly out of the daydream with another one of Eric's elbow jabs. He opened his mouth to say something but quickly closed it when she started raising her knee. While irritated at her brother's childish antics, she could not believe herself in practically drooling at a time like this. Roger finally decided to end the impasse and deliver the family's decision.

"Dr. Taylor, we have figured out a way where one of our family members can be with Susan at all times. We will make sure she is cared for and that she does her exercises." Susan first appeared glad of the news until Roger threw in that last line. She stared at him as if to say, "I'll do what I want when I want, and only if I want." The young doctor hung his head in defeat and agreed to those terms. As he prepared to leave, Donna and Emma both arrived at their mother-in-law's room.

"Dr. Taylor, imagine seeing you here!" Donna exclaimed and hugged the doctor. Amelia watched as Jason immediately became tense, wanting to watch this character with more focus. Amelia muttered that he needed to mind his temper, but he seemed to be ignoring her. "Donna Allen, what are you. . ." Dr. Taylor's words trailed off as he tied the last names together. "I never would have thought it would be your husband's family. So which one is he?" Donna grinned and strolled over to Jason and planted a kiss on his cheek. Jason's body eased slightly with this show of affection, but he was still protective. He said his goodbyes and smiled at Amelia as he left.

After Eric and Emma had left for the evening, Donna pulled Amelia over. "So, how did you like her doctor?"

Amelia wondered if she and Jason had also caught her deep in fantasy, but she decided to play dumb. "He seemed nice. How do you know him?"

Donna laughed at her sister-in-law. "Your facial expressions tell me you think he is much more than nice." Amelia had no words, and so she merely blushed. "Aha! I was right, that's great. Can I get him to invite you out for dinner?"

Amelia choked on her saliva. "Donna! I told you I wasn't ready with this Ben person, and now you want to set me up with Dr. Handsome?"

Donna grinned from ear to ear at this revelation. "Oh, so now he's handsome, is he?" Amelia buried her face deep in her hands. "Anyways, that is Ben, silly. We only call him Dr. Taylor in front of patients. I told him all about you, by the way, and I know he would be open to having dinner, especially now that he's met you." Amelia had no words for this situation. Dr. Farley was a member of the largest orthopedic group in Jackson. Donna had worked for the practice for about four years now, and she barely saw the man due to working with specific physicians. What were the odds that the doctor assigned to her mother's case would be the same gentleman Donna wanted her to date?

Amelia considered the proposition and reflected on the day. She had promised God and herself to work on amending the relationships within her family. This trip was causing her to step out of the comfort zone fully. She had offered, and was determined to stay in town much longer than planned, as a help to both her family and her father's business. She figured her mother would also talk her into helping with a few festival details. Deciding that since she had already thrown caution to the wind, she replied, "Alright. I'll do it, but just one date, and I make no additional promises." Donna squealed for joy and set off rambling to herself about all the plans she would make for the two of them. Amelia sunk back into the lumpy chair and stared out of the room's window. "Well, people always say go big or go home. I guess this time, I'm doing both."

Chapter Seven

"So let me get this straight. . ." the voice called out throughout the room. Amelia had left her cell phone on speaker while working in the kitchen. Amelia had come home early this morning after spending another night in the hospital. The doctors had agreed to let Susan go home later this morning, and so Amelia was now preparing lunch for everyone. While working, she had decided to call Brad. His voice sounded confused as he continued the train of thought. "You decided to spend the remainder of your vacation in the same hometown you like to avoid? I mean, come on, Amelia, it is lovely and caring for you to want to take care of your mother, but you are actually going to stay a full three weeks?"

Amelia laughed as she considered his question. "Director Jones already approved the time off, and while it does seem weird, I can admit that, but at least it doesn't sound crazy, right?"

Brad laughed deeper than Amelia had heard before, "Maybe not crazy, but deciding to work as a human resources director while on vacation for having too much leave? I think that is the epitome of crazy."

Amelia saw the humor in the situation but chose not to let Brad think he was right. "Well, are you going to help me or not?"

Brad continued laughing, "That's rich. You want me to go over to your house tonight and pack more clothes for you? You then want me to drive them to you, and all you offer is a meal? It sounds like I need to do some better bargaining here."

Amelia rolled her eyes at him just as he commented, "And since I can almost guarantee you rolled your eyes at me, I think you should pay a large fee for this service." Amelia wished she could get her hands on his neck and push a few pressure points, but that seemed to be frowned upon in the current world. "What did you have in mind, brat?" She could feel his lips contorting into the evilest smile one ever saw. She knew that his request would be for an arm and maybe two legs. Brad was never one to be subtle, even when doing favors.

"I think you should give me the copies of those embarrassing photos you have of my mishaps." Amelia could not believe how easy she was getting off. All she had to do was to trick him into believing those were the only copies.

She quickly agreed to the deal and began feeling the calculating gaze of Bradley Winters through the telephone. "I'm also going to need you to sign a simple statement. It only states that you agree to all the terms of said agreement, blah blah blah, and states that if you decide to breach any of the listed terms within the agreement, I get to share your childhood photos with the entire department at our next retreat."

Amelia tried to talk her way out of this issue, "Now, Brad, we have been friends for so long. Why in the world would we need a contract?" He laughed, "The fact that you, a rule abider and legal stickler, are trying to talk your way out of signing proves that you have something else planned."

She sighed and said, "Quit being dramatic. This small kind

favor is not worth all the trouble." He laughed and reminded her that she was tasking him with picking out outfits for her in addition to gathering her undergarments. He argued that constituted hazardous pay. She realized he was being extremely liberal with his comments since he was so far away. If he had been within her reach, he would be hurting in at least a couple of places. Finally, the two reached an agreement that consisted of burning blackmail and a favor to be asked for later.

"So, how are things with you and Ian?" Bradley decided to turn this conversation into one of more concern for his friend. Amelia sighed as she folded the laundry her mother had left. "It is confusing. On the one hand, I want to be mad at him for how things ended all those years ago, but then on the other, he goes and helps my mother. The lunch the other day, and everything seems to be showing sides of him that I've never seen."

Bradley continued to chat with her about Ian, and when Amelia mentioned the new doctor, he just groaned. "A doctor? Does he know you have three brothers who would take care of him in a heartbeat?" She laughed and told him to quit being dramatic. "Thanks for always being there, Brad. I'll talk with you later."

Amelia finished making the lunch just as her father opened the front door with her mother in tow. Jason was pushing her in a wheelchair. He and Eric had both taken the day off of work to help move Susan home. Their mother smiled at the three of them as they sat at the table together and served lunch; the family feasted on a taco bar Amelia made out of the items in the home. She had also concocted homemade guacamole and opened one of Susan Allen's tasty jars of homemade salsa. The family ate the delicious food with light-hearted conversation. After sharing a glance with her siblings, they decided to sit down with their mother after lunch.

Donna and Emma had been to the house early this morning

before work. They had rearranged the guest room that was downstairs. The two-story home had three bedrooms upstairs and two on the lower level. Amelia had moved a few of her things into one of the rooms in preparation for if Susan needed her assistance the first few nights. Donna and Emma had relocated several of Roger & Susan's belongings into the larger room. It would be better to keep Susan on ground level for the next few weeks and not trouble with getting her up and down the stairs.

Once the brother finished lunch, they helped their mother into the guest room's bed, which generally housed different guests closer to Festival time. "Who's going to take care of the festival preparations? Roger, you can't leave your office unattended too long." Amelia knew that her mother was scheming to be left alone. That would allow her time to test her own strength and get a few critical tasks accomplished. He had informed her that she would have care around the clock, and she kept trying to talk him out of it.

Roger took to clearing the table and dishes to allow the children to meet with their mother. Amelia took charge as both the oldest and also the bossiest. "Mom, the doctor told us why you had your accident." Susan Allen turned her head away from her children. She was not having this conversation with them.

"Amelia, remember who the parent is here." None of the three Allen kids blanched at that statement.

Amelia recognized the tactic, as her mother had often utilized it. "Mom, what did the preacher speak on last Sunday? Dad told me it was about children helping their parents."

Susan glared at Amelia and added disapprovingly, "It also says to honor your parents. The tone you are using is awful close to dishonor, young lady."

Jason decided to try and help his sister out. "Mom, we are honoring you by talking to you. We could easily try and change you on our own, but we wanted to sit down and talk about this rationally. All three of us agree on your health. You are arguing before we ever begin."

Susan muttered barely enough to where the children could hear her, "I've been trying forever to get these three to agree with each other and act like siblings. Of course, it's now at my expense."

When they saw their mother breathe out a sigh with no retort, they knew it was momentarily safe to proceed. It was like walking in a minefield. Sometimes you could test and see if there was anything ahead. While that made your path clear up to that point, you still had to watch for explosions. The Allen trio decided to take a step forward in the minefield known as their mother.

"You need to be more careful, mom. Every family member has said you've been looking pale and weaker. I noticed how frail you were that morning, and just like with everyone, you denied it. We were hoping you could let us know when you are not up to par. You don't know how scared we were when you were hurt. Mom, this accident could have been a lot worse." Susan Allen stayed quiet but with a remorseful face.

Eric decided to take his turn next. "We want you to take these next few weeks and rest. You are not to do anything that takes too much energy. You need to heal from more than just the accident. You have done so much for us and others over the years. Let us help you now."

Jason nodded his head in agreement and decided to add, "Mom, Eric, and I cleared our schedules as much as we could to help out. Donna and Emma are helping too, so everything, including the Festival, will be taken care of soon. Please, just rest."

Admitting slight defeat, Susan nodded her head in agreement. "I will try. I promise all of you that. My accident is bad timing, that's all. Your father has trouble at Allen Inc., and the Festival is so close. He will be so stressed out helping both here and there."

Amelia decided to share her news now. "Well, dad will have

some help. I decided to stay through the Festival and also help out at Allen Inc. I can help with you here, mom, with the business, Festival, whatever you need." Amelia expected her mother to be happy that Amelia was staying, but her face seemed cold.

"So you aren't headed back to Nashville tonight?" Amelia thought maybe her mother was in shock, so she assured her mother that she was here for the long haul. The look of joy never appeared on Susan Allen's face. Her eyes drifted around the room. She finally said, "So, you'll do whatever I need?" Amelia nodded her head in agreement while confused at her mother's behavior.

"Good. Amelia, I need you to go back to Nashville. Tonight."

Chapter Eight

Roger Allen was unsure what had gotten into his wife after hearing her remarks. He tried assuring Amelia not to take the comments personally, as Susan would have difficulty adjusting. He suggested she go into town and stop by Allen Inc. for a tour. Both brothers looked at their sister sadly. The family had been working towards peace, but this seemed to have halted everything. Amelia was trying to understand her mother, but in reality, it deeply hurt Amelia to hear her mother tell her to leave.

Amelia decided to take her father's advice and get away for a little bit. Her brothers were there to help her mom, and so she drove over to Allen, Inc. Emma tried getting her to talk about whatever had her so upset, but Amelia just ignored the probing. Emma eventually gave up trying and showed Amelia around the office. It had been several years since she had ventured deep into the office building. Amelia realized that the trip to see Emma just a few days prior was probably the first visit to the building in at least seven years. She was surprised to see so many warm and inviting faces welcoming her home.

Amelia stopped to chat with Harry Thompson, the head tax

consultant. Harry had always been an honorary uncle to her, and he wanted to check on Susan. The two talked for a while, and Amelia promised to do lunch with him soon. She made her way to where Roger planned to put the marketing department. A few individuals had joined the firm, and a few of the contractors even had desks there. She stopped by one desk that had a lot of character. She saw Tennessee Volunteer memorabilia, trinkets from cities across the state and region, and random paperweights.

Two of the wooden items caught her eye. Sitting on the desk was a figurine made from the library's old dogwood tree. She knew this because her mother had gotten her a snowman ornament made from the same wood. The other item, a paperweight, was also made of wood, though she was unsure of what type. It has a beautiful strawberry engraved on its face, surrounded by minor nicks in the wood. On the upper left side of the paperweight was an *R*, and just below it, on the right was an *A*. She wondered if that was the individual's initials or the special meaning behind the letters. The carving looked eerily familiar. She admired it for a moment longer, noticing a lily carved into the side along with a treble clef and what appeared to be a muffin. She was thoroughly impressed with the craftsmanship. There were such grand details in such a tiny piece.

She looked up to see that Emma had re-entered the room and was looking for her. She apologized for getting side-tracked and decided to make her way through the remainder of the tour. Emma landed them back at the Human Resources division and showed Amelia her temporary office. Inside was a beautiful painting of Twin Oaks, an old home recently repurposed into a wedding and event venue. She admired the touches of strawberries all around the building, though not prominent inside her office. She decided to arrange just a few things on the desk before heading home.

When she arrived back home, tension still hung in the air. Her brothers acted as if nothing was wrong, but she saw her father and mother look hesitantly at each other. She asked Eric and Jason to help her start supper and ignored whatever issues were going on with her mother. The trip to Allen Inc. had taken her mind off the trouble, even if only for a moment. Seeing all the happy faces and strawberry decorations, she knew that her home, at least for the next three weeks, was right in Humboldt, TN. Her mother would just have to deal with her decision.

Amelia prepared a simple salad topped with feta cheese, strawberries, and roasted walnuts and decided to make homemade chicken alfredo. Her brothers helped make the pasta and homemade garlic bread. Her father wheeled out his wife a little while later to join the family for dinner. They wanted to keep her out of bed as much as possible during her recovery. Susan Allen was a very active individual. Sleeping her recovery away in a bed would be detrimental to the woman's overall health. Donna and Emma had stopped in after work to check on Mrs. Allen and spend time with the entire family. Just as Amelia was placing the dessert on the dinner table, the doorbell rang. Amelia offered to see who was there, and she headed towards the front of the house.

Amelia swung the door wide open to see Ian standing on the porch. "I wondered if you might still be in town. I wanted to check on your mother."

Standing at the door, she was conflicted on how to react. One part of her wanted to criticize the man for suggesting that she would be gone with an injured mother, but she kept coming back to when he called the first responders. "She's doing as well as she can."

Ian nodded his head solemnly. "Well, good. I just wanted to check and make sure she was doing better."

He turned to head back to his vehicle when Amelia called out after him, "Ian?" Turning around to face her, he saw a look of sincerity on her face. "The officer told us who helped mom."

His shoulders sagged. "I asked him not to give out my name."

Amelia raised one eyebrow at him, "You know we would have seen it in the police report, or mom might have told us. Either way, I wanted to thank you, but why weren't you at the hospital when I arrived? I know they questioned you, but I arrived not long before the officer. I figured you might have come too."

Ian looked down to the ground, unable to meet her eyes. "I've caused enough stress with your family the last few days. I made sure she was in good care before giving your family space. I started towards the hospital but thought I'd visit later instead. Your sister-in-law has been good to keep me informed."

Amelia nodded her head, taking in his reasoning. Without hesitating, she asked, "Would you like to join us for dinner? I made more than enough." He started to shake his head no, but she kept pestering him to join them. "Ian, it is the least any of us can do for you. Come inside, please." He reluctantly accepted her invitation.

Once inside the house where everyone could see him, all three Allen men jumped out of their seats to shake his hand and even hug the man. Ian glared at Amelia, who slightly enjoyed his embarrassment. When Susan laid her eyes upon him, tears escaped her eyes. She beckoned him over to wrap her arms around his body. He leaned into the heartfelt hug. She murmured thank you countless times into his ears. Once everyone had spent time with the new Allen family hero, they all settled into eating dinner.

"Amelia, you did a wonderful job on this meal," Ian commented. Her brothers shouted cries of "I helped" and "I supervised." The entire table laughed at their antics. As the group was devouring the dessert, Ian asked Amelia when she planned to return home. Amelia shared her new plans and noticed how her mother seemed to look anywhere but at her as she spoke.

Ian helped Amelia clear the dinner table and noticed a few pieces of chicken lying on the kitchen counter. "Amelia, what's this chicken laying here?"

Amelia kept rinsing the dishes before loading them into the dishwasher. "Oh, that's leftovers for F. . ." Amelia caught herself before using the name Frank. She remembered how she'd informed Ian that her boyfriend's name was Frank. Realizing her mistake, Amelia dropped the plate in her hands, shocked by the turn of events. She caught it at the perfect timing as it was about to shatter into a million pieces.

Ian smirked at her. "That's for who?"

Amelia recovered as best she could and said, "My cat."

His grin was incorrigible. "You always did like cats. Where is he or she?"

Amelia glanced around, knowing with extreme certainty that the cat was upstairs in her room. "Oh, he must be napping." As if the fates were working against her, Eric walked into the room holding Frank.

"Amelia, Frank must have smelled the chicken down here. He was practically begging at your door, wanting out. Did you save him any?" Ian laughed loudly at Amelia's situation. She was flushed with embarrassment and could not meet his eye. Roger Allen came into the kitchen and saw Frank as Eric was setting him on the floor.

As the cat looked for chicken on the ground, he wandered over to Ian. He purred and rubbed against his leg. Roger smiled, "Ian, that's the famous Frank that Susan mentions all the time. It seems that he likes you." Ian laughed as Amelia's head sharply rose to watch him. Her face was a mixture of betrayal and profound embarrassment. *He's known the whole time.*

"I think he just wants some chicken." Ian reached over to grab the chicken and laid it on a small paper plate for Frank to have.

Amelia finally found her voice to ask, "You knew who Frank was the whole time, didn't you?" He laughed and nodded his head while Amelia looked for something to use in giving him a piece of her mind.

Ten minutes later, Ian was laughing with the whole family as he regaled them with the encounter at the post office. Amelia was secretly hoping lightning would strike her through the window at any time, but the skies were as clear as could be. When the doorbell rang once more, Amelia did not offer to answer the door. Instead, she bolted from the rest of the family, eager for the distraction of a new visitor. "Uncle Kent! How nice of you to stop by. Please come inside."

Kent Tomlinson walked in and exchanged pleasantries with the entire family. Seeing that Susan's brother had joined the gathered family, Ian decided that was his time to head home. He bid the family a good evening and carefully maneuvered out of the house without Amelia getting to harm him. Kent stayed for a couple of hours, visiting and scolding his sister. The entire Allen clan was happy to let someone else fight this battle with her. Kent was probably the best choice after Amelia since he and his sister were only thirteen months apart in age. Amelia smiled as she saw her uncle making headway with his sister. The two were as close as she and Eric, maybe even more. In the same way, Eric could handle Amelia, Kent was able to manage Susan.

Eventually, Susan called Amelia over to her bedside. "Amelia, if you insist on staying through these next couple of weeks, I need you to handle my responsibilities with the Festival. I know Donna and Emma will help you as much as possible." The two mentioned ladies nodded their heads in the background to show their agreement. "Now, it is going to keep you busy, so let me know if I can do anything from here." Amelia was shocked that her mother seemed to accept this so soon after talking with Kent. She also noticed how her mother still seemed unhappy with her, and Amelia wondered what she had done wrong. Amelia agreed to do whatever needed to be accomplished for the Festival to run smoothly.

"Very good," was all Susan had to say. Kent added, "Jessie

will be over tomorrow to help you out, sis." Amelia questioned why Jessie needed to stay with Susan since the Allen family could more than take care of their mother. Kent informed her that Jessie wanted to be there for her aunt, and Susan seemed happy to spend time with her niece.

Amelia still was unsure why her mother was upset with her and why she'd rather spend time with Jessie. Donna saw that Amelia's wheels were constantly spinning and decided to distract her sister-in-law. "Amelia, do you have any plans tomorrow night?" Amelia thought for a moment and said, "Well, Bradley is coming Sunday afternoon to bring me a few of my things. Other than that, I want to look over the work needed for the Festival. Why? Do you want to catch a movie?"

Donna thought for a few moments before responding, "A movie sounds great, but why don't we grab a bite to eat before the show? Jason and I would love to spend some time with you." Amelia thought it sounded like an excellent plan, so she agreed to meet them the next evening for dinner and then a movie. "Great!" Amelia's eyes narrowed at her sister-in-law's deep enthusiasm and figured with the different emotions, it wouldn't be wise to read into anything much. Jason meanwhile looked at his wife bewildered. He thought that they had plans to look at furniture for the nursery. He shrugged his shoulders and started talking with his brother again.

"Amelia?" Roger and Susan had called their daughter over to discuss the Festival in detail. She settled into a chair across from her parents as they began to go through the details. Roger grimaced slightly at his wife before turning to Amelia. "Milly, are you sure you can handle all of your mother's responsibilities at the festival?" "Of course, you both know how much I love this Festival. The work will be fun and go smoothly. Besides, it should only be the recipe contest and dinner here at the house, right?" Amelia watched as her mother gave a satisfied smile towards her father.

"Well . . . not quite," Roger replied. "You see, with an empty nest, your mother has taken on a few more responsibilities." Amelia glanced back and forth between the two parents. "When you say a few, are we talking about two or three items or an Allen 'few'?" Roger chuckled at his daughter, "I guess it would be the latter of those two options." Amelia groaned and asked for her parents to give full disclosure. It turned out that her mother hosted two dinners, one the Saturday before the Festival and another the Sunday following all the events. It was a beginning and end to the Festival for the prominent staff members. She also helped set up for the art exhibit, served at the prayer breakfast, oversaw the recipe contest, introduced one of the live acts, served on the Hall of Fame committee, judged the BBQ cook-off, and for fun took care of the judges for the last night of the pageants.

"At least I can enjoy the parades," Amelia murmured to herself. Susan perked up a little more, "Oh, I forgot! I was supposed to be Berry's escort this year." Amelia now knew why her mother was in such poor health. The woman never seemed to take a break and relax. "I guess I inherited that problem too," Amelia grumbled under her breath as she walked away from her parents. Her vacation had suddenly morphed into two full-time jobs.

"Amelia?" her father called out. Amelia decided she was ready to retire for the evening, so she kept walking. He decided to say his last words to her as she started up the stairs. "You are going to need to work closely with the general chairman. The president this year is Marcie Donald. The general chairman is Jenna Wallace, Emma's sister." Amelia hung her head as she continued to her bedroom. Tonight was not an evening to spend in the extra guest room. Tonight, she was going upstairs, where she could moan and groan without her family hearing. She was very much looking forward to working with her old rival on all things strawberry.

After Amelia disappeared upstairs, the other Allen family

members slowly dispersed to their own homes. Both sons spent extra time with their mother, hugging and wishing her well. She made them both promise to pray for her recovery. "You boys better pray for me. If I find out you've not been talking to God, especially about your mother, you'll have reason to pray when I'm through with you." Both boys blanched as she kissed them each on the cheek.

Roger made sure that all the dishes were washing in the dishwasher before taking his wife back to bed. He laid beside her for what seemed like an eternity, savoring every moment beside his soulmate. His gaze lowered towards her head. He would be thanking God with more of his heart tonight. As he watched his wife, his mind churned over the recent events. He wondered if she was still awake to discuss them. "Su?"

Susan raised her head to look at her husband. "What's on your mind, dear?"

He hesitated before deciding to bring up the problems he had. "Why did you act so healthy when you felt so weak?" Roger could ask questions like this between the two of them without her getting too upset.

"Roger, I like being able to go full force. I knew something was wrong but couldn't admit it even to myself. I put you and everyone through so much stress, and for that, I will try to do better."

Roger held his wife gently, not wanting to cause her any pain. Her answer was genuine, and he counted himself lucky to be able to have this conversation. "Su?" Roger called again with another pressing question stuck in his mind. "Why are you upset with our daughter?"

She laid her head on his chest and tried to embrace his warmth. "I have no idea what you mean, dear." She enjoyed being near her husband and thought that she could play the hurt wife card to avoid this discussion. He rubbed the side of her arm as he continued his probing.

"I think you do. Everyone tonight noticed how you treated her. You even seemed glad to pile on loads of work on her. Remember that she is supposed to be on vacation."

Susan Allen was not giving up her motives this quickly. "Well, no one asked her to stay. She could still take a vacation and enjoy it."

Roger stopped rubbing her arm and lifted her chin so that he could look into her eyes. "Dear, she offered to stay. An offer you very rudely refused. Our daughter hardly ever comes home and once she offers to stay and assist her mother, you, the very mother, ask her to leave. So, either that accident caused more than physical issues, or you are upset with our daughter."

Susan was not intimidated by him staring into her eyes. Her will was much stronger than anything he could throw her way. "Well, Roger, we don't need her help. Between Jason, Donna, Eric, Emma, and Jessie, we have more than enough help. She shouldn't have her vacation time filled with taking care of her sick mother or worrying about the work at Allen Inc."

"So, do you not like that she is finally helping me with the business? We always hoped she would consider even part-time consulting for me in Nashville. I've always wanted an Allen in the business. Emma is the closest I thought I could get until now." Susan agreed it was nice to have their daughter involved in Roger's company that he had worked so hard to build. Even then, she still stood by her decision to ask Amelia to leave.

"Roger, I think once she has to start doing all this festival work, she will decide to spend an actual vacation. We will see her later this year, maybe take a trip up there once my recovery is over. She needs to take some time for herself, and she will not do that here."

Roger thought that while there was some truth to his wife's

assessment, there were still unanswered questions. Susan was getting tired from the long day. Deciding to let her think this conversation had ended, he kissed her forehead and turned out the bedside table lamp. As Roger pulled the covers over the two of them, he grabbed her hand as they prayed together. After their evening prayers ended, he curled up beside his wife, hands still held tightly together. "Su?" Roger whispered the question this time in case she was asleep.

She groggily answered, "Yes, dear?" He laid quiet for a moment until he thought she was back asleep.

"Be careful, dear. I would hate not even to see our daughter in Nashville because we pushed her away." With his last statement said, Roger closed his eyes and drifted off to sleep.

Susan lay wide-eyed and wide-awake. She had many reasons for why she had treated Amelia with contempt tonight. Some of them stemmed from hurt feelings and others from unresolved issues. The crucial, personal reasons had more to do with herself than with Amelia. She fretted that Roger could be correct, but she was trusting in her instincts with this matter. As she closed her eyes to get some rest finally, she muttered, "I would hate that too."

Chapter Nine

*A*melia awoke the following day more exhausted than when she had gone to bed. Her mind was still pondering how everything had devolved over the last few days. She seemed unable to find rest in her old bed, but she was still thankful for being here. She dragged herself downstairs to make a fresh pot of coffee. While the coffee was brewing, she decided to make a small breakfast for her parents. Wanting to avoid confrontation this morning, she left their breakfast on the counter with a simple note. A few minutes later, she loaded one tumbler with coffee and another with her signature shake and headed down to Allen Inc.

She was surprised to find that the office was practically empty when she arrived. It was not uncommon for her to spend the weekend working as she was notorious for being at work on Saturdays while off the clock. In state government, unless there was a conference or particular project, you were generally guaranteed weekends. Amelia knew from friends, like Chase, that their offices filled with workers during the weekend in the private sector. She wondered if something was going on in town to keep everyone away but decided to get to work instead of giving in to her curiosity.

Focusing on the task at hand, Amelia was determined to review what work Mr. Timmons had left behind. She was only here for two weeks, and during that short time, her goal was to hire someone to fill these HR vacancies. Finding a few resumes on the desk, Amelia picked them up and began sorting through each candidate. She quickly sifted through the unqualified individuals, discarding their applications before making notes for Emma to set up interviews with her top selections.

As she examined the paperwork on the desk, she realized this task would not be as challenging as she first imagined. Mr. Timmons had accomplished a great deal of work before resigning. He had already prepared job descriptions for the new marketing positions. He had also organized all of the files for his successor to have an easy transition. She noticed that two employees were retiring within the next two weeks, with both already having replacements hired. The new employees would work one week with their predecessors to learn the role. She decided to pack away the new-hire orientation manual for some light bedtime reading to familiarize herself with the way Allen Inc. handled these tasks.

Amelia noted that the office was a strong contrast to the remainder of the building. Where strawberry-themed décor filled everywhere else, this office was lacking in color, let alone personal touches. That simply was unacceptable, and so she jetted out of the building and over to Berry-Exciting Gifts. An hour later, she returned with several strawberry-themed decorations, and soon the office felt like home. She wanted whoever took this spot to appreciate the small things that made Humboldt a great place to live. Deciding that there was not much else to do until more staff were available, she locked the office and headed out the front door.

Wondering what to do with her time, she decided today would be a perfect day for a trip to the lake. Her mind always seemed to be at ease near water. She could walk along a creek bed or pond endlessly and make the world's troubles seem miles away. She considered where to go to accomplish this desire when an idea struck her. She buckled her seat belt, and off she went to the outskirts of the city. It took her about fifteen minutes to reach her destination, Davy Crockett Lake. The older members of her community still called it by the old name, Humboldt Lake. The lake was between eighty and ninety acres, and on a clear day, you could feel just as serene as the water looked. As she walked along the bed of the lake, she eventually stopped to take in the scenery. Her mind drifted to days gone by, fishing with family and friends. This location was the source of family memories and even a picnic date with Ian; As she looked out on the grounds, her heart blossomed. Past heartaches had added unnecessary stress on her life, and recent events had only increased her tension. Here was a place where she could unwind and relax. She sat down by the water's edge, not caring if her pants became stained by the grass. She gazed out upon the water and let the gentle breeze take away all her issues.

Amelia stayed by the lakeside for at least an hour. Not wanting to waste the entire day, she headed back to town, noting that there were still about five hours until she was supposed to meet Jason and Donna. She drove over to the new downtown coffee shop to enjoy a simple sandwich and a chilled coffee. Amelia was enjoying her meal when someone decided to join her. "Amy? Your father told me you were back in town."

Amelia looked up to find Jenna Wallace, this year's general chairman, and her old rival. Amelia swallowed the bite she was chewing before greeting Jenna back. "Jenna, it is so good to see you. I hear we will be working together a lot in the next several days. Since we are going to be spending so much time together, I think you should know that I go by Amelia now."

Jenna raised an eyebrow at the statement but let it pass without comment. "I am so sorry to hear about your mother's accident. Your father said that she is recovering well, and that is a blessing. The festival, however, must go on, even without the help of our greatest asset. I know you haven't been home in a while, but it is always good to have an Allen on the job."

Amelia half-heartedly laughed at the last line. She hoped not to be a disappointment as her parents were so involved in the community. "Well, I am here to help! My mother gave me the rundown on the events and her role. I guess we need to nail down several of the details." Jenna smiled at her old rival. Amelia took the warm look and realized that despite teenage history, this would work out fine.

"Perfect! Let's start with the dinner. That is only one week away." Amelia appreciated that they focus straight on business. There was no need for situations in the past to hinder a relationship centered on working or wasting time catching up like the old friends they never were.

The two ladies sorted out the invitation list first. There would be about twenty individuals, including the mayor, president, coordinators, event chairs, and spouses. With all the events, Amelia thought there would be more individuals. Jenna used Amelia's family as an example since her parents were both the chamber director and an event chair. When she considered how much overlap there would be within families, it made a little more sense. The menu was a much more difficult situation. Susan Allen was famous for serving her homemade lasagna, complete with the Tomlinson sauce every year. Amelia did not want to divulge why that was not an option, but she emphatically stated there was a need for a new menu. She and Jenna went back and forth on several options before Amelia ultimately decided on breakfast for dinner. The two women agreed that an unusual choice might best represent this situation, and it would be easy to incorporate strawberries.

The two continued making plans throughout the afternoon.

Amelia finally had to ask Jenna to come by her father's business on Monday morning to finish the long to-do list. Jenna laughed and commented, "Well, that won't be a far journey." Amelia looked at her confused before realizing that Jenna must also work for Allen Inc.

"Living in a large area, you forget that most people work together around here. I'm guessing you work for dad?"

"There's not a ton of opportunities for accountants in a small town." Jenna went on to tell Amelia a bit of the work she did for the company. Jenna consulted more than she worked on the company's personal accounts. Amelia learned that each consultant split the task of internal accounting, which seemed to be Jenna's strong suit. Amelia filed these notes away in her brain and said her goodbyes.

By the time Amelia arrived back home, it was nearly half-past three. She went to check on her mother but found the woman dozing comfortably in her bed. Amelia pulled the covers around her mother and quietly exited the room. She found her father in his study and decided to ask how the first full day home had gone for her mother. "There you are, Milly," Roger called to his daughter as he saw her entering his study. "The breakfast this morning was delicious. Thank you for going to the trouble. Jessie just left after helping us a great deal today. She fixed lunch for us and did a little housework. Your mother is resting now; she was a little worn out from being up a while this morning. How was your day?"

Amelia still was not thrilled by the idea of her cousin helping out. She did consider that Jessie had helped today while Amelia was working elsewhere. Chatting about the day's events, Roger thought it was hilarious that Amelia had found someone more detail-oriented than herself when she discussed the endless planning session with Jenna. He agreed that a breakfast dinner sounded delicious and agreed to help get the house prepared for the company. Amelia started to get ready for the evening before deciding to ask a question about her day. "Dad, why was no one at Allen Inc. this morning? I would have thought several of the staff would have been there working on projects today."

Roger put down the document he was working on to stare at his daughter wildly. Amelia began to wonder if something was stuck to her face the longer Roger searched her with his eyes. Eventually, he regained some of his composure and responded to her question. "Milly, why would people have been there on a Saturday?"

Amelia was a little thrown by his question. She thought it was perfectly logical to work on a Saturday, but he seemed to be against the idea. "Well, with their busy schedules, they need to touch base with clients and prepare for the next project, or am I missing something?"

He chuckled at his daughter's comments. "You've been in the city for too long. We work Monday through Friday here. I very rarely let a business keep my workers busy on weekends. I even allow my consultants a trip home each weekend if their out-of-town project keeps them away for more than a week. Our clients know that we are available during business hours, and someone is available for emergencies each weekend. Otherwise, evenings and weekends are family time. Most of our employees were spending valuable time with their loved ones today. We are a light-hearted operation which has caused our clients to respect us and appreciate that we value family first. These companies are looking for someone who will treat them like family."

Amelia nodded her head as she considered the answer. The business model went against everything she knew and understood of the private sector, but it had worked for Allen Inc. Looking at the clock, Amelia realized it was time to get ready for the evening. Wanting an outfit still upstairs, Amelia headed to dress. While changing into a simple teal shirt and blue jeans, she heard the door below shut. She thought Jessie might have decided to help with dinner, so she decided to check her emails instead of seeing who had stopped. A few moments later, there was a knock at her door. "It's Donna. Can I come in?"

Amelia was a little confused but invited her to come into the room. "I thought I was meeting the two of you at the restaurant. What are you doing here?"

Donna smiled at her sister-in-law as she responded, "Well, Jason wanted to run a couple of errands, so I asked him to drop me off here. I thought we could ride together." Amelia thought that it made perfect sense and then noticed that Donna was wearing a stunning dress. Donna likewise was taking in Amelia's outfit. "Amelia, please tell me you are not wearing those clothes to the restaurant."

Amelia's confusion quickly returned. "I thought it was just dinner and a movie. Why do I need to wear anything different?"

Donna hesitated for a moment before stating, "I want us to take some pictures before I start looking like a balloon. Let's get you into something gorgeous. I want your niece or nephew to see what I looked like before they were born." Amelia thought her reasoning seemed a little off but thought it best not to question a Southern pregnant woman. The two spent a good bit of time going over the few items in her closet. The other batch of Amelia's clothes were not due to be here until tomorrow. The pair finally agreed on a strapless emerald green dress. The dress showed Amelia's curves without being too flashy. Amelia looked at herself in the mirror and noticed how content and beautiful she looked. She considered that maybe Donna had the right idea in wearing more elegant clothes. Donna got Amelia to put on a little extra makeup, and the two left to meet Jason at the restaurant.

As they pulled into the parking lot, Donna pointed out Jason's car in the parking lot. They went through the large black front doors and began looking for Jason. In a booth on the far right side of the restaurant was the middle Allen child. The two made their way over to him and settled into the booth. Amelia slid into one side of the booth and wondered why Donna was following her into that side. When she noticed the fourth set of silverware on the table, Jason exited the booth to allow the additional occupant to sit across from his sister. "Nice to see you again, Ms. Allen."

Amelia found herself staring into those deep cerulean blues of Dr. Ben Taylor. "Dr. Taylor, this is a surprise. I thought it was only going to be three of us." Amelia said the last statement while glaring at her sister-in-law. Donna simply smirked at Amelia. Who was going to hurt or get revenge on a pregnant woman?

Dr. Taylor laughed, "Donna said you probably would not be pleased with this plan. For the record, I told her not to do this, but she's very persistent. She informed me you agreed to be set up on a date but would likely back out. I typically would do the same, but I wanted to see your face just once more. Please, call me Ben."

Amelia melted under the warmth that radiated from his laughter. The man sitting across from her seemed to be a real charmer and a true gentleman. "Please, call me Amelia," she stated as she extended her hand. Instead of shaking it, Ben lifted the extended hand to his face and kissed its back. Amelia blushed as she took her hand back. "Maybe my sister-in-law's persistence is a good attribute." Ben laughed at her comment and remarked, "Perhaps an outstanding attribute indeed."

The four had a great evening dining and chatting together. Amelia seemed to be under less pressure on this date than she had been on many before. The double date was causing her to be more open and willing to give this a try. The four of them had chatted for so long inside the booth that they almost missed the movie. Their quartet drove over to the local movie theater in downtown Humboldt to see the latest romantic film. Jason had tried to argue for an action-packed movie, but he was outmaneuvered three to one. He complained that Ben should side with him, and Ben informed him that Donna's suggestions had yet to be wrong. He winked at Amelia as he said those words. Jason very exaggeratedly rolled his eyes as his sister's face turned bright red.

As the film started, the four sat together near the back of the theater. Jason and Donna were getting as cozy as they could in the seats. Before the film started, Amelia and Ben tried to get to know each other a little more privately. Once the commercials started, they could not whisper to each other with ease, so they instead focused on the film. As the movie progressed and began to tug on the heartstrings, Ben wrapped his arm around Amelia. She first was shocked at the gesture but quickly leaned into his embrace. The feeling was familiar and warm, but best of all, it made her smile. The film ended with a beautiful wedding scene. As the two couples left the movie theater and began walking to their cars, Amelia noticed the tear stains that glistened on the face of one of the two men. "Jason, are you crying?"

Jason Allen quickly wiped away all evidence of any tears. "Amelia, I think you must be seeing things again. Maybe you should schedule an appointment with an optometrist while you are here. Say, Dr. Ben, can you recommend one?" The group laughed at the horrible attempt to deflect the attention.

Ben commented, "I might know one or two. I can also recommend a good psychologist for you, Jason." Amelia laughed harder than she had in years. Jason spluttered as he failed to find a comeback.

Donna laughed, and as her husband continued to deny the tears, she added, "It is okay, honey. It seems the man also gets emotional during pregnancy." The group laughed again at Jason's expense, and Amelia could tell he was ready for the evening to end.

Jason and Donna left the parking lot to give Ben and Amelia a chance to say goodbye. "I had a fantastic time tonight," Ben said to Amelia.

"I did too. I greatly enjoyed spending time with you."

Ben leaned in to kiss her cheek. "I wanted to do that since I saw you at the restaurant."

She smiled and blushed at his quick move. "Maybe you will get a chance to do it again."

Ben's face illuminated, "Well, are you free Tuesday night?" She thought for a moment before replying that she was free. "Wonderful! I will pick you up about six." The two exchanged numbers, and Amelia drove back to her house in bliss. She was pretty infatuated with Dr. Ben Taylor and wondered what story time would tell.

The next morning Amelia was up early to prepare the traditional Allen Sunday breakfast. Her mother always had the entire family over for both Sunday breakfast and lunch each week. While Amelia had missed the tradition for a long time, she was ready to prepare it for everyone this time. She made homemade waffles and pancakes as well as eggs, hash browns, sausage, and bacon. The coffee was ready for everyone as she set the table. Minutes after setting the table, all of her family arrived. The Allen's dug into the feast, and Susan even commented on how delicious the food was. Amelia beamed at the praise from her mother as it had been missing for a few days now.

Eric and Emma offered to clear the breakfast table while the others prepared for church services. Amelia had considered skipping the service but realized she would feel too guilty. Jessie was coming over to stay with Susan so that all of the other Allens could attend together. Roger wanted to stay with his wife, but Susan convinced him to go as he was the adult Sunday school teacher. Amelia loaded into the car with her father, Eric, and Emma, and they headed over to the church.

Amelia spent the majority of the morning answering the same questions: "How is Nashville dear?", "How is your mother?", "Will you be here for the festival?" and her personal favorite, "Is there anyone special in your life?" Amelia thought about responding yes to the last question, but it seemed to be an awkward answer since the relationship was so new. She first wanted to make sure they were compatible before telling the world, let alone her parents' church.

Amelia enjoyed the song selection this morning. Her congregation in Nashville tended to sing primarily newer hymns. They were beautiful, with a great message, but she often missed the older hymns. The song leader chose hymns like Victory in Jesus, and It is Well with My Soul. She sang her alto notes loudly through all of the songs. When the preacher started delivering his message, she noticed how well the hymns tied into the sermon. The preacher talked about joy and peace amid trials. He reminded them of who was always on their side and where to find courage, strength, revitalization, and victory. The message sunk into her soul, and she was yet again grateful to attend the service.

As she rode home with her family, it dawned on her just how thankful she indeed was for this trip, even with her mother's accident. It amazed her that she had fought coming home for so long, only to realize that the vacation was benefitting her. She wondered if God was teaching her more about herself and how she ought to be living. It was something she wanted to examine more and more. She hoped that these next two weeks would teach her how to be content.

Jessie had cooked a delicious lunch of roasted pork chops for all of her family. The Allen kids informed Susan of the sermon today and various church news. Brad called as they were almost finished with dessert to let Amelia know he was on the way. She thought of how ironic it was that he had called at the same time her mother normally would.

About two hours later, Bradley pulled into the Allen home. He came inside to visit with Susan, who lit up at his presence. Amelia and Susan had gotten along much better today, but Amelia was slightly hurt to see her mother's reaction to her friend versus to herself. Bradley talked with Roger for a while before helping unload Amelia's belongings. Amelia got him to agree to a trip through town to see the places she often mentioned. They parked his car in one area downtown, and she walked him all around the area. Bradley became charmed by the serene setting of the little town and all the strawberry decorations. "You weren't kidding about all the strawberries. It's wonderful, Amelia."

She laughed, "This is nothing. You should see the town next week when the festival begins." He continued glancing around the town, admiring its small-town beauty.

"Is that an invitation?"

Amelia was glad that someone else saw how special this place could be. "If you want, we have the room. You are more than welcome to stay a day or the whole week."

He looked ecstatic. "I think I will take you up on your offer. I'm scheduling the vacation tomorrow."

She rolled her eyes at his antics, "I guess the two-week rule doesn't apply to you, Mr. Leave Administrator, does it?"

He gave her a lop-sided smile. "Why, of course not! That's one of the perks of the position. So tell me about the date with the doctor."

As they walked back to his car talking about the other night, Amelia noticed Ian sitting inside the downtown Mexican restaurant. She saw him laughing and giggling with someone she couldn't quite make out. As they rounded the corner, Amelia was able to get a better look at his companion. Her heart seemed to drop as she noticed the woman sitting opposite him. The feelings stirring in her only lead to more confusion. Hoping they would vanish, Amelia wondered why she was irritated at the thought of him seeing someone, especially after going on a date and consenting to another one with Dr. Ben. She decided that the problem was not in him dating but in who he was seeing. She walked briskly to the car with Brad, who was so busy taking in the town he failed to notice the change in her demeanor.

Later that night, after he had headed back to Nashville, Amelia prepared herself for the next day of work at Allen Inc. She decided to try and go to bed early and get some rest for once. As she laid in her bed staring at the ceiling, she quickly realized this would be another restless night. Her mind could not stop showing her the image of Ian Reynolds having dinner with her cousin, Jessie Tomlinson.

Chapter Ten

Early Monday morning, Amelia prepared her breakfast shake and decided to go for a run before heading to the office. Since moving to the city several years ago for college, there was less time to run and no time to play tennis. She headed up to Bailey Park to take several laps around their track. When she pulled into the parking lot, she noticed that a few individuals were playing on the tennis courts. She thought about how nice it would be to play again and headed off on her run.

As Amelia ran the track, her mind drifted to a match on that very court her senior year. *"Aha! I beat you." Amelia was celebrating the win over her boyfriend. Ian's face was merely one of elation at seeing how happy she got. She began teasing him about losing to a girl when he mentioned, "Well, I think I'm the real winner." She stopped and started looking at him, confused, "How is a loss by six points a win?" The two began walking the track and interlaced hands. "Any day spent with you is a win in my book."*

Amelia completed about two miles before deciding to head back to her house. As she neared her car, she noticed the tennis players had left. Right as she was opening her door, a voice called out, "Have a good run?'

Amelia turned around to see Ian in an athletic shirt and shorts holding a tennis racket. "I did, thanks. Were you one of the ones playing tennis?"

He smirked at her, "No, but I did happen to play some new version of basketball. It involves a racket and a much smaller ball." She nudged him for making fun of her. "When was the last time you played?"

It took her a moment to try and remember when the last time was that she had set foot on a court. "It has been at least five years."

Ian was appalled at that answer, "Well, you must play while in town. You can join me say Friday morning, 6:00?" Amelia typically slept until around that time, but lately, she was waking up earlier each day. She loved playing the game even though it was currently nothing more than a past-time. Ultimately, she agreed to meet him for a match at the end of the week. He smiled, and the two parted ways.

Amelia returned home with enough time to make breakfast for her parents and clean up before heading into the office. Amelia dressed in a smart coral pantsuit. She made sure her hair was styled professionally and drove over to the office. As she walked into the building, she noticed several individuals in what appeared to be business casual. The men wore very few suit jackets, and the women were in simple outfits. She rounded the corner to her temporary office and saw Emma hard at work. Emma looked up at the perfect time to see Amelia enter their area. "Amelia, don't you look nice today." Amelia thanked her for the compliment and headed on into the office.

Sitting on the desk in a beautiful clear glass vase was an arrangement of light pink roses. They were gorgeous, but she could find no card or note as she looked around the area. "Emma?" Emma came into her office and smiled at the arrangement. "Emma, there was no need to put flowers on the desk. I'm glad to help out."

Emma chuckled slightly, "Uh, Amelia, someone sent those about fifteen minutes ago. The card kept falling out. Sorry about forgetting to leave that on your desk. Here it is." Emma left the office as Amelia opened the card. The words scrawled upon the card were simple, *Beautiful pink roses for one strong, funny, and gorgeous lady.* Amelia smiled as she imagined Dr. Taylor saying those words. No one signed the card, but instinct told her they were from the good doctor.

Amelia began working on confirming the interview schedule Emma had drafted. Five total candidates would be coming this Friday for interviews about the two positions. Feeling accomplished, she started tackling the small backlog Timmons had left. Amelia went over the leave banks for the employees and made notes for conversations later this week. She also acknowledged a retirement letter for someone planning to move at the end of July. The employee wanted to give ample time to find a person to learn the job with them. As she prepared to move onto the next task, Jenna knocked at her door. "Amelia, I hope you enjoyed the remainder of your weekend. I was hoping that we could finish going over those details." Amelia invited her into the office and shelved the documents of the next project. Amelia had a feeling that this meeting might last a while.

Two hours later, the ladies emerged from the office. Jenna seemed extremely satisfied with the meeting and chatted with her sister before returning to work. Emma took one look at Amelia and laughed. "I guess now is a bad time to tell you that she will be helping plan my wedding, isn't it?" Amelia shook her head more than a few times to bring herself out of the daze.

"As long as you and she can handle it, I am wonderful. I never knew how much mom did for this festival. It is going to be a nightmare trying to get this all together. Can you track down Lucy Carpenter for me? We need to discuss the venue and preparations for the recipe contest."

Emma laughed, "I guess since you had to experience Hurricane Jenna, I can help you with that." Amelia nodded her thanks and went back into the office.

Amelia worked straight through lunch, determined to get the last few items done. She wanted to spend the next few days getting to know the staff and seeing what else needed accomplishing. Emma noticed that Amelia was not stopping, so she ran out to get her future sister-in-law and temporary boss a salad. She came back into the office and dropped the container directly on top of Amelia's paperwork. "Hey! I was looking over that."

Emma gave a slight shrug, "As you remember, hay is for horses. Now, eat." Amelia knew that Emma would fit in fine with their family; she could be just as commanding as the rest of the Allen women.

The two ate their lunch together, and Amelia took a few moments to relax. "Emma, why does everyone dress so casually around here?" Emma quirked her head while munching on the meal.

"Your dad has always felt that you need to look presentable yet down to earth. He doesn't want us to be considered the same as any other corporate consulting firm. We are different here, the atmosphere is relaxed, everyone works together, and we enjoy our jobs. Your dad actually had us start doing a volunteer mission each quarter as well. It is good to give back to this community and spend time working together on something more meaningful." Amelia nodded her head at the answer but chose not to comment.

She had worked in a corporate HR environment before, and it was night and day compared to this. She always imagined retiring from the state one day and diving back into the private sector. She imagined the business dinners, presentations, luxurious offices, and more of the city life. She never considered it could look like this. Her trip home started to cause Amelia to question what she wanted in life. She was brought out of her daydream by her phone vibrating. She smiled as she looked down and saw the message was from Ben. He was wishing her a great day and told her he looked forward to their date the following evening. He began using several extremely horrible pick-up lines, which made Amelia smile and chuckle. Emma picked up on the giddiness she was exhibiting, "You met someone!" The words were more of a statement than a question. Emma got up and hugged Amelia and said, "It is about time! While I'm thinking about it, what are you doing around seven tonight?"

Amelia ignored her antics and responded to the question, "Unless mom needs something, I think I am free. Why?"

Emma sported a wide grin, "Great! Come over to my house this evening. Jason and Eric watch wrestling on Monday nights, so Donna comes over with Lou sometimes, and we have a girls' night. We are having dinner and a movie tonight; you should join us."

Amelia thought it would be nice to spend some time with the ladies who had captivated her brothers' hearts. "Sure, Emma, that sounds wonderful!"

Deciding it was time for a change in scenery, she headed back to the house. As she entered, she caught her mother attempting to hobble across the floor on crutches. "Mother! You know you should be in bed. What were you thinking? Where did you send dad?" Susan rolled her eyes, frustrated that she was caught and by her daughter no less. Amelia helped her back into bed before she begrudgingly began answering the questions.

Amelia learned that her mother had been attempting to see how hurt she was. She suggested Roger go into his office to make sure everything was going smoothly in order to pull this off. To trick him into leaving, she feigned being asleep long enough to get him to leave. He had whispered to his wife that he would be gone an hour at the maximum. That had only been fifteen minutes ago.

Amelia turned to leave her mother and get some housework done, but she decided to take advantage of the two being alone. She faced her mother once more and said, "Mom, why are you upset with me?"

Susan pretended to be shocked at the question, but Amelia knew her mother's tells all too well. "Why do you think I am upset with you, dear?"

Amelia was not playing coy with her mother. "You asked me to leave and have been avoiding me ever since I decided to stay." Susan glared at her daughter but did not answer her back. It was a battle of the wills for a few moments until Amelia decided she would not stand there and play games.

As Amelia turned to exit the room, her mother called out, "For someone on vacation, you sure seem to want to work a lot." Amelia kept walking, not taking the bait. She headed upstairs to her room and sat on the bed. *Why did I even move anything downstairs?* At this rate, she doubted she would spend much time in that room at all.

Amelia stroked Frank as she considered the confrontation with her mother. While Susan was attempting to elicit a rise out of her daughter, the words had struck a nerve. She was supposed to be relaxing away from work. Oddly enough, she felt more relaxed working on the festival and Allen Inc. than she had in years, despite having several tasks that needed finishing. Her mind recalled the lunch conversation with Emma, and there she found her answer.

She was determined not to be as stressed about work and instead be more relaxed. Tomorrow she would work on the Festival preparations, such as making sure everything was ready for the recipe contest, the breakfast-themed dinner items were planned, etc. The company was in good shape and could afford a more hands-off approach at the moment. She had agreed to play tennis on Friday and had a date tomorrow night. Reviewing all of these developments in her mind, Amelia convinced herself that she was taking a step back from overworking herself.

Her father arrived home about thirty minutes later. She decided that the best payback on her mother was to tattle. Roger angrily scolded his wife for her dirty tricks while she gave Amelia the evil eye. Once Roger had calmed himself, Amelia approached him to discuss the interviews.

"Dad, I would like for you to sit in on the interviews. They will be this Friday; the first one is at 9:00 a.m." Her father tried to reason his way out of the meeting, but Amelia had prepared for this. "Jessie has agreed to stay with mom the whole day, and your office assured me they could cover the chamber without you." Recognizing that he was arguing with a strong-willed Allen woman, he gave up fighting the decision. He agreed to be in the conference room Friday morning. As he went off into his study, Amelia could have sworn she heard him murmuring about stubborn mules. She pretended as if he was reminiscing about his childhood on the farm and went off to start dinner for her parents.

After she set dinner on the dining room table, she went upstairs to change clothes. Fifteen minutes later, she waved goodbye to her parents and headed over to Emma's house. She had brought along her favorite new recipe: strawberry & cream cheese cobbler. She was not wholly sure what Emma had planned for them to eat but figured no one would ever turn down a dessert. She entered the house to find Emma finishing the main course. Donna arrived moments later, and Lou had even managed to stop by. As Emma finished setting the table, the last two guests arrived. Emma had invited both her sister Jenna and the Allen siblings' cousin, Jessie. Amelia was not aware that Jessie was close with her future sister-in-law but chose not to be too curious this evening.

As the ladies began enjoying their dinner, the conversation seemed to focus on Amelia. She started to complain, but Lou was the one to keep her from deflecting. "Amelia, I think everyone either misses you, or maybe they want to know how your life is going. Indulge them and me. I love seeing you squirm." Amelia glared at her longtime friend but chose to give the room what they wanted. She sighed and leaned back in the chair, ready for the inquisition.

"So, Amelia, how is it being my sister's boss?" Jenna asked with a hint of teasing. Emma rolled her eyes at her sister and pretended to hit Jenna in the shoulder. Amelia laughed at the teasing and told the group how much she enjoyed working at Allen Inc. It was refreshing how all the workers and their attitudes at the company made this experience highly enjoyable. The tone and setting of the office were bringing Amelia peace amid the surrounding personal strife.

"Amelia, not to pry too much, but why did you choose to take a vacation now? I know Aunt Susan's been wanting you to come for some time." This question had come from Jessie. This one was harder to explain, so Amelia took a long drink from her glass before responding.

"The short answer is that I work too hard, and my boss convinced me to take a break." The table stared at each other, considering the vagueness of her answer. She and Lou had talked briefly about the situation, but even then, Lou still had no idea about the complete picture. She decided to be the one to end the silence, "And the long story is?"

Glancing out the window, hoping to find an excuse to change the subject, Amelia realized in the silence that everyone was waiting on her response. "I had too much vacation time, and so my work required I take at least a few days off."

"So, you've been able to take time off for a while now?"

Amelia saw the hurt on Lou's face as she asked the question. "I . . . . well you see, . . . there's so much . . ." Every time she started a new excuse, the looks from her friend, family, and rival stopped her. "Yes."

The quiet of the room caused the guilt Amelia was feeling to magnify even more. Not being close with Amelia, Jenna remained silent but had the same inquisitive look on her face that all the others did.

"It was too hard to come home." Amelia decided it was time to answer the unspoken question of "Why?"

"This town was nothing more than the home of broken dreams and memories. I thought by now I'd be married, living here surrounded by all of our friends and family. When life went in another direction, I thought it was best not to dwell on the past. I never considered that I was hurting anyone else and thought I was only pushing forward. I was embarrassed that the life I had was not the one everyone thought it would be. Staying away, I thought, kept the remains of my heart protected. What I didn't realize was by doing so, I never allowed it to heal."

The room digested Amelia's words. Those gathered in Emma's house knew this part of the conversation needed to end here, so Donna decided to question her sister-in-law further, "Amelia, are you possibly taking on too much while home this time? It seems that your vacation to relax has accumulated a lot of work. How can you rejuvenate while still working hard?"

Amelia huffed and mumbled something about everyone asking the same question. "Why does everyone ask me that? I am most relaxed when my plate is full. As I'm getting back into this community more, I'm also learning that it's fine to come back here."

Seeing that Amelia was not yet ready to continue this part of the discussion, Emma decided to change the topic to a similar yet slightly different one. "Well, I ran into Ian the other day as he was leaving the Italian restaurant. He looked upset, and I know the two of you were supposed to meet for lunch. I take it the lunch was not what you planned." Amelia gave some details without divulging too much information. Lou knew the entire story, but Amelia wanted to keep some of her life private. As the mood was turning colder and colder, Donna decided to perk everyone up. "Well, why don't we leave old flames in the past and talk about new ones! Amelia is seeing a very handsome new doctor."

All eyes shot to Amelia, and Donna reveled in the fact that she had shocked the group. The barrage of questions began rolling in, starting with Lou's "Why didn't you tell me?!" to Emma's "Is that why you were so happy earlier?" to Jessie's request to know all the details. Amelia flushed bright red, and Donna decided to add to her embarrassment by beginning to tell the story of how Amelia practically ogled the tall, handsome doctor and he likewise. Amelia flushed as she described Dr. Taylor and admitted to having a date set for the following evening. The room became engrossed in the romantic life of Amelia, and she was thankful to be off of darker topics.

The film Emma had selected laid on the coffee table, long forgotten as the ladies dived more into Dr. Ben Taylor. They questioned Amelia on what she would wear for the event and where they were heading. When Amelia told them the date was a surprise and her only instructions were to be ready at six o'clock, their hearts swooned after the man. Amelia laughed and smiled more this evening than she had in years. *When was the last girl's night?* Part of the problem was other than one or two back in Nashville, she worked too much to have many friends. As the ladies talked more and more about their lives and love, her heart mellowed, and her mind never wandered into work mode.

Jenna turned to Jessie. "So, speaking of new relationships,

I heard you met someone." Jessie glanced at Amelia and smiled slightly.

"Well, the news certainly travels fast; we only started talking recently. This gentleman is extremely handsome, hilarious, and seems to be a wonderful guy. Our work schedules keep us from connecting on a deeper level, but we both have Festival week off. When I bumped into him, I felt that spark, and so I am hoping that this goes well." Amelia's stomach churned as she recalled seeing Jessie with Ian. Her mind rationally could not determine why she was experiencing this wave of emotion.

She considered how close she had been with Ian over the years. Even though she was moving onto a new relationship, she wanted Ian to be happy deep down. Her first instinct was to criticize the relationship, but her mind changed plans as she heard Jessie speak. Jessie seemed to be genuinely interested, and Amelia listened to the desire in her voice. She opted to see how everything progressed before sharing her opinions.

As the ladies made their way out of Emma's house and into their cars, Jessie asked to speak with Amelia privately. Amelia's stomach seemed as if she had just ridden the world's curviest rollercoaster. As they walked to a private area, Amelia spoke words of confidence to herself in preparation for the conversation. "Amelia, I noticed that you seemed a little off-put about the discussion on my new relationship. I assume you know that I am talking to . . ."

Amelia decided to cut her off before her stomach decided to take round two on the trip. Her mind knew if she heard his name, it would only make matters worse. "Jessie, I know, and it hurts not to be told by my cousin, but I'm okay with it."

Jessie was taken aback by her cousin's comment. When Jessie began preparing for this conversation, she imagined several scenarios with possible resolutions. This answer was the absolute least expected reaction in her estimation. "I thought you would disapprove, but I wanted to tell you. I forget how small this town is sometimes and should have known word would get out. Amelia, I'm sorry."

Amelia shook her head and mustered the best smile she could. "Jessie, I promise you that all is fine. Please be careful and be happy with him." As Amelia started to walk away, she stopped, "Jessie, do me one favor. If you see the relationship is failing, don't linger in it. Decide early that you two are right or wrong for each other and don't let the decision impact your friendship." Jessie stared blankly at her cousin as Amelia said goodnight and went home for yet another restless evening.

Chapter Eleven

Amelia awoke very early the following morning. Her dreams had left her with very little rest. She decided to take a run around the neighborhood to boost her adrenaline. When she returned to the house, Roger Allen was reading the morning paper and brewing fresh coffee. Amelia headed upstairs to change and shower before starting breakfast. The two Allen members stood in the kitchen in silence, one contemplating the day's work and the other focused on serving a healthy meal.

When Amelia set the homemade quiche in the oven, Roger decided to talk with his daughter. "Milly, I heard you pacing around upstairs for a long time last night. Would you like to talk about whatever is troubling you?"

Amelia started cutting up fruit to go alongside the breakfast quiche. "Only that several thoughts are running through my head. It can be difficult to turn my brain off at times."

Roger looked sad as they continued their discussion. "That might be true, but it seems something is keeping you up at night."

Amelia realized that she might also be keeping her father awake. "Dad, I am so sorry if my pacing is keeping you and mom awake. I promise to move into the room downstairs tonight finally. You should be able to get some rest after I do that."

"Milly, you are avoiding my question. What is the matter, sweetheart? If there is too much on your plate, say the word, and we can find others to cover." Amelia was not letting go of her responsibilities that easily. She was more than capable of handling the festival, Allen Inc., reconnecting with friends and family, assisting her parents, and even dating.

"Dad, I am fine. I've been thinking a lot about my work and how to make the best impact. When I get fired up, it can be difficult to settle down." Roger reluctantly nodded his head and finished reading the paper. Once breakfast was served, and the three Allen members had eaten until they were satisfied, Amelia assisted her mother in getting back into her recovery bed. Susan griped about not being able to do anything until Amelia put Frank in the bed with her mother. Susan immediately started cooing at Frank and scratching him right under the chin. Frank began purring loudly as this was his favorite spot to receive affection. Amelia chuckled at how easily she had manipulated her mother and returned to finish the dishes.

Roger was loading the last item into the dishwasher when Amelia emerged. She thanked her father for his assistance and went upstairs to get dressed for the day. Amelia came back downstairs and said goodbye to both of her parents. Roger called out to his daughter before she left, "Milly? I need you to send over the human resources proposals. I will assign the consultants to each project, and you don't need to worry about it." Amelia started to object, but her father held up his hand. "I am staying home with your mother today, and that is something I can do from here. You know I like to get a little work done each day." Amelia signaled her understanding with a head shake and turned to leave for the office.

"Oh, and Milly?" her father called. "Regarding our conversation earlier, you might try a better lie next time. Remember that it is difficult to tell one to someone who has known you as long as I have. You can never solve a problem by lying to those who care about you, but especially not while lying to yourself. Now, have a good day, dear, and we will talk later." Amelia stood frozen in the hallway. Her father had never called her a liar before, but that was in the basic sense what she had done. Her conscious thought she should come clean to her dad right then and there, but her pride caused her to walk out the door and into her car.

Amelia arrived at her temporary office, this time in much simpler clothing. She left the pantsuits hanging in the closet and chose to be more in tune with the Allen Inc. staff. Emma smiled at her outfit and handed her a few top priority items. Amelia breezed through the work and saw that the clock read 10:30. Amelia took time to organize festival to-do lists, but even that went quickly. She emailed over the files her father had requested and asked Emma what else needed to be done. When Amelia and Emma realized that they had completed all the pressing work, Amelia decided to start playing with a few projects.

Emma caught on to what was happening and decided to take matters into her hands. After hearing about the reasoning for this vacation, she was still concerned and wanted to help her fiancée's sister. "Amelia, these projects should wait for the new director. I would hate for you to get started on something only to see it unutilized. Instead of working on those projects, why don't you go out in town? I'll call you if anything comes up, but if not, take the day off."

Usually, Amelia would argue, but she thought a day off might be just what she needed. Her mind could not believe that only a short few days home had already changed her perception of work. She wanted to clear her mind after the conversation with her father and realized this was a perfect opportunity. Emma seemed just as shocked as Amelia felt that there would be no argument. Amelia smiled and thanked her "assistant," and headed out the door.

Amelia drove around for about twenty minutes, deciding where to relax. She decided on the public library. Any other day, Amelia would take a walk or visit a body of water to clear her mind. This time, she wanted to escape her mind, like she needed to the night before. After parking in the back of the building, Amelia snuck in through the back door. The last time she had been inside, there were so many people that knew her. She crept over to the classics and chose a random one off the shelf.

She settled into the reading area directly beside these books and began to read a story that transported her back to the author's time. Amelia was unsure how long she had sat in the chair, but her body had begun to get numb. She decided to stand up and stretch before putting the book away. She perused the shelves nearest to her and found Ian Reynolds standing in the middle of the romance aisle. "Never pegged you for the romance novel type."

Ian looked up to see Amelia standing there. He laughed and retorted, "Well, I am tall, tan, and mysterious. All of those authors wrote these books about me."

She rolled her eyes as she watched him collect an Amish story. "I definitely would never have thought you would read those books."

He laughed and observed her, "Are you the censorship police now? Do I need to pass an exam to select certain books?"

Amelia laughed at the jovial banter he was using. "I believe you need to pass a three-part test, sir." He asked for a copy of a study guide, and she whacked him with the book she was holding. The two laughed and carried on until the librarian finally shushed them. It was a rarity to be quieted in a public library anymore. The days of being filled with just books were gone, and libraries were community hubs. The two chuckled, and Amelia remembered all of the many times the two of them had gotten in trouble as kids.

"Seriously, what is with all these books?" Amelia inquired of him once she saw he had twelve books selected.

He glanced at her for a few moments before saying, "Are you busy for lunch today?"

Amelia wondered why he was avoiding the question. "Ian, just tell me already. I promise not to make fun of you . . . at least not much."

Ian laughed at his old friend's determination. "I will show you, but only over lunch. I hope you like creamed corn, creamed potatoes, and pork roast." Amelia agreed to lunch with him only to satisfy her curiosity.

Amelia followed him in her car over to one of the newer assisted living facilities. As the two made their way towards the front door, Amelia stopped him. "I thought we were going to lunch?"

He grinned as largely as he could. "We are. I hope you like their Tuesday special." She followed him inside and down the hall to a cafeteria. The two picked up a lunch tray from staff, who seemed to know Ian very well.

He guided her over to a table for two and sat down to eat his lunch. The two began eating, and Ian made small talk. Amelia returned the chit-chat for a little while before giving in to her curiosity. "Ian, it is lunchtime, and you said you would tell me."

He smiled as he took another bite of his potatoes. "No, I told you that I would show you. Just wait." The pair began catching up like old friends. Amelia wondered why they were able to act civilly this time compared to the last. She realized there was no pressure on this conversation and seemed to feel lighter without the stress. It amazed her how different she felt from what she had always imagined their "reconciliation" would be.

When lunch ended, he guided Amelia down to a community room. Inside were about eight residents whose faces shined brighter than the sun in seeing Ian. Several called out his name, beckoning him to come over and see each one. Amelia watched as he went person to person, distributing the books and collecting what she assumed were ones that had been read and enjoyed. He left the additional four titles on a table for the staff to pass out to other residents. She watched as he spent time with each resident and smiled at the kind gesture.

Amelia considered how often Ian thought of other people, and it made her heart flutter. The last time the two of them spent under the dogwood tree at the library was one of her favorite memories of Ian's thoughtfulness. *"What are you reading, Ian?" He tried to hide the book, but being trapped with Amelia on his side made it hard to maneuver. She finally got the book out of his hand. Candide? I thought you didn't like those kinds of novels. He murmured something that she couldn't quite make out. "I'm sorry, what was that?" He huffed before grabbing the book back from her. "I said, it's one of your favorites that you love to quote. I thought if I read it, I could appreciate it as you do." Amelia blushed and leaned back against him while reading her book. The two lay in silence while one read, and the other considered how sweet it was that someone would do that for her.*

As Ian was making his rounds around the room, an older woman wheeled into the room. Amelia noticed that she seemed to stare off into space after coming out of her daydream. The lady called out, "What is going on in here today?"

Amelia stepped over beside the lady and explained what Ian was doing. "My friend is passing out novels to several of the residents for them to read. Would you like for me to hand you one?"

The lady sat in the same position as she had when entering the room. "I don't think so. It would be hard to read, seeing as I'm blind."

Amelia profusely apologized to the woman, afraid that she had upset her. The woman laughed and shook her head. "Oh honey, I wasn't trying to be rude to you. I used to love to read, but a medical condition robbed me of my eyesight when I was a child. I listen to books when I can, but those are hard to come by here in this facility. Your friend must be the one who organizes books for a lot of the residents here. He worked out a plan with the local library a while back, but they only let him borrow hardback books, no audio recordings." Amelia grew sad at hearing the news. She walked over to the table and selected the shortest book, a classic of only sixty pages, on the table. She estimated it would take a few hours to read, and she pulled up a chair next to the lady.

As Amelia began to read, the lady questioned her on what was happening. "Well, ma'am, if the library cannot let you borrow an audiobook, I think I'll just turn this book into one for you." Amelia noticed a tear streak down the lady's cheek. She seemed so emotional over something as simple as a book that Amelia began to choke up herself. Amelia wiped the tears from her face and then used a tissue to dry the woman's face.

"That is the nicest thing anyone has ever offered to do for me, but you can't waste your time like that. I'm sure you have more important business to handle." Amelia glanced at her watch, 1:15 p.m.

Amelia knew that this is why she had taken off this afternoon. She was free until her date tonight and knew what to say. "I'm free until this evening, Ms. . ."

The lady had another tear stroll down her face. "Georgia. Georgia Holland. Ms. . . ."

"Amelia. Amelia Allen." The lady felt with her hands until she found Amelia's hand and clasped it tightly.

She breathed a teary, "Thank you, Amelia."

Amelia let another tear fall as she opened the book and began to read. The lady looked on with a face full of delight and gratitude. Ian was finishing his visit with another resident and turned to find Amelia. Amelia noticed he was admiring her reading to Georgia when his eyes lit up with inspiration. She watched out of the corner of her eyes as he disappeared off into another part of the facility.

Around 3:40 p.m., Amelia finished the story. Georgia was so thrilled to have been able to listen to another beautiful work of literature. Amelia glanced up to notice there were hardly any people left in the room, and Ian was nowhere in view. Amelia used the next twenty minutes to learn about Georgia's life and vice versa. Georgia was a lady who had moved to Humboldt from Chicago more than forty years ago. She had never married and had two nieces and a nephew. All three still lived in the greater Chicago area. They would come to visit occasionally at Christmas and on her birthday. She mentioned that one niece called regularly, but otherwise, she was alone.

Amelia's heart broke at seeing this lady all by herself. "Well, Ms. Holland, I am from here but live in Nashville. I'm in town for about twelve more days, but there are a lot of festival preparations. I will try to call and visit with you when I can if that's ok." Georgia smiled, although Amelia could see a hint of disappointment. Amelia knew it must be hard to realize your new friend was only here short-term.

As Amelia stood to say her goodbyes, Ian came into the room with the activities director and another hardback book. "Good you are still here! Ms. Georgia, my name is Ian, and I coordinate the book program here. I remember you wanted to read a particular book, and I was able to get it from the library for you." She thanked him and asked with more than a hint of hope if it was an audiobook.

The activities director spoke up next, "Not exactly Ms. Holland. I was able to get some volunteers to agree to read to you and a few of our other residents with disabilities for one hour each day. Ian has volunteered to be the first reader tomorrow." Georgia Holland's face lit up once again at this news. She was beyond thrilled at a chance to experience literature once again. Her face was not the only one that had illuminated. Amelia was staring at Ian in complete and total happiness. She could not believe the program he had begun for these residents but how he was going out of his way to help this lady. She wondered if he knew just how beneficial a program like this was for both the resident and the volunteer. The last two hours had given her a fresh take on life, and she felt more empowered than ever.

As the two celebrated the news, Georgia felt around for Amelia's hand once more. "This is all thanks to you, my dear. They saw what you did for me and were inspired. May God bless you, and please keep in touch with your new friend!" Amelia leaned in to hug the lady and then knew it was time to head home. She said goodbye to the sweet woman and walked out with Ian. As they made their way into the parking lot, Amelia could not quit smiling at him. "What? Still curious about something?"

Amelia continued smiling as she replied, "Not this time, just thankful for you putting up with my badgering and for you letting me experience this. It is such an amazing feeling to give back to others." Ian smiled at her as the two separated.

Amelia arrived home to find her father exiting his study. He noticed the smile on his daughter's face and wondered what had caused it. "Milly, did you have a good day?"

She continued grinning as she headed up the stairs. "The best!" He watched her climb higher and higher up the stairs and called out to ask what had made it so great. As she reached the top step, she called out, "I enjoyed a good book." Roger quirked his head at these words, but before he could inquire any further, he heard her door close.

Amelia spent the rest of the afternoon on cloud nine. "Bradley, you'll never guess what we did today!" She had called her friend once again to give an update on Susan and how things were going. "That sounds amazing, Amelia. I am glad you are enjoying life and not spending all your time at your dad's office. It seems like Ian is a perfect gentleman, but don't you have a date tonight?" That brought her down long enough to decide on what to wear for the evening. After trying on about six different outfits, she settled on the slim black dress and black heels. She added a slight amount of makeup and decided she was ready for the evening.

Just as the clock struck six o'clock, the doorbell rang. She opened it to find Ben standing there holding a box of chocolates. She accepted the chocolates and joined him outside. "You look stunning this evening," he commented as his eyes glossed over her image.

She took in his pin-stripe suit, white dress shirt with a strawberry-themed tie and smiled at him, "You are looking very festive and handsome yourself." He escorted her into his burgundy SUV, and they made their way to the date.

While on the car ride, she attempted to uncover where they would be visiting this evening. He refused to answer any questions regarding their evening, and so instead, they learned more about each other in the ride. Over the night, she learned that he was a huge dog lover, golfer, and his favorite books were non-fiction. On the other side, Amelia was a cat lover, sometimes a tennis player, and enjoyed all types of fiction. Regardless that not all of their preferences were identical, neither could deny the connection. Amelia felt comfortable with Ben, and the feeling seemed mutual. She enjoyed their car chat and was sad when they pulled into their destination.

Ben had driven all around the area just to end up at Davy Crockett Lake. She laughed when she saw the location, and he immediately fretted over his decision. She explained to him how special this place was to her and how she had visited recently. He relaxed and pulled out a blanket with a picnic basket. "So we got dressed up for a picnic on the grass by a lake?"

He laughed and laid out the blanket. "That was the plan. Why do we have to do everything the conventional way?"

She enjoyed his whimsical attitude, and the two enjoyed the meal as the sun went down. "I love a sunset, especially as you see it disappear over the water or the trees. I see it as a reminder that when the sun goes down, it is time to reset and restart before it rises again the next day."

He gazed off into the sky and nodded his head, agreeing to her sentiment. "Nature truly is peaceful."

Ben and Amelia discussed their dreams and desires. Amelia was openly honest when she said her dreams might be conflicted. He sat patiently as she discussed how she was reevaluating her life. Most men would try and fix her problems for her; however, he listened and offered sage advice for her to consider. Other than in that moment, the conversation stayed highly engaging and light-hearted. As the evening continued to dwindle, the two inched closer and closer together. Once the night had started turning dark, they loaded everything back into his vehicle and headed home.

"Ben, this was a lovely evening. I was expecting a fancy dinner, but this was a much better option." His face shone with happiness at her comments. "I had a great time as well. Maybe we can see each other again? I am on call the next couple of days, but how does Friday night sound?"

He consented by giving her another peck on the cheek before returning to his car. Amelia entered her parents' house and moved a few more items back down to the additional downstairs bedroom. She prepared the bed and eased into it. For the first night in several days, Amelia slept peacefully and soundly.

Amelia entered Allen Inc. the following day with a bright disposition. Emma noticed how happy Amelia seemed and commented, "You must have had a good evening," with an exaggerated wink. Amelia chuckled as she entered the office. The first item to draw her attention was the beautiful, ornate vase on her desk filled with gardenias. The second was a note propped up against the vase and eagerly opened the envelope. *Your beauty is more than just skin deep.* Her heart swooned at the flowers. She wondered why he had chosen not to sign the card again but appreciated the mysterious feeling. The flowers were a sweet gesture, but she wanted to act surprised when he admitted to sending the bouquet. Instead of messaging him to thank him for the flowers, she instead mentioned how much she had enjoyed the evening before. Amelia found herself engrossed in a text message conversation rather than her computer. The two bantered back and forth until the hospital called him to see a patient.

Once she had reviewed the few files on her desk, she asked Emma to touch base with her if anything was pressing. Amelia was surprised by how light the work was here. She had done a few consultations over email, but essentially the workload was lighter. Amelia was unsure if the work was easier to accomplish or if her heart and soul were enjoying the work more. The companies she had been in contact with seemed to be great partners, and she was fascinated with helping them solve their problems. She headed out to the coffee shop to meet the other members of the recipe contest committee.

The committee was able to accomplish a great deal of work over coffee and scones. Amelia was thankful that the crucial details had been handled by her mother beforehand or delegated to other members. She needed to meet with the Opera House staff to confirm setup and decorations and then staff the event. Mrs. Higgins offered to be the emcee and run interference as she had been the vice-chair for years. Amelia was happy to pass the role onto someone more familiar with the event. She was only there to taste the recipes.

Wednesday night came and went with a prayer service at her parents' local church. Amelia attended with her siblings and found the service refreshing. Her soul seemed to have needed this more than she had imagined and left the sanctuary with a smile plastered across her face. Thursday was a relatively easy day. Amelia handled several consultations for different projects and assisted the other consultants on their proposals. She dealt with a few minor necessities in the business but was still able to cut out around three o'clock. Amelia drove over to the same assisted living facility that housed Ms. Georgia. She planned her arrival to be after the book reading and found her intended target listening to the radio in her room.

Georgia was elated when Amelia visited her. The two of them sat and talked for hours. Georgia asked Amelia all about her Nashville life and her work in town. Amelia told her of the issues she had been facing, and Georgia acted as a grandmother would to her new friend. She asked Amelia what her heart desired and instructed her to reflect on what this trip was teaching her. "I will try to come to visit again, Ms. Georgia! I am unsure of when since the festival is getting closer and closer. Unfortunately, I cannot visit tomorrow."

Georgia's face was calm and peaceful as she listened to her young friend. "No worries, dear. Just remember to listen to your heart, and everything will fall into place." Amelia hugged the older lady and walked down the hall. Georgia could not tell when Amelia disappeared from the hallway, but she waited a while before commenting. "Your heart will always lead you to wherever home is."

Amelia drove home to find dinner already waiting, courtesy of Jessie. Amelia's last few days had been excellent, and so she decided to put aside all of the inward issues. She helped her cousin finish setting the table, and the four individuals sat around the table as Frank stroked against their legs. Amelia refused to let Jessie clear the table and forced her to go home and enjoy the remainder of her evening. Amelia noticed that Susan seemed to be a little warmer towards her at dinner tonight. She chose not to test the boundaries too much and cleaned the table.

Susan called Amelia into her room later in the evening to discuss the dinner. "I heard you've changed the traditional meal." Amelia could not discern any animosity in her mother's statement, but she felt herself becoming more defensive. Her mother continued speaking without giving Amelia a chance to interrupt. "I think your idea is great for the meal on Saturday." Amelia felt her mind calm with these words. "We've done the Italian meal for so long that it can get tiring. Do you have the entire menu planned?"

Amelia went over her thoughts on the menu and seating arrangement. Susan Allen gave one sharp nod when she agreed and two when she was thoroughly impressed. Seeing the two nods, Amelia decided to let her mother get some rest and started to leave. As she neared the exit, a wave of courage rushed her. "I guess it was good that I decided to stay, don't you think, mom?" Her mother stared blankly at her daughter, and Amelia decided to leave the room. She felt triumphant given the lack of expression or words from her mother. Amelia walked through the house to the downstairs bedroom, barely catching what Susan muttered. "Maybe so. Let's see how the rest of the trip goes."

Chapter Twelve

Amelia awoke invigorated for the last day before the Festival activities were set to begin. While gathering her equipment and heading over to the tennis courts, Amelia thought of how quickly the time was flying. It was hard to believe that she had already spent two weeks in Humboldt. Several upsetting moments occurred during this trip, but those were merely speed bumps along her path. This trip was restoring her love of Humboldt and its residents. She knew this was only the start of several trips home.

Ian was waiting for her on the tennis courts when she arrived. "Thought you might have chickened out," he goaded with a grin. "Not on your life!" Amelia was a little rusty in the game of tennis, and in no time, he was leading 30-Love. He began teasing her incessantly, and her motivation kicked into high gear. The rust seemed to burn off of her as she became more and more zealous to acquire the win. Ian never scored another point the remainder of their game. For losing, he was a good sport and continued grinning throughout the game. The two rested for a moment before playing another game. This time it was a landslide victory for Amelia. Her body ached, and she knew that the following day would be sore.

The two walked the track at Bailey Park, following their game to catch up slightly more. Ian told her of his work with a large firm in the New England area before he decided to return and start his own business. "What made you decide to come back home?"

They walked in silence before he began to explain his decision. "I went to work every morning, and it just seemed to be a routine. I had no passion for what I once loved. When you work for a company, you have to answer to them and their clientele. In freelance work, it is just the client and me. I was tired of going through the motions and knew I needed to change. I decided to come back here because this is where I first became passionate about my work. I used to love drawing for school projects and, well, for you." Amelia blushed as he continued, "What better way to start over than to come home?" The two kept walking, and Amelia was unsure how to respond to these statements.

Wanting to find a distraction, Amelia gazed out over the park. She noticed a tree trunk near the tennis courts and ran over to it. "Amelia, wait up!" Ian yelled as she took off. Amelia loomed over the stump of the departed tree while wondering what had happened. "What happened to the tree, Ian?"

"A couple of years ago, there was a bad storm, and the tree was struck by lightning. They had to cut down what remained. The tree wasn't too scorched, but the storm broke it into several pieces."

Amelia and Ian had been dating about two years and were beginning their last year of high school. On this beautiful day, they'd come to Bailey park for a tennis game and to sit under the shade of the old oak tree. Ian had barely won against Amelia moments prior, and they were now relaxing. The two were talking about plans and the hope of being together forever. Ian decided to make this spot a token of their love, and so he took his pocket knife and sketched a heart into the tree.

Amelia reached down to rub over the stump. "So then it's gone." He sighed and confirmed her suspicions. Amelia let a tear fall as she considered what was missing. Her inner thoughts commented that it was a representation of what had happened between them. She thanked him for a lovely game and went home to shower and prepare for interviews.

At the exact moment the clock struck nine, Emma walked the first candidate into the conference room. Amelia had assembled a team of four to conduct these interviews. In addition to herself and her father, she had asked one of the lead consultants to join them and the head of the management consulting division. Bringing a team member of the division would allow them to assess how the candidates would mesh with their potential employees. Roger considered how intuitive it was of Amelia to bring in a management consultant. Their expertise would help distinguish those who could take the task of managing human resources with the best chances for success. The first candidate was stellar on paper. His work in the private sector over the years had been with several top firms. The team was a little surprised he would be interested in moving to Humboldt.

The gentleman informed the panel that his wife's family was in Dyersburg, and they wanted to move closer to family. Amelia thought his interview was phenomenal, but she could tell the remainder of their group did not share her views. After a forty-five-minute interview, they thanked the gentleman for joining them with a promise to hear something soon. Amelia had planned each interview to take approximately forty-five minutes to allow a fifteen-minute discussion between each candidate to discuss and compare the panels' thoughts. Amelia began the process of reviewing the candidate. "I think he seems very knowledgeable and would be a terrific asset to the company."

Her colleagues glanced around at one another before the

management consultant commented, "His interpersonal skills were somewhat lacking. I don't think the majority of our firm would feel comfortable approaching him about issues in the office or with their lives." Amelia noticed how the others were shaking their heads in agreement.

The human resources consultant added her thoughts to the conversation, "His background is steeped heavily in traditional, corporate structures. His answers were very textbook and not creative. Each business is different, and thoughts and concepts need tailoring to fit each need." Amelia thought back over the recent interview and concluded that the gentleman said all the correct answers at the right times, and it did seem very rehearsed. In the end, the panel decided that this was not a viable candidate for either position.

The day wasted away with the four additional interviews. Each candidate was an excellent choice for a corporate environment but not necessarily the perfect fit. "Amelia, are these all the candidates you could find?" Her father's question ate at her more than she was willing to admit. She hated feeling as if she had failed this assignment. Her brain began working through several possible scenarios on how to overcome the issue at hand.

"Let's have a fifteen-minute break, and then we will come back and discuss the plan a little more." Amelia arose from the table and paced around the room as the others filed out. Her mind continually sorted through plan after plan until she had decided on how to move forward. She quickly sent off a text message and ran out to Emma for a little more information.

Twenty minutes after she dismissed the panel, Amelia burst back into the room. "Sorry for the delay, but we have two additional candidates to consider. I hope the four of you had no plans for the next little while. We've got two more interviews to conduct." The room all nodded their assent as Emma brought in a laptop to connect to the conference room's digital television. "I was able to get the first candidate to take time for a virtual interview." Over the next forty-five minutes, the candidate became well acquainted with each panel member through their grilling questions. Amelia thought that this time, the panel liked the individual more. The questions were more in-depth and seemed to be making progress. At the end of the forty-five minutes, she thanked the candidate, and Emma ended the call.

The panel was delighted with this candidate. Within ten minutes, Roger Allen asked Amelia to offer this candidate the position as the new head of their internal Human Resources. "Why did you save the best for the end?" Roger joked with his daughter. She smiled and remarked, "Just wait for this last applicant."

Emma handed out five packets of information and kept one for herself. "I've asked Emma to assist on this interview. Her insight on the head consultant would be valuable. She will be reporting to both the new head of human resources and the head consultant. It is worth mentioning that she was highly in favor of both candidates. Please take a moment to review the packet in front of you." The panel members showed various faces of disbelief and surprise at the packet sitting in front of them. One panel member, in particular, sat stonewalled in their chair while staring at Amelia. After the other panel members lifted their heads to show their completion of the task, Amelia smirked and asked Mrs. Williams if she had considered applying for the head consultant position.

The lead consultant from the human resources division continued to sit there with a blank face that morphed into one of utter disbelief. Only when Roger nudged her did she speak, stumbling slightly, "I considered it but decided that I was not qualified for the position."

Amelia scoffed at her response. "Mrs. Williams — Tonya — proof alone is how you have handled the interviews today. You are already familiar with several of our regular clients and the type of clientele the firm has. I asked Emma to pull your reviews and the resume on file from this year's professional catalog update. I was pleasantly surprised to learn you meet all of the qualifications of the position. Will you consent to be interviewed?"

Roger Allen encouraged Tonya to at least take the interview, and she could decide from there. This interview was much more lighthearted than the others. As Amelia had pointed out to the panel, Tonya had exhibited the skills necessary in her consultations today alone, let alone her years of service in the field. After thirty minutes, Allen Inc. was no longer seeking a Head Consultant but instead looking internally to promote someone to lead consultant and would be posting a consultant position soon.

As the panel disbursed, Roger lingered behind to speak with his daughter. Amelia and Emma finished cleaning up the room when they noticed Roger standing nearby. Emma took the files and excused herself. "I had concerns after the first two interviews. The next three candidates confirmed those fears. They all seemed great on paper for a large city-based consulting company. I was afraid that my daughter had lost the vision of what this firm was built on and wondered if you were too much like the corporate world. The two last-hour choices, however, renewed my faith in your knowledge of this world. Amelia, you did a wonderful job today. You took the time to evaluate each individual and decided on who would be the best candidates. I never considered Tonya for the position, and as soon as I saw her resume, I knew this was our new head consultant." Amelia beamed at the praise as he continued, "I was very impressed in the skill you showed in recognizing the talent of each individual."

Amelia smiled, and her father kissed her cheek as he went to leave the room. "Dad?" Her father turned around as he heard her call. "On that subject, there are a few individuals that we need to discuss. Jenna Wallace would be much better suited to handling

the company's financials and occasionally consulting. Timothy..."
The two walked through the office as Amelia captivated Roger's attention with her several recommendations. She ended with, "Allen Inc. is extremely successful but imagine how much more effective you would be with everyone in the best position for them."

Roger considered his daughter's words and made plans to set up meetings with each staff member listed to see about moving forward with these recommendations. Amelia bid her father a farewell and prepared to head to the grocery store in preparation for the next day. Before she could exit the room, he called out, "Milly, you are a fantastic human resources administrator." She beamed again at his praise. "I think, though, you are an even better talent recruiter." She considered his words as he left the office.

While Amelia drove toward the store, she was pleased with how easily everything had worked out. She spent the first few moments in the car to call and offer the position to the other candidate. She could tell how excited they were to accept the new opportunity. Their start date would be contingent on them being able to relocate to the area. In the few moments of finding exceptional candidates, Amelia's passion for human resources had been reignited.

At first, she was unable to discern the problem with each of the original candidates. Now, it was clear as crystal at how she had inadvertently picked individuals her business professors would love to see. Small towns were their own breed and not in the wrong way. It took special people to recognize the importance and the impact a small town can make. Amelia was so deeply entrenched in her thoughts that she nearly passed the grocery store.

Amelia went up and down the aisles greeting friends and family along the way. She stopped and visited with several individuals as she collected the items from her grocery list. She was nearing completion as she noticed a few strawberry trinkets over to the side of the aisle. She continued edging the cart forward while picturing the charms at different parts of the dinner table. Amelia decided to take several for decorations, but not before plowing into someone with her cart. The sound rang out through the aisles. Amelia rushed to help the individual to their feet and collect the items that had fallen from their hands. "I am so sorry! I must be more careful about where I'm going! Are you o – Ian?"

Ian Reynolds laughed it off as he stood and collected back the items. "More careful? Should I take this as more than a first offense?"

Amelia's jaw set as she did not want to tell Ian about her earlier run-in with Lou. "Well, it might have happened once before." He laughed and noticed the contents of her basket. He examined the several containers of eggs, milk, sugar, strawberries, and different meat selections.

"Just a little hungry? There's always a restaurant. No need to clear the store out of their stock."

She laughed, "Did you decide to become the grocery police overnight?" He returned her chuckle, and the two jabbed at each other for several minutes. "I've got to get going. I need to make preparations for the dinner tomorrow. We are hosting twenty of the festival leaders for a beginning dinner to commemorate the festival."

Ian smiled at the mention of the festival, "So, I guess that means you will be staying around for the reunion then." She had forgotten about their class reunion being one week from today.

"Oh, I completely forgot! I will be in town, so I need to let the organizers know, don't I?"

Ian grinned even more prominently, "You already have. If you need any help in the kitchen, remember I'm an excellent cook."

At his attempt to charm her, she merely rolled her eyes. "Thanks, Ian. I'll see you later."

Amelia finished collecting everything on her list and the

trinkets before heading home. She walked into the house to find her mother standing in the kitchen with her father arguing with his wife. "Mom, why are you out of your brace? You are going to hinder your progress." Amelia joined in on the tirade against Susan. Her mother stood in silence as the two droned on and on. Amelia finally was exhausted from the lack of response and signaled for her dad to stop.

Once both she and her father had cooled down slightly, she calmly asked her mother, "Mom, why are you up walking around when your doctor told you to take it easy?"

Her mother smugly smirked at her daughter, "No, that's not what he said." Amelia and Roger each turned their head in confusion towards each other.

"Mom, we know for a fact that he said. . ." Amelia trailed out as she saw Dr. Ben Taylor exit the bathroom.

"Susan, you are doing well! I think it's time you rested, though. We don't want to over-do your therapy." She smirked at her family as they turned around to face Dr. Taylor.

"Yes, doctor. It was so nice to do a little walking today." Amelia and Roger both looked abashed at themselves and waited until Susan was situated back in bed.

"Well, Ben. I wasn't expecting you for a little while longer," Amelia commented as she began bringing in groceries. Roger Allen went to help his daughter with the load before Ben interrupted and offered to help her instead. As the two shelved everything, they made small talk.

"I decided to come to check on my patient and see about starting a little therapy. I apologize for arriving unannounced, but truth be told, I couldn't spend another moment without seeing your face."

He leaned in to kiss her on the cheek as she blushed a deep crimson red. "Charmer," she quipped. "I need to do a few preparations before we head out to dinner. Hopefully, it doesn't interfere with your plans too much."

Ben smiled as he steered himself over to the pantry. Retrieving an apron, he put it on himself before responding, "Let me know where to help!" Amelia's heart fluttered at his desire to assist. She wondered when he would start disappointing her as every man did but decided not to try and get bogged down by the pitfalls of many relationships.

After about forty minutes, the pair had finished preparations for the next day and headed out the door for their third date. Ben had gotten them tickets to a performance in the neighboring town of Trenton. The pair enjoyed the play and a walk through the neighboring downtown while chatting about dreams and their future desires. Amelia noticed that Ben had his life planned out, and for the first time in several years, she seemed unsure about hers. The conversation rattled her slightly before turning her attention back to Ben.

Before she knew it, it was approaching midnight. Time she spent with Ben seemed to pass by in the blink of an eye. Her mind was always content and light in any conversation with him. The two-headed back to Humboldt, where he walked her up to her front door. "I enjoyed our evening, Amelia, more than I can say. I'm on call tomorrow but free Sunday. Let me take you out to dinner to celebrate the beginning of the festival."

Amelia grinned at him and nodded in agreement. "I'll gladly let you!" Ben leaned down and captured her with a long, sweet kiss. When they separated, he grinned at her with every muscle of his face. He walked back to his car, smiling the entire time.

Amelia went inside her house and dropped her purse at the door. Her fingers reached up to touch where their lips had met, and she wondered if this was a sign. People had always said that true love's kiss would set off wild sparks. Yet moments ago, she felt nothing more than as if she was kissing her friend or a brother. Her mind ran wild with possibilities. Ben checked every box off her list: handsome, successful, charming, caring, sweet, funny; the list went on and on. Amelia was conflicted on how to process this new development. Her love life had experienced more ups and downs than a teeter-totter. She decided this was just a minimal bump on the road. Amelia mumbled to herself as she went to bed, "Sparks can take a little time. Sometimes you need to jumpstart them; after all, practice makes perfect."

Chapter Thirteen

*A*melia's alarm went off at six o'clock. Stretching out to turn off the alarm, Amelia noted how exhausted she still felt. Amelia had gotten more rest than she imagined after the following evening's events, but not enough to be Amelia-on-the-spot directly on waking up this morning. Amelia pushed her long hair out of her eyes and stood to prepare for the day. The dinner may not be until five-thirty this evening, but the to-do list was lengthy. She planned to make a minimal breakfast for her parents and just a shake for herself. She had decided to do the cooking alone, refusing all offers of help. As she headed downstairs and mentally reviewed the list for the day, she realized how daunting the task would be.

Once the pot finished brewing the coffee and Amelia had downed her first cup of the day, she began working on the family breakfast. Amelia decided to make a spinach quiche which would be suitable for breakfast and lunch today. It would be easier not to stop and prepare a second meal while in preparation for the evening. Amelia heard the oven's beep to signal the appliance had pre-heated. She sat the quiche in the oven and set the timer. Amelia took a scratch pad out from a nearby drawer. She listed everything on her preparation list, careful not to miss anything:

Set Dinner Tables for Guests
Place Decorations on Table
Food: Bacon, Sausage, Ham
Eggs
French toast
Muffins — Chocolate Chip, Blueberry, Strawberry
Pancakes — Chocolate, Plain, Strawberry, Pecan
Cinnamon Rolls
Berry Salad
Fresh Fruit
Grits
Hash browns
Biscuits
Toast
Gravy
Quiche

Amelia finished writing the list and realized this would take all day to prepare to feed all the individuals coming over tonight. She checked on the quiche and noticed that the batter was still liquid, and the crust appeared raw. She checked the temperature on the oven and saw that she had set it correctly; Amelia glanced at the clock and saw that there were only supposed to be ten minutes left before it would be ready. Recognizing that everything on the device looked correct and knowing that she had followed this recipe the same as every time before, there must be a problem with the oven. Half of an hour later, the repairman was checking the stove. "The heating element has gone out. It's a simple fix, but the type it needs won't be in stock until Monday. You might find one in Jackson."

Amelia filled with dread, knowing that this would set her back if she went to Jackson and there was no guarantee. She thought for a few moments and then pulled out her cell phone and began to call in favors. Moments later, Jessie, Lou, Emma, Donna, and Eric were all on their way to the house. Jessie offered to come to sit with Amelia's mother and take care of setting up for the dinner tonight. Amelia asked her to sit places for six more individuals as there would, hopefully, be enough food for everyone. Lou was coming to pick up the ingredients for the cinnamon rolls to mark that off of Amelia's list. Emma offered to make the French toast while Jason and Donna took care of all of the meat. Eric offered to take care of cutting the fresh fruit while making their mother's wonderful berry salad. He had the ingredients for her homemade dressing to coat the berries and loved helping out. That took care of several items on Amelia's list, but she still had several things to accomplish, and they all involved a working stove and oven.

After the friends had come and gone, Amelia finished contacting different stores in the area. Just her luck that there were no heating elements available. Amelia dialed one more number, "Does that favor to help still stand?"

Twenty minutes later, Amelia was unloading a car full of supplies into Ian's kitchen. "When I offered to help you, I didn't realize my house was becoming a restaurant," Ian chided with Amelia as they unloaded everything and began to prepare the meal. Amelia decided to get to working on the muffins first.

"Ian, thank you for helping me. Hopefully, I did not ruin your day's plans by seeking your assistance."

He laughed, "Not in the slightest. Today was going to be a relaxing day, and baking will be just as relaxing, right?"

Amelia surveyed him up and down with her eyes. "That depends, Ian. Have your baking skills improved since high school?"

This time he cut his eyes towards her and gave a slight chuckle. "I guess you will just have to wait and see."

The pair worked in sync as they made their way through Amelia's list. Amelia watched how well Ian worked in the kitchen and was surprised as she remembered the fiasco of a science project in high school. *"Ian, are you sure you know how to bake?"* Sixteen-year-old Ian's chest puffed out, *"Of course I do."* *The two worked on the batter, adding in candies for different veins, arteries, and more.* *"Remember, I want to get a good grade on this project."* He scoffed, *"Amy, please, I've got this — I am a pro."* *The first trial looked more like a burn victim than any creation resembling skin, and the second wasn't much better. Amelia snatched the project away from him and handled the oven herself. He sighed and sat down to watch her. "I guess I can do the frosting." She laughed and said, "Are you a pro at that too?"*

Catching herself replaying memories of years gone by, Amelia began laughing at the memory. She couldn't help but notice that her laughter was warm and foreign. *I haven't laughed like this in years.* She caught Ian staring, and then his grin began to match hers as he asked, "Would you like to share what's so funny?" Amelia reminded him of their project from high school, and their work rapidly devolved into laughter. The two began swapping stories of their past before Amelia attempting to get them back on task. "Yes, Ms. Allen," Ian cheekily remarked as he went back to his biscuit dough.

As she watched him knead the dough and use the biscuit cutter, she was overwhelmed in thinking of all the lessons she'd given him on cooking and baking. In those moments, they'd not only had fun but grew closer together. Due to her hard work, he was now making his way around a kitchen with ease. Amelia glanced over and caught him staring at her once more. To her, it appeared as if he was admiring her. Once he realized she had seen him staring, he smirked, "You've got something in your hair."

She began checking the locks, finding nothing. "Here, let me help you out." She thanked him for the offer until his hand brought flour to her face and hair. The two had a friendly spar involving batter, flour, and utensils. Twenty minutes later, they were still behind on food preparations, and the kitchen was a mess. It reminded them both of so many fond times, but Amelia reminded him that they had to get everything done. He grinned at her, making her heart leap, and the two went back to work.

"When we saw each other on the steps of the post office, why did you pretend to be in a relationship with your cat?" Ian chuckled as he asked her the question. Amelia blushed brighter than the strawberry pieces she was adding to the pancake batter. As he took in her bright red face and slightly abashed look, his chuckle turned into a full laugh.

"Well, it had been a while since we saw each other, and something came over me. I think it bothered me that everything wasn't perfect in my Nashville life, and I didn't want to give you the satisfaction of knowing that."

Ian stopped laughing and gave her a hurt, yet serious look. "Did you think I would be happy if your life weren't perfect?"

Amelia shrugged her shoulders before responding, "Maybe?" Ian turned away and kept working on his recipe. She could tell by the way his shoulders sagged that he was less than pleased with her answer.

The two worked in silence before Ian decided to ask her another question, "How do you like working in Nashville?" He noted how silent she was in the immediate time following the question. Eventually, she decided to answer.

"I enjoy working for the state and helping my department. It is way different from small-town living, though, and I love some of the luxuries. It is nice to have greater access to a variety of recreational activities, stores, and restaurants. My co-workers are great, and our assistant director is retiring this year. The director informed me that I am possibly a final candidate for the position, which would be great for my career."

Ian nodded his head slowly as if deep in thought before responding, "That's a very logical answer, but how does your heart feel about being in Nashville?"

Amelia seriously considered his question, searching deep within for the answer. "Truthfully, I'm not completely sure. Three weeks ago, I would have easily said my heart was happy in Nashville." Ian was surprised at both her answer and the sincerity that seemed to stem from behind it. The person before him was not someone hiding an issue but rather someone laying their cards on the table.

"And now?"

She stared wild-eyed at him, conflicted with the question. She wondered how to respond without revealing too much of the struggle happening inside of her mind. "Let's just say there are some recent complications and memories that make me question if I belong in the big city. I'm still deciding everything." Ian decided to leave the answer alone, although he had several questions.

Once everything had finished baking and cooking, Ian and Amelia loaded their vehicles with the fruit of their labor. Amelia triple-checked the list before preparing to drive home. "Ian, I cannot thank you enough for your help today. This morning it seemed as if everything would go wrong today, and you helped me. I'm glad we can try and move forward from our past. Today brought back so many memories. You have helped my family in more than one way the last few weeks. Join us tonight for dinner. There is more than enough food, and it is the least I can offer as a show of my gratitude." Ian shied away at the praise, but before he could offer an argument of refusal, she insisted that he would attend. Before he could respond to her second insistence, Amelia got into her car and drove away.

Arriving home, Amelia could not believe how wonderfully decorated the house was. Jessie had done a terrific job in setting up the house for the dinner. Amelia glanced at the clock and noticed guests would be arriving at any moment. Her father informed her that all the other goodies would be over soon, but Lou would not stay. One of the twins was having a bout with colic, and she would be sending her cinnamon rolls over with Eric and Emma. Amelia was highly grateful for her friend's assistance despite the trouble at home. As Amelia headed up the stairs, Roger called out to her, "Milly, there was a delivery for you while you were gone."

Amelia decided she could wait to check on the delivery until after she had changed. Amelia returned downstairs with a beautiful white sundress without taking too long, accentuated with her favorite strawberry necklace and bracelet set, paired with simple strawberry earrings. She wandered into the kitchen and saw a vase of beautiful flowers sitting on the island. The flowers were the most beautiful yellow roses with a beautiful red hue lining the tips of each petal. Amelia opened the note in eager anticipation of what was written and to see if Ben had decided to sign his name this time. *Roses of changing colors for the woman who is ever-beautiful in whatever stage.* Her heart melted at the sweet words written on the card. She decided to continue playing along as if she was clueless as to who had sent them, just until the right moment.

Susan Allen used crutches to come and sit at the kitchen table. "Amelia, let's talk," Amelia noted the serious yet anxious tone in her mother's voice, but she did not want to have this conversation with guests arriving soon.

"Mom, people will be here any moment. Can this wait?" Susan pursed her lips, and Amelia knew this would be a losing battle. She readied herself for the conversation and sat down across from her mother.

"Amelia, you have done a good job today. When trouble came, you created a plan to overcome the issue instead of falling apart. Your dad has gone on and on about how much you have helped the company, and I cannot say how much I appreciate what you've done for me since the accident. Thank you." Amelia was flabbergasted at the statement from her mother. The last several days had been very tense between the two Allen women.

Amelia decided to take her shot once more. She first told her mother that while driving to the hospital, she prayed to God that she would work on being a better daughter if he healed Susan. Amelia decided not to stop there but also to ask the question that had been burning at her. "Mom, why did you ask me to leave?" Susan glanced off in the distance, hurt by hearing Amelia's prayer and knowing how she had hindered it.

It took Susan a few moments before she was able to answer her daughter's question. "You hardly ever come home. The only reason you came this time was because your boss forced you to take a vacation. I was afraid that if you stayed and worked the entire vacation, you would have another reason to resent coming home. I didn't want to be the new reason why you chose never to come home. This place should bring happy memories, and for so long, it has caused you pain. I hoped you would one day reconcile with Ian, but those first few days of your trip showed that was unlikely. Then, I was so glad you and Lou spent time together and thought I might have a shot at seeing my daughter in her old bedroom more. When I had the accident, I knew that you would offer to stay and help, whether you wanted to or not. I only wanted you to enjoy your time in town and feared that taking care of me or my duties would stop you from having fun. I have to admit, you've been happier the last several days than I've seen you in years. I'm sorry for treating you differently. It also hurts to feel as if I'm losing my place with the Festival. I live for this week, and now I cannot be as involved as I normally am."

Amelia crossed the table to hug her mother. "I have been happy the last several days. I let trouble from years ago keep me away from home, which was not fair to our family. Maybe in the future, we can both communicate more?" Susan Allen smiled and agreed to her daughter's suggestion. The doorbell rang, and Amelia went to let Ian in with the last of the baked goods. After she finished setting out the food, Jenna Wallace became the first guest to arrive.

The remainder of the guests arrived soon after Jenna. Eric, Emma, Donna, and Jason all came with their contributions to the meal between guest arrivals. Once everyone was seated for the meal, Marcie Donald, the festival president, rose to give a speech. "I want to thank everyone for attending our annual opening dinner this year. The 81st Annual Strawberry Festival will be the best one yet, and that is because of the contributions of everyone gathered around this table. I want to especially thank the Allen family for their continued hospitality, despite barriers this year. Susan, our thoughts and prayers are with you and your recovery. Tonight, let's enjoy each other's company and take a relaxing moment as the Festival begins tomorrow afternoon!" Everyone raised their glasses and toasted with one another to the beginning of another festival.

The guests dived into the breakfast feast before them. Around the table, everyone seemed to be enjoying the delicious spread and sharing about their lives. Amelia smiled as she took in how the evening was going. This morning Amelia had been unsure of how the dinner was going to end. Looking around at the bright smiles and peaceful people, she knew that tonight was a success. All around the table, people found deep conversations in their fellow attendees. She saw Jessie and Ian in a serious discussion, and for once, there was no feeling of dissatisfaction. Amelia realized while cooking with Ian that she wanted the best for him. Jessie seemed to keep his attention, and she seemed so involved with him by the way she had spoken at girls' night. Amelia's heart only wished that Dr. Ben was able to be here with her this evening. She had to admit that she had hoped for sparks on the first kiss but realized she had not fully resolved her feelings for Ian. She knew from the way her heart fluttered at the flowers, to the text messages they shared, and the fun times they had enjoyed, that the next time they kissed would be more significant than Monday night's firework display.

While Amelia was deeply considering her relationship, Jenna rose to give her general chairman's speech. "I want to echo Marcie's earlier words. I was skeptical about changing from the traditional Italian to a breakfast dinner, but I think I speak for everyone in saying that this food was delicious. Thank you, Amelia and the Allen family, for this meal. I am excited about the Festival this year and want to thank Marcie for choosing me to serve as her general chairman. One year ago this week, she approached me about serving in this capacity and, on the last night, changed the tradition by announcing it to finish the Festival. I look forward to making my announcement one week from today. To quickly go over the week's schedule, I decided to pass out a sheet with everything listed instead of speaking each event out line by line. Please let me know if there are any issues with your events or if you need anything additionally. Once more, let's raise our glasses in gratitude to the Allen family." Everyone around the table toasted to their hosts, and Jenna called on Amelia to make a speech.

Amelia was brought out of her thoughts by Eric nudging her to make a speech. "Marcie and Jenna, thank you for the kind words. Our family has always enjoyed hosting this event. This year, however, we could not have done it without the help of Ian, Jessie, Donna, Jason, Eric, Emma, and Lou Hart, who is home with a sick little one. I am grateful to help out this year, and I am eager to attend all of the events. It's been a while, too long, since I made the trip to the Festival. I hope everyone enjoys the rest of their evening, and let's look forward to the Festival beginning tomorrow." Everyone cheered her speech, and the crowd slowly began to disperse. Roger and his children worked to clean the tables and their house. Amelia saved leftovers for the family Sunday breakfast tomorrow as the repairman would not fix the oven until Monday.

Amelia finally plopped down onto the couch to rest from the long day. She had only been sitting a few moments when the doorbell rang. Amelia went to the door and found Bradley standing with his luggage. "I was wondering when you were going to grace us with your presence." He laughed and entered the Allen home. Amelia helped him into the room where he would spend the week. "I cannot thank you enough for letting me come visit. I am so excited to see the Festival and this town." The two spent time catching up on the day's events and developments with her mother.

"Well, at least now you know why she wanted you to leave. I want to hear more about the baking today and meet this doctor guy, but what's the first thing to do for the Festival?" She had never seen Bradley so engaged and happy before this. She smiled and invited him into the kitchen for a late snack. As he munched on a strawberry muffin, she handed him the paper Jenna had passed out so that he could see the week's events:

81*st* Annual Strawberry Festival

<u>Sunday</u>
2:00 pm — Art Exhibit

<u>Monday</u>
7:30 am — Prayer Breakfast
6:00 pm — Opening Ceremonies
8:00 pm — Fireworks Extravaganza

<u>Tuesday</u>
6:00 pm — Recipe Contest

Wednesday
5:00 pm — *President's Dinner*
6:00 pm — *Strawberry Shortcake in the Park*
7:00 pm — *Live Entertainment Downtown*

Thursday
10:00 am — *Non-Motorized Parade*
12:00 pm — *Golf Tournament: Strawberry Strokes*
4:00 pm — *Pageants Begin*
5:00 pm — *Humboldt Hall of Fame Induction & Reception*
7:00 pm — *Live Entertainment Downtown*

Friday
10:00 am — *Motorized Grand Parade*
12:00 pm — *Queen's Luncheon*
12:00 pm — *Governor's Luncheon*
12:00 pm — *Shopping at the Strawberries Market Opens until 5:00 pm.*
1:00 pm — *BBQ Cook-off Begins*
5:00 pm — *Pageants Begin*
6:30 pm — *Horse Show*
8:00 pm — *Live Entertainment at the BBQ Cook-off*

Saturday
8:00 am — *5K & 10K Race*
8:00 am — *Classic Car Show*
9:00 am — *Tractor Show*
10:00 am — *Market Reopens until 3:00 pm.*
11:00 am — *Pageants Begin*
2:00 pm — *BBQ Winners Announced*
6:30 pm — *Ending Pageant and Closing of the Festival*

Bradley took in the long list of events on the page. He glanced up at Amelia with his mouth wide open. "Your town does all this in one week?" She laughed and told him of the shops in town and the specials they would have throughout the week, the carnival located right off Main Street, and all of the food vendors who would set up across town. Amelia showed him pictures of events from years past, including ones like the chess tournament a local bank would host but were no longer a part of the event. The Festival had grown and evolved over the years, and he was impressed by the show the town would put on this week. Amelia cleaned up the kitchen and dining areas for one last time this evening and said to Bradley as they went to bed, "Who knows, you might even find a young lady to go to all the events." Bradley started to protest, but she replied before entering her room, "Welcome to my home, known this week as Berryland."

Chapter Fourteen

Sunday morning came early for at least one member of the Allen family. Amelia was up before the crack of dawn to get down to the art exhibit. She took to the task of setting up for the invitational event that began the festival week. On the Sunday of the Festival, little went on for most members of the town. Several would stroll through downtown, visit food vendors and stop in open shops. If they were lucky, the carnival crew would begin setting up for the week, and they could get a chance to glimpse at the rides and attractions for this year. Amelia could get most of the preparations done at the center before heading home to warm up breakfast.

The entire Allen family, plus Bradley and Ian, enjoyed the leftover goods from the night before. Amelia had asked Ian to join them for breakfast before church since he had made a large portion of the food. She had also invited Lou, but Kathryn was still battling colic. Amelia had also invited Ben, but he was exhausted from being on call yesterday that he decided to see her later.

As the family and friends sat around eating, Susan asked her daughter what still needed finishing for the week. Amelia went through her list again and was happy to report that nearly everything was completed. She needed a little help setting up for the recipe contest. She also asked her mother to confirm with Mrs. Higgins about the judges for the contest as well. "While you are talking about the contest, please tell me you are entering that cobbler you made the other night. It was delicious!" Donna had been the one to speak up and request that of her sister-in-law. Amelia started to object before her mother butted in, "You should enter that and a few of your other recipes, dear. The rules only state that the chair and the vice-chair cannot enter. You are technically not the chair, only filling in to help in my place. I will still be in attendance as the chair; only I'll be sitting the whole time for once."

Amelia thought about the request for a few moments before agreeing to enter at least one event category. She began cleaning up the dishes as the others headed out to church services. Amelia was staying behind as this was a special Sunday. Not only did today mark the beginning of her favorite week of the year, but it also would be the first Sunday Susan could attend services since the accident. Susan was recovering much quicker than any of the doctors had imagined. Dr. Taylor had agreed to let her attend just the worship assembly and not Sunday school for a couple of weeks, and from there, they could grow her ventures out. He especially wanted her to be cautious as this was Festival week, and they all knew she would be out for all of the festivities.

Amelia brought her mother to the church building at the perfect time; Sunday school had ended, and there was a short break before the worship assembly would begin. Amelia hugged Ben, happy to see him there for the service, and invited him to sit beside her. Several of the older ladies in the congregation happily grinned at the sight of the two individuals. In the South, the older ladies at any church were eager to see the younger individuals married. Seeing two singles together was like Christmas Day to them, and hopefully, two fewer individuals needing to find their better half.

The preacher spoke about community this morning and helping your neighbor. He pointed out that this week often brought out the best in their little town. He encouraged each person to understand why they cared for each other this week and try to imitate those feelings throughout the year.

Amelia appreciated the lesson and the draws to Jesus caring for all different types of "lost sheep." She sometimes felt like she was adrift, not knowing where her life should be or how she could best serve God, her family, and others. She stood and spoke to the preacher for several minutes following the service. She had been encouraged by his lessons and hated that she would be returning home after the following Sunday. She would miss his heartfelt, scripturally-inspired lessons that drew on real-life situations. He thanked Amelia for her excellent attention and reminded her that they would always welcome her in their assembly.

Amelia was able to get her mother home and serve a few sandwiches with leftover fruit. She was in a hurry to get back to the Art Exhibit and was thankful Ben was coming along to help since no one else was willing to come. Bradley insisted that this was his vacation, and for the first day of the Festival, he would be exploring the town. Her brothers mentioned helping their mother, who was doing just fine. She was pretty sure they were visiting her cat instead. The whole family seemed to love Frank more than her at times.

As Amelia finished setting up for the event, she thought deeply about the lesson this morning. Ben helped move everything into place, and then she asked Mrs. Ryan if she or the event needed anything else. The event organizer looked around and saw that everything was in its proper place and thanked the pair for their hard work. She asked Amelia if the two would like to stay, as her mother would often peruse the gallery. Ben seemed eager to stay and see the paintings, but Amelia had something more important on her mind.

When Amelia asked if it would be alright for Ben to stay, he protested, wanting instead to go with her. "You would really enjoy the exhibit, Ben. There's something I need to take care of this afternoon. I'll come back about three-thirty and catch the last few moments of it, and then we can go to dinner, alright?" He looked reluctant to the idea but finally agreed to her plan.

She rushed to her car and headed over to the same assisted living facility she had visited the week prior. Walking inside, she asked the activities director to point her towards Ms. Georgia. Amelia strolled down the hall, eager to spend time with her friend. She stopped just outside of the door when she heard Ian's voice inside. "It was a wonderful lesson this morning, Ms. Georgia. I wish we could take you to the service sometime." The young man was telling her all about the church service Amelia had just attended. She wondered if the sermon had the same impact on him as it had her. In thinking of caring for the community, her mind turned to the joy she got from helping Ms. Georgia by simply reading a book. It had been a small task that brought such happiness to the older lady while also renewing her own spirits.

As Amelia's mind wandered away, she was pulled back to reality when she heard Ms. Georgia ask about her. "What's the story with you and Amelia?" The gentleman sat quietly for a few moments. "Amy? Well, let's say we have a lot of history. We were the best of friends growing up. Sometimes I think I was the fourth Allen kid with as much time as I spent at their house. We dated through high school and broke up at the beginning of college. It's all old history now." Amelia stood back from the doorway, where she hoped not to get caught eavesdropping. Part of her screamed to run away, but her more curious side wanted to hear the remainder of the conversation.

"Amy? Is that her nickname?" She eagerly wanted to hear what Ian said in regards to that question. "Oh, I sometimes forget that she stopped using that nickname. I gave it to her when we first met at the age of seven. I couldn't call her Amelia without messing it up, so I just said, Amy. For years she never let anyone call her Amy except me. Eventually, everyone used the name until she decided to go back to just Amelia."

"Ian, forgive an old lady for prying, but it doesn't sound like old history to me. The two of you work so well together. Whatever happened?" She heard Ian mumble something before saying, "I broke her heart. Ms. Georgia, I never meant to hurt Amy as much as I did, but I thought what I was doing was right and honorable." Amelia was in disbelief at the words. She could never imagine how anyone could perceive the way he handled everything as right or honorable. What was more shocking to her, however, was that she was keeping calm through his statement. It was bizarre to her that the famous Amelia anger was staying at rest. She assumed it was because of how sincere and genuine the words felt. Deep down, she believed that Ian was telling the truth. She missed the remainder of the conversation but heard her say, "Ian, thank you for coming, dear. I hope to see you again soon. I'm glad the two of you can at least be friends now and put the past where it belongs."

Amelia hid in an alcove beside the hallway until Ian passed by her spot. She waited a good five minutes before emerging from her hidden location and heading into the room for Ms. Georgia. As she approached her friend, Amelia's heart was conflicted. Hearing them called friends had hurt her, shocked her by feeling that emotion since the relationship had long ended, but ultimately it also helped her focus on pursuing the relationship with Ben. Amelia walked over and sat in the same chair as Ian.

"Ms. Georgia! How are you today?" Amelia leaned in for a hug as the woman happily welcomed her.

"Amelia, dear, it is so good to have you visit again. I figured it would be later in the week before I would hear your voice. Did you happen to see Ian when you came in today? He just left."

She decided to be more than a little deceitful with Ms. Georgia. "I guess he walked right past me. Does he visit you often?"

"Yes, he has come a few times to read to me or simply to visit. Today, he read me some Bible passages and told me about the lesson at your church this morning. He told me that your mother was able to attend and all about her accident. I'm glad to know she is improving."

The kind act Ian was showing to Ms. Georgia touched Amelia. "That is very nice of him to come and read the Bible to you. The thought never crossed my mind."

"Yes, that Ian is one thoughtful young man. I hope he finds everything he is looking for in life."

Amelia smiled and continued visiting with Ms. Georgia. She was having such a great visit that she hadn't realized that it was nearly twenty minutes until four. "Ms. Georgia, I am so sorry to leave so soon, but I am going to be late for my date!"

Georgia chuckled and called after Amelia as she left, "You'll have to tell me all about this gentleman. Have fun!" Amelia hollered out her goodbyes while running down the hall. Georgia continued to chuckle, "I wonder why we have always talked about Ian, and this is the first mention of a boyfriend."

Amelia made it back to the art center with four minutes until the exhibit closed. She found Ben waiting by the front door. "I am so sorry that I'm late coming back. I got caught up and lost track of time." Ben looked disappointed but shrugged off the excuse and welcomed her back. The two went inside in time for the first event to close. Amelia realized that on the first day of the Festival, she had skipped the entire event. This was her favorite week of the year, and yet she was just as happy being in town and helping others as she would have been at the Festival.

Ben and Amelia assisted in putting away the tables and decorations once the event ended. Amelia noticed that Ben was a bit more reserved than usual. After they did all of the day's work, the two decided to take a walk through downtown. The conversation did not flow as effortlessly as it had on previous dates. The two stopped at one of the many concession stands to order food. They continued walking until they came to an area with tables set up and stopped to eat. Ben finally decided to attempt to clear the air. "Where did you go, Amelia?" Amelia told him about her visit to see Ms. Georgia. Ben smiled at her as she told the story. "I can see how easy it would be to lose track of time when visiting with her. What a lovely idea to go and be with her."

Ben was much livelier after the short conversation. Amelia had omitted any indication of Ian or the thoughts swirling around her head. While Ben was much more engaged, Amelia was still processing those feelings from earlier. Her mind logically was agreeing that this brought closure to her relationship with Ian. Her heart, however, wanted more answers. Amelia shook the problem from her mind. She could deal with endless ifs and maybes another day. Tonight, she needed to focus on Ben and developing those sparks.

As the sun was beginning to set, Amelia beckoned Ben to join her on a short venture. They went behind one of the downtown buildings, which had access to the roof through a set of stairs. The two climbed the fast path to reach the top of the two-story building. She sat down near the edge of the roof and patted for him to join her. The two watched as the sun sank lower and lower behind the distant landscape. She watched below as people flooded downtown. Amelia pointed out "Berry" to Ben and informed him that the large walking strawberry was the town mascot. While she was watching the scene below and the sun in the distance, Ben was admiring his date.

She stretched back on the palms of her hand to enjoy the last remaining bits of sunlight. "I love it from up here. When I was younger, I would sneak up here to watch the sunset. My favorite time of year to do this was always the week of the Festival. Seeing everyone happy below, as one big family, would always melt my heart. These sunsets are the most beautiful sights in the world."

Ben leaned in to rest his head against hers. She could feel his thoughts, if that was possible, with how close they were in the moment. Her heartbeat blared through her head as he seemed to inch closer and closer to her. Right before his lips met hers once again, as the sun drifted below the buildings, he whispered, "Amelia, it is beautiful but pales in comparison to the radiant beauty before me. I'm blessed that I get to see both."

Chapter Fifteen

Amelia was taken aback by the sudden kiss and was excited when she felt a few sparks. It was not a fireworks show, but it was a beginning reaction. She thought about the man who was kissing her and how kind, patient, generous, and trustworthy he was. She remembered the beautiful flowers he had sent to her and all of the romantic sayings he often said. As she considered how Dr. Ben Taylor was a perfect choice, she recaptured his lips into another short but sweet kiss.

Ben grinned broadly at Amelia before the two decided to head back down the stairs and return to their cars. Amelia was ready to head home after the long day that had been only the first day of the Festival. Ben informed her that he had gotten most of the week off to attend as many as possible. "Unfortunately, I have to work the next two days, but I promise that I will be with you the rest of the time." Once she reached her car, Ben held open the driver's side door and allowed her to climb in before shutting it. Amelia lowered her window and called out to him before he could enter his vehicle.

"Ben?" Amelia beckoned him back over to her car. "Friday night is my ten-year high school class reunion. It's at my uncle's new event barn: Tomlinson Farms out on the Medina highway. I was wondering if you'd like to attend with me." If Ben's smile were any indication, Amelia knew the next word out of his mouth would be, "Yes!" Amelia thanked him for agreeing to accompany her, and the two decided to talk details later. They wished each other a good night before heading to their own homes.

Amelia dropped quickly onto her bed as soon as she entered the room. Tomorrow was an even longer day, starting bright and early. She told Frank all about her day as she settled into the bed. Frank seemed to stare at her without a care in the world. Amelia went on, not caring that her orange tabby was indifferent to her love life. The earlier troubles with Ian were long gone at this moment. Dr. Ben had utterly captivated the remainder of her evening, and as she stroked and rubbed Frank, Amelia droned on and on about the handsome Dr. Ben Taylor.

Monday morning of the Strawberry Festival comes pretty early for those working the Prayer Breakfast. Since arriving in town, all Amelia had known was early mornings, not that she minded as this was always one of her favorite town traditions. She enjoyed seeing everyone start the first primary day of the Festival in prayer and fellowship together. The Allen family always volunteered as servers in this event, and so both Roger and Amelia would be assisting. Amelia arose early that morning to prepare a light breakfast on the stovetop for Susan and Jessie. She filled two travel mugs with as much coffee as they could hold for her father and herself. The pair drove over to the hospital conference center, where the breakfast would commence soon.

The two Allen family members worked diligently in setting up the tables for each guest to sit. Once her family accomplished that, they began assisting with gathering the serving supplies. Around seven-thirty that morning, the majority of the attendees started arriving. Marcie Donald welcomed everyone to the event and said a few words before inviting the town mayor to come to speak. He told the community members in attendance how blessed he felt to serve through another festival. He introduced this year's invocation leader, the preacher from the Allen family's congregation. Amelia was pleasantly surprised to see him as the speaker. She was looking forward to hearing his prayer, as she was confident it would be refreshing for her spirit. The preacher took the microphone and asked the room to bow their heads in prayer.

"Almighty Father, we stand here praising You and Your presence. Father, we are so blessed to be able to live, work, and be together with each other. Father, we pray for Your blessing over our Festival this week. Let this week be a reminder to all of us about the true meaning of community, friendship, and fellowship. May we seek to serve our neighbors, as You have taught us, not only this week but in every week. Almighty God, we pray that You bless our city not only during this Festival but throughout all of our history yet to come. May we recognize what is truly important and love each other. We pray that this week will restore our spirits and souls and help our hearts seek what You desire for each of us. We pray that You will be with the leaders of this event. May they work together to bring us more united this week. Father, we pray for those who are in special need of Your care. May Your hand be on them, and may we seek to serve them. Father, we are grateful for another year to serve in Your work. May You bless this food, that we may use its strength to be more fruitful to You. We ask this in Your Son's most precious name. Amen."

Around the room, there was a chorus of "Amen"s. Amelia was correct in assuming his prayer would touch her. It was very reminiscent of the sermon he had preached only the morning prior. Amelia resolved to understand God's will more this week in her life and be there for the people of this beautiful town. As everyone started moving around, the volunteers began to become busy serving the different attendees. About nine o'clock, the crowd dispersed, and the volunteers rested for a few minutes, enjoying the leftovers.

Amelia and Roger rushed home to change and head to their different offices. Amelia was handling a little of the transition paperwork today at Allen Inc. After today, she would likely no longer be working in the building. She would drop by if there were any issues, but the company would be closed after tomorrow to celebrate the Festival anyways. Amelia was looking forward to savoring what time she could there today, as this had been the best several days of her career in a long while.

Amelia drove slowly over to the office, wanting to extend her time as much as possible. After she pulled into the parking lot, she sighed to herself. She imagined what it would be like to work in a smaller atmosphere, but that was only a distant fantasy. In a matter of months, it was likely that she would assume the assistant director position. Amelia did not want to jeopardize what she had worked so hard to achieve with silly wishes. She strolled through the office, talking with various individuals and catching up on their weekends. Eventually, Amelia found her way into the temporary office.

The desk was littered with files, marking the start of the transition for the new director of Human Resources and the promotion of Mrs. Williams to Head Consultant. In the stack of files, she found a few transfers and job title changes based upon the conversation Roger and Amelia had shared. She was glad to see Jenna's promotion to the head of internal accounting. The last part of the files included open positions to be posted for the new marketing division, the need for a new junior human resources consultant, and a few new positions due to the transfer and a needs assessment. It took Amelia no time to work out the details of these files. She ensured that there was nothing left pending before signing out of the computer.

Amelia was about to leave the office when Emma brought in a dozen red tulips. The flowers were bright, colorful, and such a sweet surprise. Emma had barely left the room when Amelia tore open the card. *Your smile is more beautiful than all the flowers in the world. It warms my heart more than the sun and brighter than the stars.* Amelia took this as confirmation in Ben sending all of these flowers. He had practically said the same statement in comparing her to the sunset the night before, so surely he was adding to the sentiment. As she gazed adoringly at her red tulips, Amelia remembered that they were significant but could not place why.

Amelia decided to stroll through the office one more time, in case this was her last trip for a while. She waved at different employees and happily chatted with those who were grateful for her discussion. Several commented on how happy they would be in their new positions and thanked Amelia for the latest opportunities. She lingered at the desk cluttered with different paperweights and figurines once more. So many of the items showed the character of the individual that used this desk. She realized that the desk owner was still a mystery, although it was not crucial to know who it was. Her hand hovered over the paperweight bearing the "R" and "A" initials. Her mind could not shake the familiar feeling it gave, but every time she seemed closer to an answer, it would disappear. Amelia turned to head out of the office when her eye caught a book lying on the desk. She ran her fingers over its cover as it had been years since she had seen a copy of the *Language of Flowers*.

Her mind immediately signaled for her to check red tulips in the book. As she turned the pages, she remembered that red tulips were a signal of one's declaration of love. She sat down in the chair and began flipping through the pages of the book. Susan Allen had taught her children the secret language found through flowers. The lessons were all flooding her memory now as if the small book had opened the floodgates. She began to run through her mind of all the flowers, the timing, and their messages. They added together to paint a picture as if out of a fairy tale or an age-old love story. Her heart melted in finally piecing together all of the clues. Amelia took a piece of nearby scratch paper and wrote everything out to have it memorialized.

The Language of Flowers — Ben

1ˢᵗ Flowers — Given after the first date — Light Pink Roses (Admiration) — "Beautiful pink roses for one strong, funny, and gorgeous lady."

2ⁿᵈ Flowers — Given after the second date — Gardenias (Hidden Love) — "Your beauty is more than just skin deep."

3ʳᵈ Flowers — Given after the third date — Yellow Rose with Red Tips (Falling in Love) — "Roses of changing colors for the woman who is ever-beautiful in whatever stage."

Now — Given after the fourth date — Red Tulips (Declaration of Love) — "Your smile is more beautiful than all the flowers in the world. It warms my heart more than the sun and brighter than the stars."

Amelia was on top of the world to finally see the big picture. Through these flowers and hiding his identity, he was romantically telling her how he truly felt about her. At this moment, she had never been so glad to have invited him out, even if it was only to her reunion this week. This written detail was all the proof Amelia needed to know to decide that she had met the right man for her. Years of self-wallowing and being trapped in the past were gone. This Amelia knew what she wanted, and that was Dr. Ben Taylor. Amelia headed out the door with the largest smile Emma had seen in years. Emma called out after her, but Amelia was unable to hear anything. Her head was in the clouds, and she decided on an impulse to head downtown.

Amelia strolled through downtown, buying several strawberry-related gifts and goodies. She stopped at the local coffee shop for a sandwich and a drink and practically ran into Bradley on the way through the door. "Brad! There you are. I wanted to show you around town but noticed you were gone after the prayer breakfast."

Bradley rubbed the back of his head with his hand. Amelia knew that he only acted this way when he had something to hide. "Oh, hey there, Amelia! Maybe later this week? I have a few things I need to get done in town." With that, Bradley was gone.

Amelia called out after him, "But you don't know where anything is!" He either ignored her or could not hear those words, but he quickly vanished from her sight. Amelia shrugged her shoulders, deciding that her good mood was way more important than any suspicions about her best friend.

After visiting with Mrs. Gretchen at the gift shop again, Amelia headed through the remainder of downtown. She stopped and chatted with strangers and old friends. This town could be so unique during the Festival that she hoped it would never end. On a whim, Amelia stepped foot into the Chamber building, not to see her father but rather to take a tour through the festival museum again. She saw her Grandfather Tomlinson in one photo and how he had been Grand Marshall of the parade that year. She moved through the exhibit to see a photograph of past festival presidents, where her mother and father were both pictured. This town and Festival were more than just her home. Here was her history and, most importantly, her family. Caught up in the sentiment, Amelia made a quick phone call to discuss a few ideas for the Festival with Jenna. She ended the call happier than when she had dialed. Deciding to embrace the impulse rather than the practical, she decided to make one more stop during her trip downtown. If everything went well, she figured her happiness would only increase more and more.

Two hours later, Amelia emerged from the building victorious. Amelia was going to hold the news for Ben until the absolute perfect moment. No one else could know, not even her family, until she had the chance to surprise him. He was the driving reason behind her decision when she considered how kind and considerate he had been. The sweet notes and gifts were prime examples of why she wanted to do something this nice for him. She only hoped he would enjoy this new development.

Amelia got a message from the new human resources director informing her that he had found a home in Humboldt with a target close date of May 23rd. Amelia was shocked at how quickly he could plan it, but he informed her that Humboldt is where he wanted to be and promptly. He would submit his two-week notice to his current employer this week and looked forward to meeting the staff soon. Amelia decided that the only reason this day could not be called perfect was that Ben was stuck at the hospital in surgery all day.

At five-thirty that evening, the entire Allen family headed over to the town stadium for opening ceremonies to begin. Amelia saw Lou and Ian and a few other friends from high school all assembled. Since this was their class reunion, everyone would have multiple opportunities to get together throughout the week. She hugged old friends and took time to meet people's significant others. Everyone was sad to hear that Justin was deployed and would not be joining them this year. Amelia had told Lou about inviting Ben to the reunion after getting home the evening before. Lou decided to take the magnifying glass off of herself and turned it to Amelia. "Well, at least Amelia is bringing her new beau, Dr. Ben Taylor," Amelia answered the barrage questions, but for once, she welcomed them. She knew that Lou hurt to think about her husband away for so long. One of the best events of this trip was reconnecting with Lou. She had missed her old friend, and now she was resolved to stay close forever.

The group headed up the stairs and filled in a section of the stadium. At six o'clock, the mayor of Humboldt welcomed everyone to the start of the 81st Annual Strawberry Festival. He went over the brief history and a few personal comments before turning the microphone over to Roger Allen. Roger introduced several of the guests, including the pageant royalty, members of the festival committee, the chamber staff, and of course, the president and general chairman. Marcie Donald took over from here and began telling all about the week's events and this year's honoree, a ninety-nine-year-old Humboldtian who had been a part of the Festival in so many ways over the years. Jenna rose to follow the information with an introduction to tonight's entertainment. The local school of dance had sent over several students to do a few routines, followed by local solo musicians. The performers would go until it was dark enough out for the fireworks extravaganza.

As the entertainment began, Amelia began talking with a few of her former classmates. Ian nudged her on the shoulder and motioned towards the press box. She knew what he wanted and headed up to the top of the stadium with him. The two sat in silence as the sun began to set in the distance. In high school, the two would often come up to this location and not say a word while the light faded into darkness.

One time, Ian had chosen to talk through the evening instead of sitting in silence. *"Amy?" Ian called to the girl whose head was on his shoulder. "Yes?" He waited a few moments as they watched the sun settle down. "What do you want to do after high school?" She exhaled with ease as she commented, "Well, we will go to college, graduate, and find the perfect jobs. Hopefully, we can make a large impact in people's lives, but as long as we are together, that's all that matters to me." He smiled but only slightly. "You know I would give you anything in the world, right?" She grinned at him, "All I want is you."*

As the sun sank lower and lower, Ian whispered, "Thank God for sweet strawberry sunsets." Amelia's eyes lit with fire at his words. No one said another word as they watched in peace until the sky was dark. Amelia started to move back to their original location, but Ian stopped her. "You know this is the best spot in the stadium to watch the sky. Stay here with me and pretend it's like old times." *I already am* - Amelia nodded her head in agreement and sat back against the wall of the stadium.

The fireworks would take several minutes to prepare before the show would begin. Amelia decided to recount memories of years past while waiting, "What was your favorite firework as a kid?"

Ian thought long and hard before responding, "The planets. Remember that year when they set off different fireworks that resembled each planet?" Amelia laughed as the two of them began recounting all the different designs they had seen. When this town called something an extravaganza, you better believe it was worth every penny. Over the years, the residents had seen favorite cartoon characters appear in the fireworks as well as planets, fruit, shapes, designs, stars, flowers, etc. Amelia and Ian would have kept talking, but the first loud "Boom" stopped their conversation.

Over the next twenty minutes, the stadium and surrounding area watched a magnificent fireworks show. The city of Humboldt had yet to fail on a spectacular event, and tonight was no exception. The crowd let out several "ooh"s and "ah"s at the display. When the event ended, Ian and Amelia walked down to the open area beside the stadium. There they joined Bradley and Jessie to discuss the show. "Amelia! When you said extravaganza, I thought, well, maybe to a small town, this will be something large, but this was amazing! Why have you hidden this place for so long?" Amelia laughed at Bradley's over exaggerations but was glad her friend was having a wonderful time.

Moments later, Amelia found herself wrapped in a warm

embrace from behind. She turned her head to find Dr. Ben, still in scrubs, holding her. Everyone watched as the sight of Dr. Ben illuminated her face, and she leaned into his embrace. "I thought you had to work." He smiled as he informed her that his shift had ended, and he drove straight to see her. Jessie made a slight sound of approval at how sweet he was.

"We are still on for Friday, right?" Ben asked, and when she agreed, Ian immediately asked Jessie if they were still good for lunch tomorrow. Jessie was a little taken aback by his question that seemed to come from left field but confirmed their plans for the following day. As the five individuals stood staring at different places, no one saw the two disappointed looks on the faces of a few male members of the group.

Bradley, Jessie, and Ben all excused themselves to head to their respective cars. Ian and Amelia walked to the parking lot before attempting to say good night. "Ian, tonight brought back some enjoyable memories. It is always good to remember times as good friends."

Ian smiled at her and stopped her from getting into her car. "So, tomorrow is the big day. I know you well enough to believe that most everything for the recipe contest is done or planned out. So, here is the real question. What are you entering?"

Amelia laughed at him, "Maybe you do know me pretty well. I've decided to enter my strawberry cream cheese cobbler, but I think that's all."

Ian smirked as he voiced his disagreement, "No, no, no. The daughter of the talented Susan Allen cannot enter only one category. You should at least enter two others."

Amelia scoffed at him, "With what time? I will be prepping all day tomorrow for the event and then rushing home to make a dessert and get back in time."

Ian challenged her to think outside the box. "Tell you what,

Amelia. I'll make a bet with you. If you win more than one category, I get to call you Amy again." Amelia weighed her options. While she never wanted to back down from a challenge, this one was different. Emotions ran high as she considered the risk of the despised nickname and the conflicted feelings in her heart. She wondered if her feelings need a vacation from all the changes she'd introduced the last few weeks.

"And if I only win one challenge or less?"

Ian thought for a few moments before a light bulb went off in his head, "I remember how much you enjoy blackmail material. I will give you copies of poems I wrote when I was in high school, attempting to become a famous poet."

Amelia was confused, "Sorry, but Ian, I don't see how that can be blackmail."

Ian laughed before responding, "I think one of them was about a toilet. Ironically it was a metaphor for where that career went."

Amelia laughed hard before saying, "You've got a deal."

The two began to head home before she called out, "Oh, Ian, you also volunteered to help set up tomorrow morning, help with my prep work, and cleanup in the kitchen tomorrow afternoon. When Ian began to protest, she put up the palm of her hand and said, "No arguments! It's your fault I'm losing time tomorrow. The least you can do is help. See you at eight o'clock in the morning. Bring coffee." Not wanting to give him a chance to argue, she took off fast out of the parking lot. Ian stood there realizing that Amelia Allen had played him as she had in so many old times. He chuckled once to himself and muttered, "Fair enough, Amy, fair enough."

Chapter Sixteen

Tuesday morning started not quite the way Amelia intended. At seven o'clock in the morning, sunlight crept through the window curtains to rest on Amelia's face. She had spent the better part of her late evening deciding on what to cook for today's contest and making a shopping list that caused her to be undoubtedly tired. The sunlight continued to bear down on her face, causing her to stir. Amelia began to swat at the sunlight as if to make it disappear. She rolled over in the bed to check the time on her phone. Unfortunately, she had forgotten to charge her phone last night, and since it was now dead, her alarm never sounded. Seeing that the cellphone was blank, she glanced at the clock on the wall.

Amelia looked at the time and closed her eyes to roll back over and sleep some more. Mere seconds later, her eyelids flew open, and she raced out of bed. If trophies were being awarded this morning for the fastest time getting ready, Amelia would have won first place. She hurried down the steps, makeup bag in hand with her hair still damp from the swift shower. Her father laughed as he handed her his travel coffee mug before she could fly out the door. Roger continued chuckling as he went to pour himself a new cup.

Amelia made it to the Opera House with two minutes to spare, only to find Ian waiting at the front door with a box in hand. He held the door open for her as the two entered the building. Ian's eyes took in the picture of the Amelia that stood in front of him. He realized she was running late, a trait not generally associated with Amelia Allen. He filed this information away into the back of his brain to keep for another time. Ian may not have been on the best of terms with Amelia the last several years, but he still knew when to leave certain situations alone, at least for the moment. "I picked up some donuts this morning. All strawberry glazed, of course."

Amelia looked longingly at the box. "That was nice of you, Ian. I typically don't eat donuts and have a shake instead."

Ian saw how long she gazed at the box. "You know, it wouldn't kill you to eat one every now and then."

Amelia looked at Ian and laughed. "So I've been told. Bradley says it to me all of the time." She reached into the box and grabbed a donut, taking one bite before letting out a sound of sheer pleasure. Ian laughed at the way she sounded.

"You act as if you've never had a donut in your life." She waved off his jab at her and continued to enjoy her quick breakfast treat. Once she had eaten two donuts, Amelia decided to get to work. She assigned different tasks to the volunteers who had agreed to help and those like Ian, who Amelia had voluntold (as her father liked to call it). She glanced around the room.

"Where is Bradley? He agreed to help this morning, but I couldn't find him anywhere at the house. I thought he might already be here. He would never believe I ate a donut unless he saw it with his own eyes."

Ian was moving chairs around to open the room more when he heard her question. "Are you going to put an out-of-town guest to work on their first festival? It would be better if you let him enjoy the trip. Someone who has never lived here before needs to enjoy their first strawberry festival. When they return for future ones, though, sign them up to work everything." He finished his statement with a grin.

Amelia found herself laughing at his matter-of-fact yet insightful statement. "I guess you might be right. He can get off this time, but only once."

Ian decided to keep picking at Amelia, "Did I happen to hear you say I might be right? Can I get that written and signed, in blood, preferably? On second thought, repeat it after I hit record on my voice recorder app."

Amelia rolled her eyes as she walked away from him. Years may have passed since the two had been so close, but Ian was the same as he had ever been. "Of course not. Clean out your ears and get back to work, Ian."

With the number of volunteers Amelia had been able to assemble, the room was ready for the main event in a mere couple of hours. The workers had displayed decorations and established areas for each of the five categories. Amelia set out clipboards for the judges to be given with the score sheets already attached. She wanted to have as much work done as possible before the group left to save her from having to do so much this evening. Amelia made signs for each area and had Ian draw strawberries around her lettering to make them more visually appealing. After the group set out chairs for guests who wanted to taste-test, their work was done.

Ian and Amelia were the last two to leave the building. After she locked the front door, she thanked Ian for his assistance. "I will see you at one-thirty. We need to get everything ready for tonight's contest."

He shook his head to signal that he understood and wondered out loud, "So, what did you decide to enter?" Amelia glanced around to see if any other competitors were around. Ian couldn't help but laugh. Tonight was only a strawberry recipe contest, and she was treating it like a trade secret.

"I am going to enter three categories: cake, miscellaneous, and salad. I decided not to enter my strawberry cream cheese cobbler. I think I will hold that recipe for another year." Ian raised his eyebrows at her mention of a future festival contest, but she kept explaining her menu before he could question her. "For miscellaneous, I am entering my strawberry salsa. For the salad, I am going to do a spinach salad with feta cheese, toasted pecans, and homemade strawberry vinaigrette."

Ian waited for her to explain the cake recipe, and when she stood there staring at him, he finally asked, "And about the cake?" She shrugged off his question, "You'll have to wait and see!" He sighed and agreed to hold his suspense.

"That sounds like a great plan, Amelia. On that next entry, we should do my grandmother's strawberry rhubarb pie." Amelia looked at him, confused with the word "we." He saw the look on her face and decided to try and play it off, "Since you like volunteering me for different projects, I am volunteering you to help me with the same competition you decide to enter the cobbler." Amelia considered before nodding, and the two separated, intent on meeting right after lunch.

Amelia drove over to the local grocery store and gathered all of the ingredients she had written down the night before. She headed home to refrigerate the perishable goods and set out the items that needed to warm to room temperature. Amelia noticed that it was only eleven-thirty. Her body felt completely out of sync due to waking up so late this morning. Seeing that she had extra time, Amelia wondered how to utilize it best. She pulled out her laptop and started to go through emails and suggestions in her work inbox. She hoped Director Jones was not aware that she had been working through emails the entire vacation. The thought of coming back to an inbox of three weeks' messages unread terrified her. She justified this to herself as keeping her stress low upon her return.

When Amelia opened the inbox, she realized that the messages had been untouched since Thursday. She had given little thought to her regular employer throughout the weekend and yesterday.

Amelia's inbox showed more than seventy-five unread emails in that short period. While the number was not unusual for that long of a period, it was for someone's inbox that was supposedly on vacation for three weeks. Amelia noticed several tedious situations that seemed to irritate her nerves. Her mind was getting more and more agitated as she worked through her messages. She had nearly finished when a new email came in from Director Jones. Amelia debated whether to open the email and finally settled on seeing what he had to say.

> *Amelia,*
>
> *More than likely, you are checking this inbox while on vacation. I will not scold you for doing so, but I do hope you are enjoying what time you have off. When you get back to Nashville, I'd like to go over a few new proposals. We've got a lot of work to be done in this department.*
>
> *The other directors believe you are a good candidate for the promotion, and we will evaluate the effort you show over the next few weeks for the final recommendation.*
>
> *Best Wishes,*
> *Tom Jones*
>
> *P.S. Tell Bradley, he owes me lunch. I bet him you would be checking your emails, and he disagreed. I reminded him that even with change, some things simply stay the same.*

Amelia laughed at the last line. She had been surprised to hear about Bradley's estimation of her journey while at home. As she considered this trip, the time spent in Humboldt was a journey in and of itself. Bradley had not been around much during his stay so far. Amelia could not place her finger on the situation, but he was acting suspiciously. Amelia deflated, realizing that she may not get the chance to share her town with Bradley due to his frequent disappearance. While he had business to attend to at the beginning of the week, Amelia wondered if it was taking all of his time or more to the story. This morning, he had texted that he was visiting with a new friend he had met. Amelia decided not to continue down the rabbit hole and instead pulled out her phone to make a call.

"Director Jones?" Amelia asked when he answered the line. "This is Amelia. I wanted to talk with you about the vacation time I have accrued. . . ."

At one-thirty, Ian walked right through the front door. "Decided not to knock or ring the doorbell, did you?"

He looked around and pointed at himself, "Are you talking to me? I practically grew up here. The last several times were not to shock you so much. You told me to be here, but I can leave if you don't need the help."

Amelia's eyes continued to roll as they had this morning. She threw an apron at him, "Hilarious, Ian. Put this on and begin capping strawberries, slicing several for the salad, and chopping several more for the salsa."

While Ian began working on this first task, Susan Allen exited her room on crutches. Amelia moved to help her mother, but Susan shooed her away. "I'm only moving to the couch to read, dear. I am going stir crazy in that room." Once Susan was situated on the couch, she pulled over a book from the end table and began to read. Frank had followed her into the room and hopped up on the sofa to lay beside her. Susan had been so thankful for Frank over her recovery. The cat had laid with her and brought her comfort when she thought about how much the accident hindered her. She glanced over at the two young adults working in her kitchen. Amelia caught the raised eyebrows and the look that her mother gave. *What's she thinking?*

Susan Allen may have the deadliest glare in the county, but she also had other well-known looks. *Is she calculating and considering something about Ian? I wonder what he could've done.* Susan continued glancing at the two from over the top of her book. Amelia was neglecting her recipes as she considered her mother's stares. Eventually, Amelia quit noticing her mother's looks and focused on the food in front of them.

Ian had moved onto the next task Amelia assigned when he asked about this morning. "So, why were you running late?" Amelia was busy finishing the vinaigrette and stashing it in the refrigerator so that she could serve it chilled, her favorite way. "Well, I forgot to charge my phone before heading to bed last night. I was up late deciding on what to enter into the contest and writing out my supplies." *Just like old times.* Amelia's mind took a short trip down all of the evenings she and Ian had spent late into the night working on a project only to wake in a panic at the thought of being late.

"So, what is this secret cake recipe?"

Amelia's grin spread across her entire face, "Strawberry Cinnamon." Susan Allen heard her daughter's cake idea and was pleasantly surprised at the unusual yet probably tasty idea. She would not mind trying a piece of that, herself.

Throughout the afternoon, Ian and Amelia worked together in the kitchen in peace. They moved as one machine accomplishing their tasks. Ian offered to help mix, bake, and more, but Amelia only wanted him to do her preparation work and be a taste tester. She wanted to do these recipes as her own but needed help at how last minute she had started. Susan watched as the two laughed, joked, and even played with each other in the kitchen. She smiled as Amelia's eyes light up and sparkle and Ian's face shine brighter than ever before. Amelia caught more glimpses of her mother's view and now smile and figured she was reading an extra significant part of the book.

Amelia thanked Ian for all of his assistance once he helped finish everything and load the food in carriers. She gave him a ticket for the event tonight and promised to see him shortly. Amelia ran upstairs to change into a more festive outfit, complete with her strawberry earrings and pendant. Amelia reminded her mother that Roger would be by shortly to collect her for the event, and Amelia headed off to the competition.

Contestants were to arrive one hour before the doors would open to the public. This extra hour was essential for setting up your display, and it gave the judges a chance to walk around without the public crowd in attendance. Amelia surveyed the room and saw that there was extensive participation this year in the competition. While tonight should have felt like a big evening to her in "chairing" the event, Amelia was more excited at the prospect of being a contestant. She was grateful that the committee had stepped up in her mother's absence to handle many details, which allowed her to enjoy more of the festival. As the judges made their way around the room, Amelia began to get butterflies in her stomach. She reminded herself that nothing would matter if she won or lost and remember what is important — have fun.

Once the doors opened, the town members and visitors began to pour into the building. People made their way around trying samples of different dishes and visiting with old friends. Ian made his way through the building before stopping at Amelia's table. "You've got these categories in the bag. No one else's food looks nearly as appetizing as your creations." His over-confidence made her chuckle as he bent to take a bite of the food. His moan of satisfaction is what she had been hoping for, and she was delighted in achieving her goal. She began thanking him for his help today in both setting up and in the kitchen.

"It was nice of you to agree to come for support as well."

"Of course, Amy, we are a team after all."

She playfully scowled at him, "You haven't won the bet yet, sir." He smirked at her as he lifted a chip filled with her salsa. Taking the tasty treat in one big bite, he commented, "Oh, but with this, I definitely will."

Amelia started to retort when she saw someone coming down the aisle of people holding the most beautiful red carnations. "Ben?! I thought you were on call all evening." Ben presented the flowers to Amelia before kissing her on the cheek. Out of the corner of her eye, she saw Ian's body tense and a slight snarl appeared on his lip. *Why is he upset over a tiny kiss and a few flowers?*

"I was able to trade tonight for a day next week. Tonight's your big evening, and then hearing what you decided to make made me decided to come even more." Her heart leaped at the carnations she was holding. Her mind remembered this one quickly: carnations were a symbol of deep love and affection. Here was undeniable proof in her mind that Ben had sent all of the flowers.

Ian faded into the background to allow the two to have their moment together. Amelia looked for him after a few moments but was unable to locate him again until the competition results were ready for announcement. "Thank you all for attending this year's recipe contest," Marcie Donald began. "It is my great privilege as the Festival President to announce this year's contest winners. In the Kid's category, with homemade strawberry brownies, we have Julie West." The crowd cheered as eleven-year-old Julie went to collect her prize.

"In the Salad category," Amelia's heart began to pound as this was the first category she had entered, "This year's winner with a spinach strawberry salad and homemade strawberry vinaigrette is Amelia Allen." Ben kissed her on the cheek, and Ian loudly cheered for her as she went to collect her prize and stand beside little Julie. "In the pie category, with a delicious strawberry crumble pie, we have Marsha Hyatt." Amelia clapped along with the rest of the crowd. "In the cake category," Marcie continued, "with an innovative strawberry cinnamon cake, is also Ms. Amelia Allen." Amelia was shocked at having won two categories that she had entered. It seemed maybe her mother's genes had passed onto her after all. Ben and Ian both were cheering for her as she accepted the second award. As Marcie announced the miscellaneous category, Amelia wondered for a moment if she could win all three.

Marcie Donald smiled when she opened the envelope to show the winner. "Well, folks, it looks like the genes in this family run deep. The winner of the miscellaneous category with an impeccable strawberry salsa is Ms. Amelia Allen!" The last time any individual had won more than one category was Susan Allen several years ago. It was then that she took over the competition instead of entering it every year. It had taken Susan several years to win that number of awards, and here Amelia had done it in her first year.

Amelia graciously accepted the awards and looked out over the crowd. She saw the shock and thrill on her brothers and father's face. Lou, Donna, Jessie, Emma, and Jenna all were ecstatic and mouthed congratulations to her. She saw her mother's look of pure joy and swore she saw a tear stain on Susan's cheek. She glanced over at Ben, looking at her with deep admiration, and then her eyes landed on Ian. He seemed so pleased with himself and with her. She saw him mouth the words, "Told you so, Amy."

She smiled and nodded to him as he exaggerated her nickname. He had earned the right to call her that once more. He started to mouth something else, but she couldn't catch it as Ben moved towards her to congratulate her with a kiss. The ladies all looked pleased as the crowd watched the two kiss. One lady in the room, however, had been watching another young man. Her heart ached for him when she saw the word he mouthed, "I love you," and hated that Amelia never caught them.

Chapter Seventeen

Amelia started the following day by having breakfast with Jenna. The two had such a wonderful time sharing memories from the night before and laughed about so many shared experiences from years past. Amelia could not believe how quickly this trip was coming to an end. There were so many events and feelings that she had never imagined happening to her again in this town. Slowly but surely, she had fallen back in love with her community. The people continued to remind her of the joy of small-town living.

Today was supposed to be a more leisurely day, schedule-wise. Ben would be resting today following his recent shifts, and they were going to meet up this evening during the live music. Amelia only had to get a little planning work done today for the remainder of the festival and introduce the band at tonight's live music downtown. She also wanted to go to the Shortcake in the Park event. This was a new tradition that had not existed when she lived in Humboldt. She was curious to see how popular the event would be. Both of her parents would be attending the reception for past festival presidents this evening, as both had served in that capacity.

Amelia returned home to find her uncle Kent sitting with her mother and enjoying a pleasant conversation. "Uncle Kent, so good to see you again." Kent hugged his niece and sat back down across from his sister. Amelia noticed the long look on his face. "What's wrong?" Kent sighed and leaned back against his chair. "There are some problems with hosting your reunion on Friday night. With only two days left, I'm not sure what to do. Jessie is arranging a few volunteers to help out, but there are still some more issues to solve." Susan reached across the way and patted her brother's knee. "Don't worry, Kent. Lots of people will be happy to help." Amelia quickly agreed to her mother's statement. Seeing her daughter's nod, Susan let out a gasp as a light bulb went off in her head.

"Kent, I think I know how to solve your biggest problem. Amelia and our family will help." Amelia raised her eyebrows at how her mother had volunteered her for the "biggest problem." Amelia was more than willing to help as it was her reunion, but would she have time this week to deal with the most significant issue? Kent's face was brighter than the sky had been in the fireworks show two nights ago.

"Really? Are you sure it would be no trouble?"

Susan laughed and said, "No trouble for the Allen family, right Amelia?"

Amelia half-heartedly chuckled and responded, "I think I should know what the problem is before answering that question."

Kent and Susan shared a look filled with a silent struggle of who would break the news. Susan Allen may have the deadliest glare in the county, but her brother held the prize of the guiltiest stare. His eyes bore into his sister before she relented, realizing that by speaking up, she would have to explain the situation. "Well, dear, you see, there was a mix-up with the caterer, and now there is no food planned for your reunion. We need to make enough food to feed the one hundred and twenty-five RSVP'd guests." Amelia let her mouth hang wide open. Susan saw the look in her daughter's eyes and tried to schmooze her daughter before the Allen/Tomlinson temper reared its ugly head.

"Now, Amelia, you and the family with your friends did a wonderful job with dinner last weekend. I am certain that by working together we can have everything done before Friday evening. I'll get Jason and Donna to handle the pies and cakes, Eric and Emma to handle the salad and sides, and we can handle the main course: Chicken Alfredo and Lasagna. I can help make my secret five-hour sauce. The sauce can easily make it in slow cookers, and so we will borrow several."

Susan's attempt to persuade Amelia was not going that well. "Mother, are you crazy? We can't pull this off. The dinner last weekend was for twenty-five people, and it took several of us all day to present the dinner we did. Do you think we can feed five times as many people in this short of time? Are you sure there are no possible caterers?" Amelia said the last bit with slight trepidation. Kent confirmed what she figured was the truth. "No one is willing to cook for that many on this short of notice. Nothing within the committee's budget, that is."

Amelia buried her head in her hands and slumped down into the nearest seat. She moaned and groaned, but like any true Southerner, she agreed to help her family. Susan clapped her hands, happy at being successful, while Kent looked on with slight apprehension. "Jessie, myself, and a few others will handle the chicken alfredo. I've made mom's alfredo sauce a million times. You worry about taking care of the Lasagna." Kent hugged his sister before turning to give his niece a big hug. "Thanks, Amelia. I'm sorry to dump this all on you." She nodded slightly before he left.

She glared at her mother for a while after her uncle had departed. Susan finally huffed and turned towards her daughter. "Surely you aren't still upset with me. Family needed us, and isn't that what you taught me a few days ago?"

Why do mothers always have to make too much sense? Whenever her mother turned the logic back on her, it always defeated her inside, so she decided to ignore the statement. "So, this was the big problem. What else is wrong?" Susan smirked when her daughter ignored the question, proving to her that she was right.

"Planning a reunion during the festival isn't the best idea. All of the ordered decorations are at other events around town. He won't have them until Friday at three o'clock, and your reunion starts at six. Jessie has recruited several people to help with the setup, so that has at least is being handled."

Amelia was not surprised that the situation had its ups and downs, and she started to head into town when she remembered what they would be preparing. "How am I supposed to help you if I'm not allowed to know the secret recipe?"

Susan thought for a moment about how best to respond to the question. "Let's just say, Amelia, that once you see the ingredient, my grandmother added to the family recipe, you'll understand why the tradition has lasted and why I feel comfortable sharing it with you now." Amelia wanted a better answer than that, but she decided to take the answer her mother gave. It would only be a few days until the full answer came out anyways. Amelia said goodbye to her mother and headed out the front door.

She drove around town for a while, looking at all the last-minute preparations. She finally decided to pick up two bowls of strawberry shortcake and headed over to the assisted living facility. She found her intended target talking with Ian as she entered Ms. Georgia's room. "Amy, how nice of you to stop by," Ian called. She rolled her eyes at how happy he seemed to be in calling her by the nickname. Truthfully, it didn't bother her one bit this time and made everything seem like the olden days. "Amelia, come join us. Ian was telling me all about your triumphs last night. Congratulations, my dear." Amelia sat down beside her older friend and passed the strawberry shortcake to her.

As Georgia began to eat her treat, Amelia glanced over at Ian. "I had no clue you would be here, or I would have brought an extra one." Ian smiled and walked over to the bedside table before pulling out a plastic spoon and leisurely walking over to Amelia.

"No apologies necessary, Amy." Ian made that statement while sinking his spoon into her bowl. She gave him a slight, playful glare before inviting him to sit beside her and enjoy the treat. After a bit of small conversation, Ian excused himself to go and handle a little work.

Georgia and Amelia talked all about her date and Dr. Ben. Georgia was shocked by how Amelia talked about the good doctor, seeing as there was usually silence regarding a date. When Amelia brought up the flowers, Georgia reached out her hand to stop Amelia. "Are you sure, dear, that he is sending them to you? It seems strange to me that he would not own up to it after the carnations if that's what they truly mean."

Amelia thought her friend might have a point but didn't want to go down the unending rabbit hole. "I'm sure he is being mysterious and romantic."

Georgia murmured, "Maybe," and Amelia kept talking. The two visited for a long time, with Amelia even reading a little of Ms. Georgia's favorite book. She hugged her friend goodbye and promised to send or stop by with homemade goodies to sample the winning treats for herself.

At six o'clock that evening, Amelia met with Ben. She could tell that he was still somewhat tired but doing his best to stay with her. The two enjoyed the Shortcake in the park, although Amelia omitted that this was her second helping of the day. It was pleasant to be surrounded by both friends and strangers, celebrating this community in a way that resembled how sweet the strawberries could be when paired correctly. Her eyes glistened as she enjoyed the sweet strawberries and watched as the sun began to set behind the stage.

One hour later, Amelia was on stage, full of Shortcake, to welcome tonight's entertainment. She introduced the local band, headed by both a fantastic singer and baker. She climbed down the stage to find Ben not feeling as well as he would like. She finally encouraged him to get some rest and see each other in the morning, either during or after the parade. She knew that the next two days would work off all that Shortcake by walking through the parade with Berry. At first, she thought it would be upsetting to miss so much of the parade, but then she remembered that Berry came near the very beginning, which would allow her to view everything. She noticed several of the past presidents had joined the crowd; their dinner now ended. Amelia pulled aside a couple of them for a little idle chit-chat.

She noticed that Bradley was laughing and smiling at someone hiding behind a metal berry, but she never could move to see who. Now it all made sense. Bradley had been pretty well missing for the majority of this trip. Every time she would bring it up with him, there would be a new excuse, typically about seeing the town. That had made sense since he always drove himself, was never at her house, and could never be found anywhere nearby. He must have met someone in town and was secretly seeing them. Amelia decided to let it slide for now and utilize this blackmail at the most opportune time. Seeing him begin to walk towards her, she grabbed the nearest person and had an elementary conversation with them.

"Amelia, there you are!" Bradley saw Amelia as he began to rejoin the crowd.

"Bradley? Where have you been all day?" She enjoyed watching him squirm as he attempted to come up with a new excuse. He mumbled something incoherent out, but she acted as if it made perfect sense.

"Oh, well, ok. You are going to help with the reunion preparations, right?"

Bradley smiled and said, "Sure. Your cousin has already asked me to help out, and I agreed." Amelia was a little surprised Jessie could have already gotten to him but figured they ran into each other in town. Getting an excellent idea, she beckoned Bradley to follow after her.

Bradley climbed after Amelia to her favorite spot on top of a downtown building. "I want you to see this spot." Bradley was unsure of what could be wonderful at the top of a downtown building, but the view took his breath away.

"I love to watch the sunset from up here. We have unfortunately missed that tonight, but look around." From the top of the building, Bradley could see much of the town. The bright lights of the carnival located only a few blocks away illuminated the dark sky. Bradley had no clue that a small town like this could be so beautiful. After the two climbed down, Amelia took him over to the carnival.

After a few hours at the carnival, Bradley and Amelia headed back to the Allen home after receiving a message from Susan. Inside, the two sat on the couch and reflected over all the fun they had experienced. The rest of the Allen family was inside the house, even though it was late at night. The doorbell rang, and Eric moved to let both Jessie and Ian into the house. Susan welcomed everyone and asked them to sit around the table. "Thank you all for coming so late and on such short notice. There is much to be done in time for the Humboldt High School class reunion this Friday night. I know some of you have committed to helping decorate there at three o'clock this Friday. Anyone else needs to be cooking. Amelia and I will handle the Lasagna. Kent and Jessie are making the chicken alfredo, Eric and Emma, you two have the bread and salad, and Jason and Donna are in charge of desserts."

All of these individuals knew that these were their roles as Susan had already assigned them. "Mom," Amelia started, "you've told us this already. Is there something more, or why do Ian and Bradley need to be here?"

Susan scoffed at her daughter, "Forgive me for waiting a few minutes before continuing, my child." The others laughed at Susan but too wondered what was going on in the house.

"We are going to need a few extra hands to help with all of these preparations. Bradley, you will help Jessie and Kent with their food preparations, while Ian will help Amelia and me. Roger, you are going to help Jason and Donna. Jenna could not make it tonight, in preparing for tomorrow's parade, but offered to help with whatever you and Eric would need, Emma." Having a few extra hands should make the work go quicker, Amelia reasoned in her head. This revelation was not groundbreaking news, so Amelia was confused at the late-night meeting. When she saw Susan nudge Bradley with her shoulder, she realized the real reason for the meeting.

"Yes, well, while everyone is here," Bradley said hesitantly, "Susan has decided that I have some news to share now." Everyone laughed at his comments, as he literally had been pushed into announcing this. "Last Friday, I accepted the invitation to become the new head of human resources for Allen Inc. This morning, I closed on the home two doors down. I am moving to Humboldt in a few short weeks." Everyone was thrilled at the news and moved to congratulate their friend. Being Amelia's best friend for so long, he seemed a part of the family. More than one person around the table hoped this announcement would be coming from Amelia, but alas, they were both disappointed and happy at the same time. Two candidates had now filled the two open positions at Allen Inc., and the only remaining one was as a junior consultant. None of her family would expect her to move home for that position.

As hugs and congratulations went around the room, Amelia smiled and wondered what everyone was thinking. Her eyes landed on Ian's face, and she saw a mixture of happiness and sadness. He was the most unfamiliar with Bradley, except maybe Jessie, so she was unsure of how to take his expression. Staring too long at Ian's face, Amelia missed the look of total delight on the face of one member of her family.

Chapter Eighteen

The parade may not have begun until ten o'clock in the morning, but Amelia still arose early. She was exhausted from getting into bed so late the evening before, but her excitement would not let her stay resting for even a moment longer. She hopped out of bed and into a cold shower, hoping the frigid temperature would awaken her. After the quick wash, Amelia went downstairs to prepare the traditional parade breakfast.

As her family was often in the parade itself, the Thursday and Friday mornings of the Strawberry Festival were usually toast, scrambled eggs, and a few bites of fruit. It took Amelia no time to have the delicious, simple breakfast ready for the family's enjoyment. While the breakfast was nothing phenomenal, it was an excellent light breakfast before heading onto the parade route. The thought and thrill of seeing the junior parade once more could hardly contain Amelia's excitement. For many years, this Festival's Thursday parade had held the record for the largest non-motorized parade. The junior parade was always full of mostly middle school bands, and floats pulled, not driven. Today's attendance would be nothing compared to the following day, although there would be thousands of people in the city this morning. Some years, the town could see over one hundred thousand guests throughout the week. Today was the beginning of the culmination of it all.

Amelia wondered what types of floats she would see today. Her father had kept everything extremely tight-lipped, wanting not to ruin the surprise. She could hardly wait to finish the route with Berry so that she could sit and watch the remainder of the parade with her family. Her mind remembered floats of year's past. Some had lions, dogs, trees, underwater themes, birthday cakes, fire hydrants, etc. The people in this area would create some of the most inventive art pieces for kids and beauty queens to travel down the street. There would be such wonderful music and performances, all while making the trek down Main Street.

The Friday parade would include motorized vehicles, a visit from the governor of Tennessee, high school bands from multiple states, beauty queens from miles around, and even more innovative creations. She wondered if the Clydesdale horses would reappear this year. They had been absent for so long until a recent return. Another favorite pastime that had not been seen until recently was the Gibson County Mass Band. This took the marching bands from all of the county high schools to march as one collective unit down the festival path. Amelia hoped to see it again, if not this year, then in the future.

One thing this trip had proved for sure was that she was not missing another festival. This week held so many memories and elements that defined her as a person, and she could not bear to lose that again. Her homecoming had been the most rejuvenating experience she had experienced in a while, and for that, she would always be grateful.

Amelia looked at the time she had taken in following the trip into her mind of festivals gone by and saw that there were another seventy-five minutes until the Festival started. Seeing no harm in being early and unable to calm her excitement any longer, Amelia headed downtown. She found Jenna and Marcie standing near the beginning of the parade talking with Ben. She smiled to see that he was feeling better and went over to speak with them.

"Ben, I thought it would be after I walked through the parade before I saw you." He smiled back at her and leaned down to kiss her. As the two separated, he explained how Jenna needed an extra judge for the floats, and he had agreed to assist. As he went off with Jenna and Marcie, her fingers lingered up to touch her lips. The spark that he had slowly ignited had disappeared once more. She was unsure why this would have happened again but figured her sleep deprivation played a factor.

Amelia spent the next sixty minutes traveling up and down the parade line, chatting with old friends and making new ones. Noticing that there were only ten minutes left on her watch until show-time, she headed back to the front of the line. There, she found Berry ready to go and tried to get him or her to speak with her. Finally, Berry gave in and said hello. Amelia recognized the voice immediately. "Eric!? What are you doing in the suit?"

Eric hushed his sister, "You aren't supposed to reveal my identity, remember? The suit is passed on at different times, and last year mom assigned it to me. She planned to be my escort so I would know who was guiding me. You better do me right, Amelia! Mom would not be happy if her youngest ended up hurt." Amelia rolled her eyes at Eric's dramatics. "Sure thing, Eric." The sound of the sirens blared to signal the beginning of the Festival. Amelia's face became as bright as the sun before tackling Eric, barely stopping from knocking him over. "It's show-time!"

Amelia walked down the center of Main Street, waving at all the attendees and smiling at all the happy faces. She had never been this peaceful, at least in the last several years. Her heart fluttered as she saw old friends, local business owners, but primarily upon seeing Dr. Ben Taylor sitting across from the old Main Street School alongside other judges. He grinned broadly at her, waved, and then blew a kiss her way. She blushed at the way he was always so sweet and caring. A little ways down, she could see her parents and family sitting by the side with two open seats, one for her and one for Eric. She waved with much enthusiasm in seeing her mother attend the parade, even if in a wheelchair. Ian was sitting with her family and smiled largely at her as she passed by.

In what seemed like no time at all, Amelia and "Berry" had reached the end of the parade route. She helped him enter the chamber building discreetly and waited for him to emerge while taking part in the parade. She waved at the mayor, grand marshal and noticed that the high school band was doing better this year than they had in the past. She knew that one of her former classmates had returned to town to revitalize the music program. Though small as they were, the sound of the band was evidence enough of the new band director's hard work and determination.

Eric emerged from the building as the first float was arriving. The pair of Allen siblings admired the beautiful strawberry patterns lining the back of the float, honoring the hometown princess. There were two leading beauty pageants: The Hostess Princess and the Territorial Queen. One float and pageant belonged to the hometown beauties, and the other was made of queens from all around the area.

The Territorial Queen for next year's Festival would be selected this Saturday night, and Amelia looked forward to the event and seeing what begins the next Festival. Amelia and Eric leisurely walked back to where their family was sitting, taking in the various floats and bands as they passed by. Amelia made Eric stop to collect a few batches of freshly deep-fried Oreos to share with their family before finally arriving at the empty chairs.

Amelia plopped down in the empty chair beside Ian and began

to share her delicious treat with him. The two remarked about the beautiful sounds coming from area marching bands, commenting when they saw the banner of a school from more than an hour away and pointing out their favorite floats. Amelia and Ian played a contest to relate as many of the floats as possible to ones from years ago. One of the local charities had entered a float about celebrating birthdays. Amelia reminded Ian of the picture she'd seen of the giant birthday cake float the group had entered years ago. They waved at other mascots, such as the library book bear or the real-life Dalmatian on the fire station's display. After about ninety minutes, the parade finally drew to a close, and the Allen family (plus Ian and Emma) began to pack up their belongings save the chairs. Individuals would stake out the best parade seats on Main Street days ahead, and the Allen family were leaving their seats along with a roped-off area to mark their territory for the following day.

She had initially planned to enter the golf tournament, Strawberry Strokes, but she was unsure of how that would affect her getting to the Hall of Fame reception on time with the time restraints. Ben and Ian were both entering the golf tournament, and she thought Bradley might want to as well. She went off in search of her friend, realizing that she had not seen him at all during the parade route. Searching her parents' home and coming up empty yet again, she decided to pull out her cellphone and give him a quick call.

"Hello? Amelia? What's up?" Amelia barely heard his voice over several voices in the background.

"Bradley, where are you? I didn't see you along the parade route today."

Bradley spoke up a little more to overcome the noise. "I'm at the country club getting ready for the golf tournament. I saw you on the parade route today, and you were right. This Festival is magical. I was with . . . Oh, sorry, Amelia, I've got to run." With that, the phone line went dead. Amelia realized that he must have been with his secret crush, which was why she could not spot him along the route today. She decided to look harder tomorrow and uncover the hidden person.

Amelia decided to use her afternoon to make a few plans. She had already spoken with Director Jones about her upcoming decision on the extended vacation, and now she had some serious work to get done. Amelia made a detailed plan before heading out the door to accomplish a few goals. Trying to get someone to work on the afternoon of a parade in the town of Humboldt was more difficult than pushing a car alone up a steep hill. Amelia called in a few favors, however, and she finalized her plans quickly.

She glanced at the watch on her arm and realized that it was almost time to begin setup for the Hall of Fame reception. In the chaos of everything the last few weeks, she had not even taken time to review the nominees. One was a doctor, another a singer, and the last an attorney, all who had made significant contributions to not only the country and the state of Tennessee but the people of this local community. Amelia helped to decorate the tables and set out all of the needed items for the event. She was offered the opportunity to stay and attend the event, but she decided instead to head downtown.

As she walked away from the church that had always hosted the event, her mind considered the beauty of the downtown area. It had changed so much throughout the years, and she saw the closed dry cleaners as she walked up the hill to Main Street. While several things were different, the scene she stumbled upon reminded her that this was still the downtown of her dreams. The town she remembered as a small child was still here, maybe a little more advanced in some ways and regretfully a little more behind in others. Her eyes glistened as she took in the city once she arrived back on Main Street.

The city was livelier tonight than any night yet. Downtown filled with people, and while some would be across town at the first night of pageants, several were here in the heart of the Festival. Strangers were laughing and carrying on like life-old friends. People were sitting together that usually would pass each other by on the street. Right before her eyes, the best characteristics of her hometown and this Festival were being displayed. It was hard to criticize this town during the first full week of May, and she was glad to experience it once more. As she sat and smiled brighter with each reminder of the good in people and her community, she realized that this is what her heart needed. Amelia Allen had found what rejuvenated her, what cleansed her spirit, and restored her soul. Here, in this small Festival that she had avoided for so long as the inspiration, she needed to tackle the world. Coming home had opened her mind, heart, and senses back to the beautiful world around her. Her biggest regret is that she had waited this long to find what her heart indeed sought.

Amelia was caught off guard as someone sat down beside her and reached over to give her a slight peck on the cheek. "Did I disturb your daydream?" She glanced over to see Ben with a lopsided grin, eager to share the funnel cake he was holding. She laughed and leaned over to kiss his cheek before taking a heaping portion of the cake with her. The two continued laughing at each other and began enjoying the treat before them as people all around passed by them.

Just as Ben had been sitting down, Amelia saw Ian head her way. In a quick moment, he had turned and met Jessie by the concession stand. The crowd was too loud to hear what they were saying, but Amelia watched as they sat on a nearby bench, deep in conversation. The music began to play, and she swore she saw Ian mouth, "Jessie, can we talk about that dinner the other night?"

She began to sour when Ian lifted Jessie's hand to pull her off of the seat. As the band started to play a little slower, romantic music, Ben beckoned Amelia to dance with him right in the middle of Main Street, surrounded by friends and strangers. Amelia eagerly leaped at the distraction and began to slow dance with Ben.

The two swayed against the lights of downtown to the music of a local band, and Amelia's heart took in all the beautiful events surrounding the man currently holding her. She still had no answer for why the sparks seemed to come and go, but Amelia was confident that she was falling for him. As the two danced the night away, they stopped as Ben noticed the sun going down. "I thought you might want to take in another strawberry sunset. I know I will miss them."

Amelia watched the sunset on the horizon before catching his last statement. "What do you mean miss them?" Ben pulled her aside to have a more private conversation.

"I wanted you to be the first to know. I recently accepted a position at a major hospital in Chicago."

Amelia took a step back at this revelation. "What about us?"

"Well, I thought you might be interested in a position at a large Human Resources Firm there. It would be a great step for your career. We can attend several mixers and build a name for the two of us in one of America's largest cities."

"Move to somewhere even bigger than Nashville? Why not stay in a smaller town like here?"

"Small town living is nice, but it isn't what I always dreamed for my future. You live in the city and can agree, right? Sure, the Festival has its perks, and I am so thankful to have met you, but this is the life for small-time individuals." His words threw Amelia. She had thought he was a simple, down-to-earth gentleman. These words were of someone who believed much higher of themselves.

"Ben, I can't say that I agree. City life has its perks, I'll agree, but it has nothing on the community of a small town. I would much rather be in a place where I have a purpose and a special meaning than to be in the glamorous city life."

Now it was Ben's turn to take a step back, "I know we haven't been dating long, but I was sure that you appreciated the small things here as a vacation typesetting, not as a place for a future. The Festival would be a nice visit, but you have a life in Nashville, right? You've talked about how involved you are with the young professionals and going to all the city premier events, and isn't that what you like?"

Amelia was surprised even more by his comments. She had admitted what all she loved about city life to him but realized he had misinterpreted her words, "Ben, I have and do like those events, but they are very surface-level. Here, I feel a deeper connection to my work and family."

Ben nodded his head and glanced off at the now darkening sky, "So I guess you would not be interested in a human resources position in Chicago and move with me?"

Amelia sighed, "Oh Ben, I could never move that far away from my family again. I left them once before, and then I was only hours away. I'm sorry, but that's out of the question."

"Maybe we can make it work long-distance? We can have virtual dates and figure it out as we go."

As much as she had enjoyed her dates with Ben, her heart tightened, knowing that this was not the right choice. "Ultimately, I think we want different things in life. I'm not sure more time will change that. In the last few weeks, I've realized how much I miss the smaller, simpler life. You want bigger and better, and well, that's not for me."

The two stood in silence for a while before Ben finally leaned over to kiss her cheek. "I understand, Amelia. I think I'll skip the reunion tomorrow and go ahead and say goodbye." He walked away from the conversation as a tear began to roll down Amelia's cheek.

Neither person had seen Ian appear as Ben said, "human resources position in Chicago." When he heard Amelia say, "Oh, Ben," Ian's heart decided that he would be unable to stay and hear the rest of her answer. Tomorrow he would be helping Amelia in the kitchen and make the best of it without informing her he knew. He would wait until she decided to tell him and then would try to be as happy for her as he could. Ian decided to head over to the assisted living facility as there were still forty minutes until visiting hours would end. A conversation with Georgia was what his soul needed.

While Ian and Ben were both leaving, Amelia stood shocked and confused. How could the gentleman who had given her all of these beautiful flowers, watched sunsets with her, and seen the passion of this small town, end up leaving her over this? How had she misjudged his character? Her brain had known that he was not the right man for her with all of the "spark" debacle, but how could someone who seemed so romantic end things this quickly? Amelia walked back home as her heart wept inside over the last few moments. In what had only been a few minutes' worth of conversation, three hearts had left the Festival with an outcome other than what was expected. What should have been a sweet strawberry sunset had turned into something sour.

Chapter Nineteen

Amelia returned home Thursday evening sadder than any night before. Susan tried to comfort her daughter but was unable to find the root of the problem. Not knowing what else to do, Susan called Lou over, who arrived after finding a babysitter. Lou headed up to Amelia's room and entered without knocking. She found her friend lying on the bed in tears. Lou texted Donna and Emma to come over and join her. All four ladies were sitting around Amelia's bed in a matter of no time.

Amelia told the others about her conversation with Ben, and Donna was appalled to hear how things had turned out. "I'm sorry for pushing the two of you together, Amelia. I thought that it would work out between you two."

Amelia nodded her head and dried her tears. "I still don't understand the flowers, though." She muttered. When the others inquired about the flowers, she explained about the flowers she'd received and their hidden meanings.

Emma piped up, "I thought you said that no one signed the cards."

Amelia nodded her head and commented, "True, but then he

brought red carnations, which mean deep love and affection. I took that as my confirmation that he had given all of the arrangements to me."

Donna hung her head. "Oh, Amelia. I ordered those carnations for him. He was so busy that he asked me to run over to the florist and get you some flowers. They were out of red roses, so I chose red carnations."

Amelia was not mad at Donna, but she seemed unable to process this statement. If the carnations had no meaning at all, then who was behind these flowers? Had she only imagined that the flowers had any purpose at all? Amelia seemed to settle down on learning this news as she slowly began to understand Donna's statement. If Ben was never behind the flowers and had even resorted to getting her sister-in-law to buy the last bouquet, she never really knew him. Her idea of Dr. Ben Taylor had all been only a fantasy.

'Amelia finally convinced her friends to go home and get rest before the next festival day. "I will be ok. Thank you all for coming." Amelia sat on her bed as Frank tried to distract her. She finally pulled him close, rubbing her orange tabby. "Oh Frank, I guess I was wrong all along. I think deep down I knew, but yet I wanted to fall for him." She kept stroking him, wondering who had sent the flowers before finally drifting off to sleep.

The following day came much quicker than planned, especially after the evening Amelia had experienced. She readied herself for the festival and headed down to the beginning of the grand parade. She climbed on top of the fire truck, as Berry would be riding in style today instead of walking. She helped "Berry" climb up on top of the fire truck and sat down beside him, awaiting the beginning of the festival. As she waited, Eric's voice was soft but firm. "If you'd like, Jason and I can have a nice talk with Dr. Taylor."

Amelia playfully laughed at how protective her brother sounded. "It's ok. Really, Eric. He was a good guy, and we just wanted different things in life. I am glad, though, that I learned about his true self before we became more serious. He asked me to consider moving to Chicago." Eric stayed quiet for a while, and Amelia looked confused at the Berry costume. "Eric, you know that I would never move that far away again, right? I promised to be more involved in this family, and I will honor that."

Eric sighed, "I know, but I needed to hear you say it again. I'm getting married next year and want my sister more involved in both the wedding and my life." Amelia hugged the Berry, and the parade began. The two waved at the much larger crowd that had gathered for the grand parade. Amelia tried to use her eagle eye view to find Bradley but was having no luck. She glanced up to see different business owners and their friends watching the parade from the tops of their shops. There, Amelia found Bradley hanging out the window waving at her and Berry. She didn't see anyone with him and was so surprised to find him above a shop that she failed to look and see whose store it was. As the parade ended, Amelia and Berry disembarked from the fire engine, and she waited again on her brother outside of their father's office. The first vehicle she noticed was that of the state governor, waving at the surrounding crowd.

It was always lovely to see that the state's governor attended. It was a long-time tradition that the sitting governor would come on Friday, and there was a "governor's luncheon" thrown in his honor. Amelia had tickets that would allow her to attend, but instead, she would be cooking with Ian and her mother for the reunion that night. The reunion brought a slightly sad look to her face in realizing that she no longer had a date for that evening, but she brightened at the thought of seeing her old classmates and planned on enjoying the evening.

Eric and his sister headed back a little more quickly, this time to their family's spot. Amelia sat down beside Ian and watched the parade a little more solemnly. Ian did not try and make jokes or brighten Amelia's day, and she chose to stay silent. A few of the floats really piqued her interest, including ones displaying cartoon characters, honoring the servicemen, and playing on words of businesses. Amelia sat straightforward, though, to watch the Gibson County mass band, a feature that she had only seen in videos. Watching the different county high schools join together in one large collaboration was beautiful and reminiscent of the entire county getting behind one project. She also enjoyed seeing the Clydesdales, who had returned for another year. The festival's highlights had brightened a darker day, but eventually, the parade came to an end.

As the family headed home, Amelia commented on the number of out-of-state high school bands that had marched this year. It was refreshing to see people from the entire Mid-South coming together and celebrate with their city. Susan smiled as she realized that her daughter was brightening up from the gloomy stance she had shown most of the day. Ian parted ways from the others with an agreement to be at the Allen home in an hour to help with the food preparation.

Each family member went off on their respective assignments for the class reunion this evening. Susan waited until the coast was clear before pulling out the recipe from her secret hiding spot. "Now remember, Amelia, you cannot share this recipe. As this is your first time making the sauce, you'll be relying on me so that Ian doesn't find out the recipe. Not even your father knows the Tomlinson secret. You know you'll be expected to add one ingredient to the sauce at some point, but not today." Amelia looked over the recipe and saw the tattered old card that must have belonged to an ancestor. On the card in different handwriting was one or two ingredients here or there. Amelia realized that this was her grandmother, mother, aunts, and other relatives who have all made contributions to the recipe. As Amelia admired the card and turned it over and over, one problem stuck in her head. "Mom, why again can I see the recipe now instead of when I'm engaged?"

Susan smiled at her daughter as she took the card right from her hand. She turned it on its side and pointed at a small scribbled word. "My grandmother decided the recipe needed two additions: a pinch of Parmesan melted into the sauce and this." Amelia's eyes followed to where Susan was pointing. Scrawled in pencil, barely legible was the word, love. Amelia looked up at her mother, confused as Susan went on about the recipe. "Grandmother decided that only the love one has for another individual, and then their family could create the best pasta sauce. Amelia, when you love someone, you want the best for them. Love makes you change yourself and your desires for that person. Cooking is similar. In preparing food for my family, I use the love that I have to make everything a bit more tasteful. Cooking with love is essential, my dear, and so since my grandmother, only women who are engaged to be married can learn the sauce. She figured that was the only way to ensure they were in love."

Amelia took in her mother's words, still confused about why she suddenly inherits the sauce recipe. "Mom, I appreciate that you are sharing the secret, but my love was unsure and ended up being wrong." Susan helped prepare the tomatoes and herbs as she hummed in the kitchen, ignoring her daughter's statement. "Mom? Did you hear me?" Amelia called once more.

Susan looked up and motioned for her daughter to begin preparing the items for the sauce. "I heard you, dear, but I think I know best. I saw the two of you the other day, and my heart knew that you had found love."

Amelia scoffed, "My heart thought so too, but it seems that the good doctor is nothing more than a fantasy."

Susan smiled as they continued working. "Well, I knew that from the moment he entered my hospital room. I saw the way you looked at each other and knew it would never work. Call it mother's intuition, even if that is cliché."

Amelia almost cut herself with the knife she was holding. "Do be more careful, dear," Susan called as she moved slowly in the kitchen to prepare the next batch of tomatoes.

Amelia looked up at her mother, "I'm even more confused now, mom. If you aren't talking about Ben, then . . ." Susan loaded tomatoes into one giant stockpot before dividing the mixture into several slow-cookers.

"We need to get moving. If we cook on high, the sauce will barely be ready in time for tonight. Remember, there's a lot of sauce to be made." Amelia moved to help her mother before the doorbell rang. Amelia went to answer, but Susan held her back. "The other day when the two of you were working in the kitchen, you moved in perfect harmony with each other. I saw the glances you made at each other and knew that my daughter had finally found her long-lost love." The doorbell rang again, and Amelia moved to answer it once more. This time, Susan did not stop her daughter but instead let her get to the door.

"Who is she talking about? The only person I cooked with was. . ." Amelia opened the door while mumbling to herself when it became clear who Susan had mentioned. She glanced up to meet the person at eye level. Standing there was Ian, who swiftly moved in to the house to help with the preparations. Amelia turned around, staring down the hallway at the man who had breezed past here. Here was the man who was once a friend, then a lover, and now a source of confusion.

As Amelia stood at the door, she thought if she could be in love with him again. *It would certainly explain why I feel the way I do when he's with Jessie. Maybe that's what my heart has been trying to tell me?* The flowers did not add up to Ian, though, as he had never cared for floral anything. She had grown up with him and knew that there was not a fiber in his body that would lead him to share flowers with special meanings. "Amelia, are you coming back in here?" Her mother's voice snapped her out of her wonderings, and she walked back into the kitchen.

Ian was quiet as Susan had him stirring the first pot of sauce. After helping Amelia get the pasta sauce on, Susan decided she needed to rest a little bit before helping with assembling the lasagnas later that afternoon. She left them in charge of the pots, reminding them to stir and taste often. For a while, the two sat in silence as they worked on the sauce. Ian finally decided to break the ice and try to have a friendly conversation. "The parade was spectacular today, wasn't it, Amelia?"

"You didn't call me Amy," Amelia said in a quiet voice. Ian looked away before turning back to her, "Sorry Amy, I forgot that I'd won the bet, is all." Amelia was not convinced but chose to ignore the blatant lie. She decided to try and see what her heart was telling her. The only way to get to the bottom of the issues was to expose why she felt like never trusting Ian again.

For a while, the two made small talk about the festival and their friends. They guessed at who would have changed the most since high school and who might skip the reunion. Ian informed her that most had chosen Amelia for the top of that list. Amelia was glad to know that several would be surprised to see her tonight. As the sauce neared completion, Amelia knew that her mother would be rejoining them soon.

Before she lost the courage, she decided to take her chance. "Ian, why didn't you show at Belmont?" Ian had been in the middle of tasting the sauce when she asked the question. The man standing before her almost choked on the tiny amount in his mouth at her question. He froze, unable to speak, so Amelia decided to continue, "I want to forgive you and try to be close friends again, but I need to know why you never showed and why you ended things the way you did."

Ian decided that the tile on the Allen family's kitchen floor was the most exciting pattern he had ever seen. At least, that would be a good reason as to why he stared at the floor for the longest time. Eventually, he began to speak without reaching Amelia's eyes, "You always knew what you wanted to do. From the time that we were little kids, you had your entire life planned out. We were going to college, graduating, getting married, and working in our favorite fields as leaders. You are the smartest, kindest, hardest-working woman I have ever met. Amy, your skills could take you anywhere you wanted to go. I had no clue what I wanted to do. I could draw, and as your parents always said, I could give a used car salesman a run for their money. Looking back, it was logical that I went into marketing and graphic design, but back then, I was a lost kid. Here I was, someone unsure of everything but that I loved you, and you were ready to tackle the world. I decided that I would only hold you back, and I thought maybe you'd want to live here and build a life together, but I figured you might only do that for me. The hardest decision I have ever made is going to Knoxville without you. I couldn't see you and talk to you, so I wrote you a letter to end things. I knew you'd be upset but knew you were strong enough to move on from a little 'ole me to something far grander. I wanted then, and still now, what is best for you."

Ian finally lifted his head to look Amelia in the eyes. His brain warned him that she would likely be upset, mad even, and if she had anything in her hand, especially a skillet, to duck. What Ian found was a tear-stained face. "You loved me? Someone who loves truly loves me wouldn't have abandoned me."

Ian shifted his head away once more. He hadn't meant to make that statement, but it slipped out. "Yes, Amy, and because of that love, I had to let you go." When he met her face once more, he saw the anger begin to build.

"That wasn't your decision, Ian. We could have talked about this. I would have been happy working as a receptionist as long as I was with you. I wanted to conquer the world, but only with you at my side, and you took that option away from me."

Susan Allen had returned when Amelia started to get upset. Seeing her mother present, Ian decided to leave this in her capable hands. "Amy, I am sorry for how I did it and regret what it caused, but I did it for you. I hope we can move past this and be friends even if you are leaving, but I understand if not. Mrs. Allen, thank you for letting me into your home once more, but I think I better be going. Jessie needs help setting up the tables for tonight, and it might be better for me to leave." Susan nodded her head and watched as Ian left.

She hustled over to her daughter, as best she could on crutches, before sitting down and grabbing Amelia into a tight hug as the tears freely rolled down her cheeks. "Remember that I told you what love could do to you, honey. Ian made a decision that he has regretted for years but stands by the motive. Can you honestly tell me that back then, you wouldn't have done the same for him?" Amelia dried her tears and thought about her mother's words. She started to respond when the doorbell rang once more. Amelia made sure she looked presentable before answering the door. There was the same flower delivery gentleman with a vase full of Azaleas. "Delivery for Amelia Allen."

Amelia returned to the kitchen and set the azaleas down on the table. She opened the card and read, *"Best Wishes Amelia. May you find all your heart is seeking."* She shared the card with her mother and wondered who could have sent the flowers. If not for the fact that Ben had already been ruled out, these flowers would have solidified her guess. This one was easy to remember as azaleas were beautiful flowers with a sad meaning — *Take Care of Yourself for Me.*

Amelia struggled with her feelings throughout the remainder of the day. She slipped away to the BBQ cook-off to meet all of the competitors. Tomorrow afternoon she would return to the venue to judge and help declare a new winner. On returning to her parent's home, she helped her mother cover the pans of lasagna and load them into her car. She rushed upstairs to change into an elegant red dress with green emerald jewelry. While grabbing the jewelry, her fingers closed around the promise ring tucked away in the box before slipping it absent-mindedly into her purse. She curled her fading brunette locks and slipped back downstairs.

Amelia arrived at Uncle Kent's barn with perfect timing to deliver the final food. The event had come together better than she expected, and she was delighted to see how everything had turned out. The event barn was beautiful, and she knew that people would be lining up to book events and weddings here. She helped greet guests and hugged so many classmates that she had not seen in years. At the event, no one could believe how their classmates and family had made such delicious food. Amelia glanced around, looking for Ian, and failed to find him. She finally caught a glimpse of him and wandered over to his area.

As she approached, her eyes took in how off-centered he seemed. His eyes were slightly pinkish, and his pupils seemed filled with strife. Her mind was moving faster than a roller-coaster through her emotions. One moment she was sad and anxious, the next angry at the situation and the memories.

She often wanted to stop her feet from leading toward him, but as if being pulled by a string, she was drawn closer and closer to him. Her heart began to beat so loudly that it was almost recognizable above the music playing. She took another step, wondering if the floor was a treadmill, and she'd never reach her destination. Finally, she'd arrived at his area. She opened her mouth to speak, but he quickly deflected to another classmate of theirs, pulling him into a boring conversation.

She started to walk away but noticed how his eyes followed her slight movements. The eyes had become filled with agony, and her anger began to dissipate. As she stood there, near her old friend, she wanted nothing more than to find peace. He had stopped talking, and now the two stood in silence. There was much she wanted – no needed- to say, but the words couldn't seem to come. There, as she was finally about ready to speak, the music changed to what was once their song.

The two shared a look of sadness and anticipation before Ian extended his hand. "Care to dance?" She nodded and grabbed his hand as the two went out onto the dance floor. The two moved in sync, like old times, through their song and several more. With each passing moment, the anger and strife dissolved more and more. After a few more melodies, they began to look into each other's eyes. On his were written sorrow, regret, and longing. If she could have looked into a mirror, she imagined that her own eyes displayed confusion, desire, and hints of forgiveness.

As they danced, neither cared that the others were talking about the former couple. Instead, tuning out everything around them allowed them to move as if they were in perfect unison. There, on the dance floor, two broken hearts found peace in the close company of each other. They began moving closer together, and Amelia's emotions began to change. Now, she was overwhelmed with a great desire to kiss him. She inched closer towards him, and as the current song came to an end, she pressed her lips together with his. The reaction in her brain was brighter than the opening ceremonies. The sparks coming from his kiss could have lit the entire barn on fire but instead moved her with passion, love, and a firm desire.

The two separated, and Amelia's smile began to vanish when she saw the look of confusion on Ian's face. "What about Ben?" Amelia began to respond when Jenna tapped her on the shoulder. "Amelia, you've done a wonderful job this week." Ian offered to get the three of them drinks as Jenna wanted to ask Amelia a few questions.

"Sorry to bring up work questions while here, but I needed to ask a few things." The two went on talking before Amelia shared some news of her own with Jenna.

"It is a big deal, Jenna, and a great opportunity for me. I can't believe that I'm moving away from Nashville, but I'm so excited about the opportunity. Please keep it quiet, though, as I haven't made any announcements yet."

"Your secret is safe with me. Oh, thank you for the drinks, Ian!" Amelia turned to see that a look of sadness had returned to Ian's face. He handed each their drinks as Jessie came walking by. "Jessie, care to dance?" Jessie started to protest, but Ian laid the glasses on the table and took her out onto the dance floor. Her heart broke at the sight before her. *Did that kiss mean nothing? Why did he ask about Ben?*

Deciding that she couldn't stay here any longer, she started to head out the door when she ran into Bradley. "What's wrong, Amelia?" She decided to ignore his question and instead cleared her eyes.

"Bradley, what are you doing here?" She took in the nice suit that he was wearing. As he saw her calculating eyes roam over him, he knew that his excuse of being invited after helping prepare dinner was not going to work.

"Well, I started seeing someone, and they invited me here as their date." Amelia was surprised to learn that his date was from her class but decided her curiosity could wait. She wanted to leave this place immediately. "That's nice. Well, I will see you later."

"Amelia, wait! I know something is wrong." She stood in silence, unable to express in words how she was feeling. "I know, I should have told you, but I wanted to make sure we were completely compatible. We've only known each other a short time, but we're getting close." Amelia's head nodded as if on auto-pilot. "Don't be upset that I kept this from you. I wanted to talk with you like you were me and your date, but I figured with the connections, it would be awkward."

"It's ok, Bradley, really. Now, if you excuse me, I need a breath of fresh air." Bradley nodded sadly at his friend, and Amelia hated that he felt terrible. *It's not his fault, but I'll explain it to him later.*

Amelia finally reached the outside and saw Ian had made his way there. Her mind reasoned that he must have slipped out while she was talking to Bradley. "Amelia, I hope you have a good evening."

Amelia would walk on by without saying anything to him, but this comment had thrown her. "I am sorry for overstepping, Ian."

He laughed, inwardly hurting at the pain he felt. "That's ok. It was nothing but a simple kiss and didn't mean anything, don't let it hold you back from your dreams. Have fun with your new life, Amelia. I hope you enjoy your new scenery. Goodbye, Amy." Amelia hoped that was the end of what he had to say. His tone was hateful and hurt, but it cut her with a deep gash on her heart. As Ian headed back indoors, Amelia stood confused at his statement. He had obviously overheard her conversation with Jenna, but why would he react this way? As he closed the door on her, she stammered out, "Goodbye, Ian."

Chapter Twenty

$\mathcal{A}$melia returned home Friday night earlier than expected and went straight to bed. She decided to run in the 5K the following morning, so her decision ended up being wise. She arose early and took a quick shower before heading downstairs to stretch. Her parents were both awake and waiting to head over to the park for the beginning of the race. Eric, Emma, and Jason would all three be running as well, and the Allen parents would support their children.

Her mother's glances and minimal comments let Amelia know that she was tightly keeping herself from prying. The family made their way over to the starting point in silence early Saturday morning. Amelia hopped out of the car once they arrived and went off to stretch again in solitude. She finally decided to join the others and saw Bradley readying himself beside Jessie. "I never would have guessed you would run in a race, Bradley."

He laughed and put his arm around Jessie. "Well, she talked me into it," Bradley replied as he bent down to kiss her cousin. Amelia was taken aback by this display of affection and started to ask questions before the race directors had them lining up. Moments later, the shot rang out, and the race had begun.

Amelia figured the early morning run would clear her mind and help her focus on the last day of the Festival. Seeing Bradley and Jessie kiss, however, had thrown several new red flags in her face. She was distracted as she made the run around town and almost ran into shrubs on more than one occasion. Eventually, she made her way to the finish line to join the remainder of her family. As she walked over to grab a banana and water bottle, she saw Jessie and Bradley kissing again.

"Hold on a moment, you two!" Amelia yelled out at them. "Jessie, I thought you were dating Ian! How could you do this to him?"

Jessie separated from Bradley and wiped her lip before laughing. "Me date Ian? Be serious, Amelia." Bradley was simply confused at whatever was going on here. "Amelia, you said that you were okay with Bradley and me talking at the girls' night." Amelia thought back to that night and remembered that she had cut off Jessie before hearing her new fling's name.

"I did no such thing. I told you that I was fine with you seeing Ian. The two of you have had lunch several times and talked at Main Street, and then danced together last night."

Bradley looked accusingly over at Jessie with the dance mention. "I knew nothing about the dance, Jessie."

Jessie looked a little sheepishly at both of them, "Wow, this is one huge misunderstanding." The three sat down on a park bench as Jessie began to explain.

"Ian and I have been having lunch because he is doing marketing work for a client of mine. I went back into acquisitions at a Jackson firm, and we contracted out to Ian to help our situation. I also landed him several graphic design clients for logos and banners, which he thanked me with a nice dinner. We talked the other night on Main Street about the client acquisition we are currently working on as the owner is his friend. Last night, he took me on the dance floor spontaneously to share his friend's thoughts on the newest proposal. Everything we've done is all about business. There is absolutely no romance between us."

Bradley seemed convinced with her explanation, but Amelia still had her doubts. "How did the two of you meet before the girls' night? Bradley didn't come to stay until the next week." Before they could answer, Amelia turned to Bradley, "Where were you watching the Festival? I didn't catch whose building it was or see Jessie up there either."

When it seemed her questions had ended once more, Bradley decided to answer both. "I met Jessie online a few weeks ago. Her profile said Jackson, and so I never imagined she was from Humboldt. When I brought you clothes that Sunday night, I caught her outside. We were both completely shocked to see each other, and that's when I learned the connection. She had to run, but we made plans for the two of us to go out in person sooner than planned. That's where I've been this whole past week, spending as much time with her as I can. She's been helping me find a home, and the realtor invited us to the top of their building to watch the parade. Jessie was getting refreshments when you passed by."

Amelia was a little more convinced but decided on one more question, "Why so secretive?"

Bradley and Jessie looked at each other before shrugging their shoulders and Jessie responding. "I thought you knew, so I haven't been very secretive. After that talk at girl's night, I figured there was no need to bring it up constantly."

Bradley nodded his head, "I thought it was very awkward for you, which is why I avoided you some and haven't talked with you about it. Jessie told me the two of you talked, but when you didn't mention it to me, I thought I wouldn't say anything until I knew how much I liked her."

Amelia muttered an apology at the two, and Bradley eagerly

joked with her about that. "I'm sorry, Amelia, but can you repeat that after I hit record?" Poor Bradley never saw the blow to his stomach coming, which Jessie happily laughed at before helping her new boyfriend up from the ground.

Amelia headed back home with her family, more conflicted than before. If Ian was not dating Jessie, then why did he act that way the night before? She took a long hot bath, trying to relax and consider all of the evidence of the last few days. She wondered if her heart had misread the signs entirely or if she had offended Ian somehow. One thing she knew for certain, this trip home, would never be forgotten.

The BBQ cook-off judging was due to take place in less than an hour, so Amelia headed on over to the venue outside of the local high school. The Festival had planned live entertainment throughout the day. She visited with Marge, the chair of one of her favorite events, which displayed Tennessee walking horses from all over the Mid-South. She wished that the schedule would have allowed her to attend, but unfortunately, it coincided with the reunion last night. In her head, she figured it would have been a much more enjoyable evening. As she made her way around the booths, Marcie Donald stopped Amelia to share her gratitude for all of Amelia's help this week. "The pageants last night were wonderful, and tonight will be no exception. Please be there around six o'clock. You will be sitting with the judges for the senior revue. I hear that tonight will be very exciting." With her statement spoken, Marcie Donald disappeared into the crowd.

Amelia joined the other judges and collected her clipboard. She sampled all types of barbequed food that made her mouth water at the flavor of each dish. The judges huddled together, and the decision was unanimous that the Berry Brothers' BBQ was the 81st Annual Strawberry Festival BBQ Champions! She stayed around for a bit to congratulate several of the contestants. Lou and the twins were there, and they sat under the amphitheater to pass a little time. Amelia sat feeding Daphne while Lou was taking care of Kathryn. She shared the story from the night before, and Lou looked on with sympathy.

Amelia shared the news that Jenna knew, and Lou leaped out of the seat to hug her once again best friend. The few short weeks at home had rekindled their old friendship as if no time had ever passed. Lou finally sat back down once Kathryn began crying for more food and glanced over at her friend. "You need to talk to him. I'm sure this is all one giant misunderstanding."

Amelia waved off her friend's suggestion, "No, Lou. He wants nothing to do with me, I'm sure."

Lou waited a while before responding, "Are you going to let someone with that much spark slip away?"

Amelia hesitated as she had reasoned the same issue with herself earlier. "He made his choice nearly ten years ago, and it's the same choice today." Lou gave her a hesitant nod and collected Daphne before heading home.

Amelia had about two hours before she needed to report to the beauty pageant. She was conflicted on how to spend the time, opting to visit her father in his study. "Milly, what's got you so down?" Amelia collapsed into a chair and began to tell all of her problems to her father. Like most daughters, she expected her dad to chase away all of her issues. "Milly, it seems as if the two of you need to talk it out." Amelia huffed and began to rise and leave. "Amelia Susan Allen, you stay and listen to your father," he called out to her. Whenever he used her middle name, it either meant she was in trouble or acting like a disgruntled child. She sat back down in the chair and stared back his way. "That's better. Let me continue, dear."

Roger leaned back in his chair and sighed. "Milly, did he tell you why he left you the first time?" She shared with Roger what Ian had told her. "He asked me about Ben, and then after I told Jenna my news, he went and danced with Jessie, ignoring me."

"Do you think that if he misunderstood what you told Jenna that this could have been his way of letting you go again? Think about it, dear." Roger looked up at the large clock on his wall. "Amelia, it's almost time for you to head to the school." Amelia left her father's study and mulled over the words he had spoken. She dressed in a simple white dress and headed over to the school where the pageants were happening. As she pulled up to the parking lot, she saw the sunset in the distance.

She pulled the ring from her purse, as she had been unable to put it back in the box. Holding the symbol of promises past up and saying a short prayer, she asked the Lord for guidance. She opened her eyes as the sun faded away and thanked God for another strawberry sunset. Taking a leap of faith, she slid the ring onto her finger, deciding to take each moment as they came and hope for the best.

Amelia found Marcie Donald, who showed her where the judges were staying. Jenna stopped by to have a last-minute discussion with Amelia before the revue started. At five minutes until time, the emcee asked Amelia to bring the judges out to their seats. Amelia saw that her entire family had attended, thanks to her mother's request. The brothers had no idea why they were at a beauty pageant, but when their mother requested, they came. The pageant began with twenty-nine area contestants. Amelia noticed that several seemed polished while others were still new to the circuit. However, this was the cream of the crop as each contestant was already a queen of another pageant.

Amelia helped the judges into their deliberation room, where they slowly took the group down, eventually to a top ten. As the top ten began to be questioned by the judges, Amelia noticed the crowd around her. Several of her parents' church members were here, the entire planning committee for the Festival, the mayor, and many others. Tonight was not only the final pageant but also the closing ceremonies for the pageant. Once the round was over, Amelia once more took the judges back for deliberation. From here, they would decide the queen and her court. It took them a while to reach an agreement, but eventually, the panel made their decision. Amelia led them back out to the judges' table, and the closing ceremonies began.

Marcie Donald approached the podium first. The crowd cheered her before she gave her final speech. "This has been a whirlwind of a year, and I cannot believe it's already over. Two years ago, when I was asked to become the general chairman, I was so touched and honored to be selected for this position. I have met so many wonderful people all over West Tennessee and am blessed to represent our wonderful town. As my time at the Festival draws to a close, I will fondly remember all of the wonderful strawberry treats, people, floats, and more. I want to thank everyone for their work in helping to make the 81st Annual Strawberry Festival a huge success. In a few moments, the 82nd Annual Strawberry Festival Territorial Queen will be crowned. To do the honors, I turn the reins over to the new Festival President, Ms. Jenna Wallace."

The crowd cheered as Jenna came out to take her place on stage. "Thank you, Marcie, for those words and for the leadership you have shown me over the last year. One year ago, I stood here as Marcie announced me as her general chairman. I was shocked and thrilled to be selected to work on this Festival, not only because of all the fun memories but also because of my ten-year high school reunion. Working for this Festival has reminded me of the true beauty in our town, and I hope that all of our out-of-town guests tonight have seen this side of Humboldt as well. Before we crown our new queen, I want to take a moment to introduce my general chairman."

The entire town sat forward as no one was certain who would be the new chairman. Many names had been tossed around, but no rumor seemed to have enough truth behind it. "I will admit that as of two weeks ago, I still had not made up my mind. The person that I wanted for the role did not meet the requirements. I was surprised last week to learn that I was incorrect and that they were, in fact, eligible for the role. This person embodies the heart and soul of our Festival and will do a wonderful job as general chairman and then as festival president. Their determination shows through their efforts, life, and experience. This person holds a special place in the town of Humboldt, and likewise, our community holds a special place in their heart. I am thrilled beyond measure to announce that the general chairman of the 82nd Annual Strawberry Festival is our newest resident, Ms. Amelia Allen."

As Amelia headed up the stage, she surveyed the shocked crowd before her. Roger Allen was grinning as widely as possible while Susan turned to face her husband in total dismay and shock. Her brothers leaned over to their mother, "Mom, is this why you invited us?" Along with Lou, Emma, and Donna's, their faces were all a mixture of happiness, joy, and disbelief. Bradley was grinning alongside Roger, which caused Jessie to look at him suspiciously. Susan finally came out of her shock to answer her son's question, "No, your father suggested everyone attend. It seems he was in on it." As they began to question him, he quietened them all down, "Shh. Your sister is on stage." The entire family turned back towards the podium.

Amelia shook as she began to speak, more nervous than in any speech she'd given before today. "I want to thank Jenna for choosing me to serve in this role. I know that this comes as a surprise to many of you, my family included. We planned this surprise, and it seems we did it well! For the last several years, I have avoided this town and this Festival. It was not the fault of anyone here in town but rather a part of my past that I could not put aside. When my mother was in an accident a few weeks ago, it allowed me to stay and confront my issues. I remembered how special this town was and the people of it. I saw the beauty that so many miss of our little community and felt touched by all of the happiness here. I wish that everyone could see Humboldt the week of our Festival and that our feelings this week are mimicked all year long. This place restored my soul, and when Jenna found out that I would be moving home, she asked me to consider working in this role. I jumped immediately at the opportunity, although it will keep me busy with my new job. I am excited to be moving home as the new talent director for Allen, Inc., and thanks to some of this town's best realtors, I've already made an offer that was accepted on my new home. I cannot say how happy I am to be moving back, and now let's crown our queen to begin the next, wonderful Festival."

The crowd cheered as Amelia exited the stage. She saw the happy looks of her family and friends and murmured that they would talk after the pageant. She looked around the room, hoping to find Ian and see if this solved any mysteries, but realized that he was never there.

Chapter Twenty-One

The fallout from the festival announcement was more significant than Amelia had anticipated. From the moment the pageant was over, and the photographer took the pictures, her family and friends hounded her. They were all asking questions centered around two issues — why didn't she tell them, and could they help her move faster. Amelia got them all to agree to wait until they were home before she would explain everything.

As everyone sat eagerly awaiting the story around the Allen living room, Amelia went upstairs to change into something more comfortable and gather Frank. She came back downstairs to realize most of her family were still in the same outfits, not wanting to take time and change. She sat down and began to explain the story. She decided that what motivated her was right here in Humboldt— her friends, family, and community. She told them of her discussion with Director Jones, how she would come back and work two weeks to ensure the transition process went smoothly. He wished her well while grumbling about some small town stealing two of his best employees. She told them that she was buying a house only half a mile down the street and already had three offers on her Nashville home.

Jason was the first one to hug his sister, glad that she was returning home. Each family member shared the sentiment, and Lou went on and on about how happy she was to have another babysitter. Amelia smirked at her and said, "Anything for my nieces." Susan was the only family member who stayed quiet primarily until everyone left. She gestured for Amelia to join her on the couch as the two began to talk.

"Well, mom, what do you think of my announcement?"

Her mother caressed her face, "Oh, well, first I'm surprised your father kept a secret that well from me. I must be losing my touch." Amelia laughed at her mother's silliness. "I think it is wonderful that you want to be home, and I cannot be happier that you found peace here. My dear, sweet Amelia, it all seems too good to be true that you will be moving home in a matter of weeks."

Amelia gazed out the window of their living room and said, "I know. Everything seems to have happened so fast."

Susan looked a little apprehensively at her daughter, "Not reconsidering already, I hope."

Amelia laughed lightly, "No, nothing like that. I never imagined moving home to work here and help run the festival."

Susan nodded her head and grabbed her daughter's hand. "Everything has worked out quite nicely, I think."

Amelia glanced over at her mother, "Not everything, but that's ok." Susan started to tell Amelia what she thought, but Amelia decided to head onto bed. She grabbed Frank to move him off of her pillow. "Ready to move out of the city?" In response, she received the most enthusiastic "Meow" yet!

The following day, Amelia came downstairs to find a gift bag sitting on the countertop. The card said Amelia and inside read, "My darling daughter, I found this at the woodshop several years ago and bought it for you. I knew then that you would not want it but thought one day you might. I hope you remember what this item is.

Love, Mom." She opened the bag to find a wood paperweight. The right-hand side had the initials "I" and "A" carved into the wood. Amelia felt how familiar it seemed but was unable to place it.

Her mind could not focus on the item in her hand, so she slipped it into her pocket. Wanting to take a tour of her now new workplace, she headed to the office before church services. Amelia saw where her new office would be and began to plan all of the ways she would recognize and utilize the talent of their current workforce while finding the best and most unique individuals. She strolled past the desk that had always intrigued her and sat down in its chair. She saw the ornament made from the dogwood tree of the library, the trinkets representing Belmont and Tennessee universities. She glanced at the copy of The Language of Flowers before her eyes settled on the wooden paperweight. She saw the carved "R" and "A" in the top left-hand corner of the paperweight, and her eyes widened in recognizing the wood and carving.

She pulled the paperweight from her pocket and put both on their sides where one's top right-handed corner rested perfectly beside the other's left-handed corner.

I. R.

&

A. A.

Amelia dropped the two pieces as she realized this came from the tree that once stood by the tennis courts. Ian had carved their initials into the tree that the giant storm had split. Ian said that some of the wood was salvaged for trinkets, but she never imagined how someone would use this part of the tree. She took in the charms on the desk, ones that represented memories of theirs, favorite hobbies, and places of his, and took out her cellphone.

After three rings, the intended target answered the phone. "Emma, it's Amelia . . . yes I know I'm missing the Allen Sunday breakfast . . . listen, the desk I showed you that kept standing out to me, whose desk is it? . . . I see, thanks for the information." Amelia hung up the phone as she considered that this was Ian Reynolds' desk. Her mind processed through all of the last several weeks' events and realized that he had been behind the flowers. She wondered now, more than ever, why he was upset with her. She glanced at her watch and knew that visiting hours had begun only moments ago at the assisted living center. It was a long shot, but she had to give this plan a try.

Amelia found Ms. Georgia eating breakfast in the cafeteria. She sat down beside her friend and asked to interrupt her meal. Georgia invited Amelia to sit, and the two chatted about the reunion. Ms. Georgia looked sad at Amelia as she searched for her spoon. "So, I guess you've come to say goodbye?"

Amelia helped her with the spoon and yogurt before responding, "Why would you say that?"

Georgia swallowed her food and waited to see if Amelia would offer any information, "Ian told me that he heard Ben offer you a chance in Chicago. He hoped you wouldn't go until he heard you the other night talking about a big promotion."

Amelia had found the problem, and everyone had been right. The last few days had all been one giant misunderstanding. "Ms. Georgia, I am moving back to Humboldt. I took a job at my father's company and also will be the general chairman for next year's festival."

Georgia's face was so happy to hear this news. "That's wonderful, Amelia! Congratulations. I guess Ian heard wrong."

Amelia told Georgia about that evening and was surprised to learn that she had also broken up with Ben. Georgia explained to Amelia how broken Ian seemed the night after the Chicago question. Georgia reasoned that Ian was trying to let Amelia go without causing too much pain to himself. Amelia wondered how she could show Ian that she loved him, and then it dawned on her. "Ms. Georgia, I have to go. I will see you later." Georgia clapped as she heard Amelia leave. "Go, my friend. Go and find your man."

It took fourteen calls before Amelia was able to arrange her plan. She arrived at the church service fifteen minutes late, with a stern look from her mother and a curious yet happy one from her father. She mouthed apologies and tried to focus on the service. As soon as it ended, Amelia jetted out the door and to the Allen home. Susan tried to lecture her daughter on being punctual, especially in the house of God, but Amelia was paying her no mind. "I said I was sorry, mother, and I truly am. I had to make amends, though, and the Bible tells us to go and make amends before we come before Him." Susan stopped lecturing, unable to argue with her daughter's reasoning, and helped in preparing the meal for that evening.

At five o'clock, the festival board gathered into the Allen home to celebrate the ending of another successful year. The traditional Italian dinner laid on the table, but this year with an added chicken alfredo option, courtesy of Bradley and Jenna. The table was extra full as Amelia had invited her friends and family to fill it. One spot was empty, and Amelia filled with dread, hoping that this would not be the new normal.

Different guests shared ideas with Jenna and Amelia for the next festival. The two needed to get a head start on preparations, or else they would be playing catch-up the entire year. A one-week festival took months of planning to ensure that the staff pulled off each event in the proper fashion. As the guests mingled and lingered, Amelia never heard the doorbell ring. Eric, however, was near the front door when it went off, and he let the late arrival enter.

Amelia rose to give a speech to the festival organizers, "I again want to thank all of you for the faith you had in me this week in filling my mother's shoes. Not everything went to plan, but I hope this week has been as rejuvenating to you as it has been to me.

This week celebrates everything our town does well: friendships, family, and community. New friendships are made, and family bonds are strengthened. The community recognizes the value and appreciation of each neighbor. May we take these values and use them every day and not solely during festival time." Amelia glanced around the room as she made her speech until her eyes fell on Ian, the late arrival.

She halted for only a brief moment, and several let their eyes follow her gaze. Seeing him standing there, the Allen family and friends smiled as they turned back towards Amelia. "As I was saying, this week reminds us of the love we have for each other, and ultimately for this town. I love this festival and everything it stands for, but most of all I love the people of our town. As this year's festival has ended, we already look forward to what next year will bring. Farewell to the 81st, and may the 82nd be even more thrilling." Everyone raised their glasses in agreement. "Thank you all for coming this evening, and please enjoy yourselves here as long as you like."

Amelia attempted to make her way over to Ian but became hindered by several individuals welcoming her home and commenting on her speech. He waited in the background as she struggled to reach him. *He's not going anywhere this time.* She drew closer, only to be caught by another individual. In a small town, everyone has to comment, unfortunately for her.

The house was filled with the aroma of Italian food, strawberries, and a hint of uncertainty. *What if he only wants to be friends?* As she drew nearer, he began to smile. She searched his eyes. Gone were the looks of sadness, strife, and torment. Now, she saw the fire burning in his eyes, a deep desire. Her heart fluttered, and she thought maybe it would all work out.

Eventually, she made her way over to him. She took in his scent and how it captivated her senses, much more than the food. She breathed in the familiarity and noted that the uncertainty still lingered, but only slightly. "Hi," was all Amelia could say to him. "Hi, back to you. Can we talk outside?" Amelia followed him out to the front porch of her parents' home.

As they exited, each took in the other. She watched as his eyes drifted down to her finger, pausing for what seemed like an eternity there. She brushed the ring with her finger, the motion drawing his eyes back to hers. The fire was now fully blazing in his eyes.

"I went and saw Ms. Georgia after church today," Ian started. "She told me that the next time I eavesdrop, I better hear the full story." He chuckled.

This time, words poured forth from her. Her heart wanted to tell him everything that she had discovered. Amelia began attempting to explain what he heard, and he stopped her, "I know." The uncertainty vanished more, but she had to know without a shadow of a doubt. People and disappointment had broken her heart too many times that once more might cause it to be irreparable. Here stood the man that had broken her heart, and yet through all of that history, it was ready, willing, and desperately wanting to love him once more.

"Amy? Amy?" His calls to stop her fell on deaf ears. Her heart was pounding so loudly she could barely make out that he was speaking. He finally found the right way to ease her fears. Ian took her by the chin, and immediately she quit talking. He lifted her chin to where it shined in the sinking sun. He muttered a few words, but her heart was beating so fast that she heard nothing he said. He lowered, slowly, as she filled with anticipation and captured her lips with such force. The trepidation, the uneasy feeling, had utterly vanished. She returned his kiss with one just as passionate before finally breaking away. "I didn't catch what you said."

He laughed, and her soul warmed at the sight of his eyes filled with light and love. "I said that I know. This morning, everyone at church talked about how you were moving home and becoming the new general chairman. I knew I heard something wrong, and then Ms. Georgia filled me in on the rest of it. Then I got home and saw your flowers and finally decided to head over here."

Amelia tried to play coy and asked, "My flowers?" He laughed as he pulled out the card that had accompanied them — *Love is never unsure.* "I knew who sent them by the words on the card, but the choice of flowers solidified my answer. The beautiful purple hyacinths, meaning I'm sorry, with a single daffodil sticking in the middle of the bouquet — you are the only one. I remembered how much you liked the language of flowers when your mom taught us as kids. I had hoped you'd figure it out, but when I saw the good doctor's carnations, I realized there might be a problem."

Amelia gazed adoringly at the man standing before her. "There was some confusion, but my heart was never with him. I think all along I knew that it was you. I was jealous seeing you with Jessie, and even though I was mad at you, I still wanted to see you."

Ian raised her hands to his lips. "Nothing is going on between Jessie and me. I thought everyone knew she was with your friend Bradley."

Amelia rolled her eyes, "I know that now, at least." She tried to take her hands away from his face, but he caught the ring on her finger. "You still have it." It was a statement that had a hint of disbelief, and Amelia found no accusation in his words.

"I always kept it because it was a promise of you, remember?" He kissed her hand and pulled her closer to him. "Say, Amy, do you have a date for next year's festival?"

She thought for a moment and said, "Well, there might be a cute attorney moving into town."

He groaned at her antics before she got serious, "No, I don't, but please tell me I can have a date before then." He grinned at her as he captured her in a sweet, short kiss.

The two broke, and he said, "Well, how about your first night back in town?"

She grinned against his lips and whispered, "It's a date." He captured her once with a kiss that confirmed everything she needed to know. The two broke apart as the sun made its final descent for the night. His eyes glistened, and his lips curled into a bright smile as they held hands and watched the sun sink lower and lower into the ground. As he put his arm around her, the two gazed at each other and then at the sky. He whispered to her, "Thank God for sweet strawberry sunsets."

Epilogue

Two Years Later

Amelia Allen was running around the school as if everything was on fire. It was the last night of the 83rd Annual Strawberry Festival, and her time as Festival President was coming to an end. Ian came up behind his girlfriend of now two years and massaged her shoulders. "Relax. Everything will be ok. Everyone is here and can help if needed." Amelia breathed in and out and let the stress leave her body.

She glanced out and saw the audience filled with her family and friends. Justin was sitting beside Lou, being stateside once again. Eric rubbed Emma's belly while his wife's hands caressed the large bump, both with eager anticipation of what could happen at any moment. The couple kept it a secret what they were having, opting to be surprised at the birth, which would happen any day. Jason and Donna had fifteen-month-old Jackson sitting in Roger's lap while Susan had held onto two-year-old twins Kathryn and Daphne Hart. She saw the ring glistening on Jessie's finger with the matching band on Bradley's. The two had been married for less than two months, and she wondered if Ian would ever ask her to marry him.

The last two years had primarily been extraordinary for their relationship, with them growing closer and closer together. It had taken time at the beginning for the two to trust each other again fully. Letting the past go is often more complicated than it seems. This time, the two of them were ready to put in the work to ensure their happiness.

Ian had taken over the marketing department for Allen, Inc. and still was able to do a lot of graphic design. Amelia loved meeting new people and recruiting them to her father's company and the city of Humboldt. She hoped that she and Ian could examine their future after tonight with no longer being a festival chairman or president.

Amelia decided to put all of those thoughts away while she focused on the task at hand. Her general chairman had gone into labor about two hours ago, only moments before the final pageant began. She was scrambling to remember everything her chairman had planned until she saw the envelope sitting on the podium.

When the doctor had informed Sally West that her due date fell during the festival, Sally prepared an envelope for each day's tasks for Amelia to pull off everything smoothly. She opened the envelope to find a sealed note and two letters. The first informed her that Sally hid the new general chairman's name and not to peek until the right time, and the other was her speech.

The pageant went off smoothly, as Amelia remembered that the pageant chairs handled most of the event. It finally came time for her farewell speech. She walked up to the podium and waited for the applause to die down from the emcee's introduction. "Thank you all for being here tonight. It is hard to believe that I was up here to announce my return home and acceptance of becoming the general chairman two years ago. I am so grateful for my friend, Jenna Wallace, who invited me to be a vital part of the festival. This town has taught me so much these last few years, but they all center on three points: family, friends, and community. Thank you to the residents of Humboldt for always striving to make this week the best in our state. Now, I would normally invite my general chairman on stage to turn over the reins. She, however, is currently in labor. She remarked earlier this afternoon that the baby had agreed to wait until after the festival. I warned her not to jinx it, but we do hope everything is going smoothly there.

Sally did leave me her speech and asked me to read it and announce the new general chairman." The crowd listened as Amelia read Sally's speech and cheered at the end. "And now, the general chairman of the 84th Annual Strawberry Festival is. . ." Amelia opened the sealed envelope and was shocked at the name. She recovered quickly, not to leave a long pause, "Ian Reynolds."

Ian joined her on stage with a giant grin and a whisper of "Did we surprise you?" He thanked Sally, in absentia, for choosing him as the new general chairman. He gave a brief speech and then ended with, "Before we crown our new queen, I have a quick question for our current festival president." Amelia turned towards him, surprised, as this was unusual. She nodded that he could ask her, and he proceeded to drop on one knee. Her hands flew to her lips, utterly shocked at what was happening. The room filled with "aww"s and "how sweet"s.

"Amelia Allen, I wanted to ask you during your favorite week of the year. The last two years have been the best of my life, and while I wish we hadn't let so many years go by, I wonder if it wasn't leading us to this moment. Amelia, I want to spend every day of the rest of my life with you, working and loving together each day. I never want to see another strawberry sunset without you by my side." Ian opened the jewelry box to show a beautiful, glistening ring. He took the promise ring and moved it to another finger. Ian slid the new ring onto her finger and said, "Will you, Amelia Allen, be my wife and experience this wonderful Berryland with me forever?"

Amelia's emotions were moving so quickly through happiness, exhilaration, shock, and more that she didn't trust her voice. Her heart swelled with her deepest desire coming true. She nodded her head, cementing her love for the man who knelt before her. He slid the ring onto her finger, letting it rest next to the promise ring from many years before. She'd waited for this day ever since teenage Ian had made the promise, and now it was coming true.

Ian rose from the ground, took her hands, and rested his head against hers. She looked up into his eyes, finally finding her voice. As the couple tuned out the crowd around them, caring only for the individual standing in front of them, Amelia uttered the words Ian had two years before, "Thank God for sweet strawberry sunsets."

Printed in the United States
by Baker & Taylor Publisher Services